the dog farm

Published by Beatdom Books

Copyright © 2011 by David S. Wills

Cover illustration by Isaac Bonan

This novel is a work of fiction. All characters,
locations and incidents are the product of the author's
imagination. Any resemblance to actual people,
locations or events is entirely coincidental.

View the author's website:
www.davidswills.com

View the publisher's website:
www.beatdom.com

Printed in the United States
Third Edition, 2021
ISBN 978-0-9569525-1-6

Contents

Introduction

Part One
1

Part Two
149

Note on Romanisation
289

INTRODUCTION...
OR: AN EXPLANATION FOR RE-RELEASING A FAILED FIRST NOVEL

In 2011, my first book was released to some measure of controversy. Part of me had always wanted to write an infamous novel, but when *The Dog Farm* came out, it appeared that both the fans and critics seemed to base their views upon misunderstandings of the story and its author. The ones who loved it rallied behind the anti-Korean sentiments espoused by the novel's maudlin protagonist, and those who hated it attributed these sentiments to me. At first, I felt aggrieved at these reactions; I felt people just didn't *understand* the book I had worked on for so many years. But later, I felt that perhaps they had a point, and that there were some problems with what I had written. After all, if few people understood what I was trying to do, it was more likely my fault than theirs.

Much of this misunderstanding came down to the fact that the book was a novel but its readers took it for a *roman à clef*; in other words, they mostly believed it to be a thinly-veiled account of my own exploits in South Korea. In the beginning, I was offended and upset by this, for I had deliberately written the novel's protagonist, Alexander, as a pathetic loser, intended to elicit almost no sympathy. He had been a device for representing the very worst of young Westerners on their first visits to Asia: a selfish fool with a limited worldview, who creates trouble for himself and then blames it all on others. I did not foresee my readers and reviewers interpreting it as a celebration of bad behaviour.

Of course, this was largely my own fault. While the resemblance between myself and Alexander is minimal, there are a few superficial similarities. In writing my first novel, I took to heart the advice all young writers are given: *Write*

i

what you know. Having spent several years teaching in South Korea, I wrote about that particular life, and specifically about Daegu, the city where I lived for more than three years. I did this because it seemed to me a very good source of inspiration for a novel, a suitable template onto which I could layer various fictions. Even when I had left the country, I could close my eyes and vividly recall the sights and sounds and smells of Daegu and the surrounding mountains, so it made more sense to write about these places than to set my story somewhere else.

Into the midst of this fascinating setting I placed a character whom I thought would make an intriguing guide to the story I ultimately wanted to tell – that of a young man who blames the world for his own idiocy. I gave Alex my own background because I wanted him to be believable in spite of his awfulness, so in the book he is – like myself – Scottish. Previous versions of the novel (and there were many) featured female protagonists, Canadians, and Korean-American adoptees returning to the land of their birth. None of these were particularly convincing, though, and so I made the mistake that largely doomed this novel to minor infamy.

The problem I faced was that I attempted to get to the heart of why so many young people travel to South Korea to work and end up becoming disaffected, bitter, and even racist. I attempted to investigate this by presenting the story of a young man who moves across the world to escape his own demons, but who simply projects his own issues and insecurities onto his new environment, ultimately blaming South Korea and its people for the unhappiness he feels. He makes foolish choices and often jumps to erroneous conclusions, all while engaging in self-destructive activities.

To me, this was always a novel about an unreliable narrator whose flawed view of the world becomes obvious to the reader as the story progresses. It was meant as a cautionary tale and an examination of what I perceived a common yet unknown phenomenon. Alas, as most readers assumed this to be mere autobiography, they mistook my portrayal of Alexander's idiocy as a celebration of my own actions, as though Hank Chinaski or Raoul Duke had been cut loose in Asia. Whilst some parts of the novel were indeed humorous to me, Alexander's behaviour and attitude were never something I intended to celebrate, and his occasionally racist and frequently sexist statements were always meant to reflect his own deeply disturbed worldview.

Of course, very few people understood what I had tried to do, and by 2014 I was tired of being confused with Alexander. I requested that the book be removed from sale and thereafter *The Dog Farm* slid from infamy to obscurity. Disillusioned, I put the book behind me and wrote it off as a failure.

However, in 2019, while moving house, I stumbled upon an old copy of *The Dog Farm* and flicked through the pages. In the intervening years, I had moved on to writing non-fiction and hadn't given too much thought to my old novel. Embarrassed by it, I had convinced myself it was an awful piece of juvenile nonsense, and that the critics had been right about it. What I found, though, was an entertaining story with some pretty good writing holding it all together. It was funny, it was moving, and I thought it had actually answered the questions I set out to ask.

I decided to dust off *The Dog Farm* and give it another airing in time for the tenth anniversary of its publication. I read it through and laughed aloud at some of its absurdities, and I hope that you will do the same. Whilst I was embarrassed by some poorly written sentences and a handful of typos that had somehow gotten past my editors in 2011, there was much there that captured a time and place and provided insight into lifestyle and mindset that – to my knowledge – has never been explored in fiction anywhere else. A few hundred words of pointless sentences have been cut since the first and second editions, but the story that you are about to read is the same one was published ten years ago. It was a different world then and I was a different person, but I am proud to look back on this novel. I called it, at the time, "A warped love-letter to the Korean peninsula" and I stand by that.

David S. Wills
2021

PART ONE

CHAPTER ONE

I was drunk when I first heard about Korea. It was a typically brisk night in Edinburgh, and I was sitting out back of a little artsy bar with my friend, Sarah, hiding from the rain under an umbrella. We were smoking foul roll-ups, trying to keep the drunkenness at bay. It had been a long night of drinking. *Another* long night. A whole winter had gone by in unemployment. We didn't even enjoy going out anymore.

"Aye, Seoul," she said. "The job starts in July. Emma's been out there almost a year. Says it's brilliant."

"Why?" I asked. I simply couldn't imagine why anyone would go to Korea. It wasn't exactly a well-known destination. I'd heard friends talk about going to America, Australia, or even China, but Korea? What did people do there?

"Lots of money."

"Seriously?" It sounded more like the sort of place a person would go to volunteer.

"Aye, she makes double what she spends, so she's going travelling after with what she's saved. Vietnam maybe."

I snorted in disbelief. "Sounds good."

"Seems it."

"So how do you plan on getting out there? It can't be cheap."

"It's free. The school pays for you to fly over."

"You're shitting me!"

Sarah grinned, then pushed her glasses back up her nose. They tended to fall down when she smiled. "No," she said. "Seriously."

"What's she doing out there?"

"Teaching."

"Teaching!" I laughed. Teachers were meant to be responsible folk, the sort of people you'd trust so much you wouldn't think twice about leaving them in charge of wee kids for a whole day.

"Aye, teaching. Says it's easy, though. Anyone can do it."

"I'm not sure I'm exactly *teacher material*," I said. "And no offense, but I can't imagine you in charge of a bunch of snot-nosed wee bairns, either."

Sarah took a sip of her Guinness and looked me in the eyes. "What else am I going to do?"

She was right. There wasn't exactly an abundance of jobs available. We'd both graduated the previous summer with utterly useless degrees in literature. Since then Sarah had been working occasionally in a bar and living with her parents. I'd been crashing on friends' sofas, scoring free drinks and not eating, and working weekends as a cleaner at a hotel I'd worked at five years earlier, back when I *didn't* have a degree to my name.

I stubbed out my cigarette, finished my drink, and we walked back into the bar. The night dragged on as an amateurish indie band played on a tiny stage, but my mind was wandering towards a faraway place – a place I couldn't even begin to imagine.

When I stumbled home at three in the morning, I was alone, as always. My friend's flat was unlocked and I tried to enter stealthily and get to his sofa without waking him. I kept thinking about Korea. It was perhaps the first time I'd been interested in anything since before Christmas. After spending my final year in university looking for a job, as well as several months following my graduation, I'd almost resigned myself to terminal unemployment. Now I was thinking about teaching, and with every passing hour I was becoming a little more convinced that I could do it. I certainly didn't seem like an ideal teacher, but I could settle down and do the job. I could stop drinking, act like an adult for a change, and make something out of my life.

I sat on the sofa with my laptop, lit a joint that I'd abandoned earlier, and Googled "teaching in Korea." Though I had never heard of it before, it seemed that teaching in Korea wasn't exactly an uncommon thing... There were thousands of webpages devoted to the subject. Blogs, newspaper articles, forums, and all sorts of references littered my screen.

It didn't even occur to me to look around more. I was overwhelmed with information, but my mind had already worked too much out on its own. Rather than study the language or learn about the culture, I told myself that it was the right choice for me. Only a massive jump to the other side of the world would straighten me out. Only that could finally put me on a path to somewhere.

I wrote a quick introductory letter and updated my pitiful excuse for a résumé to include some grossly exaggerated – not to mention irrelevant – qualifications, such as helping out at a local newspaper and having a couple of poems in a literary journal. They were lies but no one would know. How could anyone check up on me from Korea? I was surprised they even had e-mail over there...

But evidently they did. There were hundreds of recruiters offering all kinds of jobs, from kindergarten to university. Very few of them required any sort of teaching qualification, and those that did only wanted a certificate you could earn or buy online in no time. All they really wanted were graduates – people with degrees that were in no way related to teaching. The pay varied from job to job, but it was always more money than I could have imagined, and rent was almost always paid by the school. Everything sounded too good to be true, so I sent my résumé to forty-seven different recruiters, hoping at least that one of the less desirable schools would take me.

As I lay on the sofa, I thought about the future. There would most likely be no reply and I would continue to get drunk on other people's money and sleep on strange sofas. No doubt I would find a job working for minimum wage in a single-price retailer and trudge through life always wishing I'd done something interesting.

I thought about Sarah. She was a good friend and I'd always been attracted to her. I thought she might feel the same way, but I hadn't bothered to ask her... Loneliness had become such a part of me that I had no courage. Maybe if we were in Korea we would find ourselves pushed so close together that we'd become more than just friends. Maybe. Maybe I would meet a nice Korean girl, settle down, and never come back to Scotland...

I smiled at the thought and fell asleep.

When I woke up, I checked my inbox and found I already had a reply from one recruiter. He offered me a job in Daegu, working for an academy called "Charleston Language School." The money was pretty standard, with airfare and accommodation thrown in. The name sounded prestigious, and when I Googled "Daegu City, South Korea" I was shown a beautiful place – a sprawling, overgrown village in the mountains, with temples and trees littering the landscape. A written description even suggested that the aroma of ginseng and incense filled the air at every turn.

I accepted the job immediately and set about the list of immigration requirements – criminal record check, copies of my degree, sealed university transcripts, a signed copy of the contract. Everything had to be sent from Scotland to Korea. The criminal record check even had to be taken to a lawyer's office, then sent to London, and then forwarded on to Daegu. I had to beg and borrow money to pay for all this from my disapproving parents and my amused friends, who thought I was mad to even contemplate such a thing, and who fully expected me to be the resident alcoholic crashing on their sofas in another year.

The whole process seemed to drag on forever, but I was lucky. Whereas some people experience delays that cost them months in waiting, I received my passport complete with immigration stamp after only a month, and two days later I was booked on a flight to Incheon.

Sarah drove me to the airport in her mother's car. My own parents were at work and I didn't know anyone else with a vehicle, and I certainly couldn't afford a taxi. I didn't want her to drive me there because she was the person I was saddest to leave, the girl I was beginning to think I loved. I kept shaking my head at the thought, trying to remind myself what lay ahead.

We sat in absolute silence all the way to the airport. Sarah didn't even put on any music. I wanted to say to her that I loved her and that we'd be a couple when she came out in the summer, but I couldn't. I could feel that she wanted to say something, too.

At the airport we hugged and she helped me carry my bags to the check-in desk. Again, silence. It became so awkward that she hugged me once more and walked away. I stood in a line, hoping it was the right one and hoping I had what I needed. International travel wasn't exactly my area of expertise. There were so many people, and so much information on little black and green monitors. My eyes were getting misty and I couldn't stop thinking about friends and family. Nothing made sense.

CHAPTER TWO

At the layover in Frankfurt I saw Korean people for what was probably the first time in my sheltered life. At my transfer gate there were about three hundred people standing around, waiting for the flight. I was the only white person among them, which was a strange new experience, particularly coming from a place like Scotland. They all stared at me intently, looking me up and down and seeming unfazed when I looked back. I wondered at first if I had something on my face, or if I had dropped something. What was I doing to cause all the attention?

As I looked around, I got a strange feeling. Aside from the staring, everybody had something else in common: clothes. All the women over forty wore long visors, white gloves, and tracksuits. They were dressed like Stormtroops. The men all wore suits that looked cheap but were probably quite expensive, with clip-on silk ties and most had slicked-back hair. Almost every one of them wore surgical masks, and often they would remove these to spit on the ground. The language they spoke was completely alien to my ears. It was different from a European language and I couldn't imagine ever learning it. They jostled around, too, pushing each other and vying for space near the door. Every now and then a member of staff had to come over and tell them to calm down and to stop shoving. But it was useless. Minutes later they'd be at it again.

On the plane, I found myself sitting in a window seat with two slightly over-weight, middle-aged Korean men beside me. Both men took off their shoes and fell asleep as I read my book, watched shitty movies, and stared at the barren landscapes of Siberia and Mongolia below us. About once every hour the drink cart came around and I'd order a beer. I must have drunk at least a dozen of them. Sobriety could wait.

I had my first taste of Korean food and learned my first words of Korean as dinner came. A little menu told me about "kimchi" and "bibimbap," and informed me that "annyeonghasseyo" meant "hello" and that "kamsahamnida" meant "thank you." Those all seemed like long words to me, and with the exception of "kimchi" I would close the menu and instantly forget them.

The reason I remembered "kimchi" wasn't that it was described as being Korea's national dish. It was because when I opened the little container, I was immediately hit by its pungent stench, a smell as overwhelming as blue cheese. It wasn't a pleasant odour, either. I questioned the wisdom of serving it on a plane with recycled air. The smell certainly wouldn't disappear during the flight, being farted and belched back into the air over and over.

Kimchi had smelled bad as a fermented cabbage, but after rotting in someone's gut for an hour it was even worse.

When we arrived at Incheon airport, I was terrified that something would go wrong and I'd end up back on a plane, deported before I'd even gotten into the country. But everything went smoothly and I was suddenly standing with my luggage in the arrivals lounge, wondering what to do. I had a piece of paper in my pocket with the word "Dongdaegu" written on it. That was the name of the destination I had to reach before calling my boss.

I looked around and found a "Limousine Bus" that was heading to Dongdaegu and purchased a ticket. Whilst certainly more comfortable than any bus I'd previously seen, it was not exactly a "limousine." It was basically just a bus with nicer seats.

I was excited to be on my way to Daegu and I spent the whole four-hour bus ride staring out the window. There wasn't much to see, though. Korea was mountainous but monotonous. The mountains weren't particularly beautiful, and all along the roads were ugly little buildings, fields littered with machinery, and a tedious stream of traffic comprised of seemingly one model of car. After being awake all through the flight and the previous day, I was so tired that my head kept dropping and banging on the glass.

In Daegu I was awoken by the bus driver as I must have fallen asleep again in the last hour of the journey. He shouted a word at me that I later came to recognise as "waegookin," which means "foreigner." I stood up and tried to apologise, but he waved me away, sucking air through his teeth and muttering angrily.

I stepped off the bus and into the afternoon heat. It was a far cry from the cold Scottish spring, and I realised that I should have done a bit more research. In Scotland it had been cold and so I'd naturally worn a heavy jacket and a thick jersey, and when I stepped into the stagnant, unmoving humidity of Daegu, I immediately began to sweat. I could feel my eyes bulging and the hair on my legs matting down beneath my jeans. As I grabbed my bags from the baggage compartment, I realised the smell of kimchi was strong in the air. It wafted up from the sewers and just sat there, waiting for a breeze that never came. The heat seemed to warm up the stench and make it far worse – like a clogged public toilet in the middle of summer.

When I looked around, I became immediately depressed. The journey from Incheon to Daegu hadn't exactly been inspiring, but Korea wasn't *that* ugly. I told myself that I wouldn't necessarily see the country's finest sights from the window of a bus travelling along a highway. But looking at my surroundings as I stood in the fetid heat was a crushing blow. Not only did the air smell more like faeces than "ginseng and incense," but the streets and buildings were uglier than I could have ever expected. Every building looked the same – a Soviet-style block of concrete with a convenience store planted inside it. Giant piles of trash crowded the already congested pavements, split open and spilling filth everywhere. Huge signs with poor English clouded the sky, and I wondered how stupid people had to be to print something that size with such obvious errors.

Everyone that walked past stared at me, and I wondered again if I had something on my face. Sure, I stood out with my big nose and curly hair, but I couldn't be *that* much of a spectacle. They looked at me the way I would look at an alien if it dropped from the skies – a mix of shock and fear and perhaps even revulsion. Had they never seen a white person before? Some of them even turned their heads and watched me as they walked away. Some pointed. Some whispered. Some said that word I was already coming to loathe – "waegookin."

I looked around and found a payphone near where the bus had stopped and dialled the number I had written on a piece of paper. A young woman answered, saying something in Korean that I didn't understand.

"Hello?"

More Korean.

"Hello? Mr. Park? Is Mr. Park there?"

The woman said a few more words of Korean, and then hung up. I dialled again and got the exact same response.

I began to panic. I was in a strange new country and it didn't seem friendly. People were staring at me and I didn't know a word of the language. Everything was ugly and intimidating.

I dialled again and this time I shouted into the phone, "Mr. Park!" My shouts drew even more attention as passers-by began to slow down. Two old men even stopped to watch me. "Let me speak to Mr. Park!"

There was a short silence, and then I could hear the woman on the phone talking to someone else. She said "waegookin" three times. Then there was more silence.

I waited, hoping that the few coins I'd put into the phone were sufficient to keep me on the line until I found someone that spoke English. I had no more coins in my pocket, and only a small stack of green ten thousand Won notes that I'd exchanged at the airport for the little cash I'd managed to scrape together back home.

"Hello?" a voice on the other end of the line said. Another young woman.

"Hello, I need to…"

"How can I helping you?"

"I'm looking for Mr. Park."

"Mr. Park?"

"Yes, Mr. Park. Is he there?"

"Mr. Park?"

"Yes, is he there?"

"No."

I paused. "Er, this is Alexander... The new teacher."

"Alexander?" She stretched my name out strangely – "Eh-leek-send-uh-ruh."

"Yes. I'm at Dongdaegu station. I just arrived. Can you tell Mr. Park, please?"

There was silence as she spoke to the other girl, and then said, "Waiting." She hung up and I stood confused by the payphone. I was just meant to wait? For how long?

An hour later I was soaked in my own sweat, sitting on my backpack, when Mr. Park appeared. He pulled up in a big white Hyundai, driven by a tall, thin, awkward man called James.

"Alexander!" Mr. Park shouted as he stepped out of the vehicle. He stretched my name out even worse than the secretary. I decided that in future I'd simply introduce myself as Alex.

"Hello," I said, not sure what to do. Was I meant to bow? To shake hands? Korea was a mystery to me.

Mr. Park grabbed my hand and shook it. His was greasy, just like the rest of him. He was fat and sweaty, with gelled back hair, and a hideous Cheshire Cat grin drawn from ear to ear.

"Why you look so bad?" he asked, still grinning. His voice was as unpleasant as the rest of him – high-pitched and whiny. "You have so long journey?"

"Yeah, I've been travelling a while."

"You look so bad," he said again, sneering. His smile was fading a little. "You should cut the hair." Clearly he hadn't expected my long hair, which I'd tied back in the one photo I'd sent.

"Ok."

We got in the car and James drove off. He still hadn't said a word to me, and I hadn't yet been introduced to him, although he'd politely bowed and put my bag in the back. All the time he had a nervous smile on his face.

They talked, or rather Mr. Park talked and James listened, as we moved through the busy city. They kept saying that one damn word – "waegookin." They were talking about me as though I wasn't there.

As they talked about me in the front, I looked out the window and took in the sights and sounds of Daegu. The city was *hideous*. I'd half hoped that the rest of it would have looked different from the area around Dongdaegu station, but it was all the same. I wondered how James navigated because I couldn't tell one street from the next. It was all one monstrous grey nightmare, populated by pushy people and millions of cars with blaring horns.

When we arrived at the school, I was pleasantly surprised. Although I hadn't known what to expect, from looking at the rest of the city I'd come to think that Charleston Academy was probably a cluster of desks and chairs in a vacant lot. Instead, Mr. Park pointed at the second floor of a very modern building. On the bottom floor there was a Baskin Robbins, a French bakery called Tous les Jours, and a coffee shop. Charleston sat above them, and above Charleston were two more floors, although I couldn't see what was inside.

The building was on a corner of a busy junction, where a tiny little road met what appeared to be the main highway running through the city. A constant sea of identical cars flowed by, as more poured in off the little side street. Cars constantly pulled onto the pavements to park or to skip the traffic, and it seemed that every motorcycle was doing the same. Pedestrians jumped out of the way of these vehicles, managing to crash into each other instead.

We crossed between the moving cars, apparently trusting that they'd slow enough for us to make it to the other side. There were no lights or crossing signals. It was a matter of pure faith, but Mr. Park and James seemed entirely unfazed. I was certain that I'd die in Korea, run down by a car that no one would ever trace, on account of it looking exactly like every other car on the road.

Inside, we took an elevator to the second floor. "You don't use again," Mr. Park warned me. "You young man can walk up stairs." Apparently I was allowed one free ride in the elevator. I needed it, too. The fatigue and heat were getting to me.

Upstairs we entered the school through sliding glass doors and removed our shoes. It hadn't occurred to me that I'd have to take my shoes off... I didn't even own a pair without laces. Moreover, after almost an entire day of travelling, the noxious gases coming off my feet were almost as bad as the air outside.

Thankfully the school was air-conditioned and looked as modern inside as it did from the street below. This was no dilapidated shack for poor kids. This was a rich kids' school. Everything in the foyer looked new and was designed to look expensive. It was like the set of a low-budget movie – nothing seemed functional or particularly valuable, but you could tell it was meant to look nice. From the fake pebbles to the fake waterfall, it was a vain attempt to look classy. Or, more likely, to look American.

"Welcome Charleston Language School!" Mr. Park boomed, that damn grin creeping across his face. He was proud of his school. He reminded me of a middle-aged man showing off his gaudy new sports car. "I show you."

He gave me the tour of what turned out to be a very *compact* operation. I'm tempted to say "small," but "small" isn't really a term that applies to Korea. Space is so limited that everything is crammed together tightly but efficiently, and Charleston was no different. The floor space was comparable to that of the first floor of my parents' modest house in Scotland, yet there were six classrooms, a library/playroom, a kitchen, a bathroom, a conference room, a foyer, a teachers' room, and Mr. Park's office. It all felt incredibly claustrophobic.

Each of the classrooms was brightly lit and filled with tiny tables and chairs. They were all named after famous scientists – Kepler, Bell, Einstein, and so on. The children looked too old for these things, as they squatted over the little colourful wooden furnishings, staring at their teachers, who wrote on big white boards and gestured wildly. The walls were all colourful and covered in posters written in bad English – things like "Sentence of the Week" or "Word of the Day" that contained the most awful errors in spelling and grammar.

The bathrooms were open-planned with cameras and tiny little toilets behind doors that were no more than three feet high. There were showers in the middle of the room and a sign on one wall said: "Save water; Shower with a friend!" I wondered if I could get through my entire time at school without having to use the facilities.

Mr. Park took me into his office – which was a tiny room partitioned off from the teachers' room and had a sign on the door that said "Mr. President" – and motioned for me to sit down in a comfortable chair. He disappeared and left me to look at the hundreds of teaching books that littered the walls. I wondered how many of them were actually used. Did I have to learn everything in these books? Did I have to know how to teach this stuff?

As I sat staring at the walls, I fell asleep. I don't know how long I was out for, but I was awoken by Mr. Park calling my name: "Eh-leek-send-uh-ruh!" I woke up and smiled in embarrassment, which seemed to amuse him. "Come here," he said, and gestured towards the teachers' room.

When I walked through, I saw that the previously empty room was now full of teachers – the ones who'd been occupying the classrooms as Mr. Park had given me the brief tour. He shouted something in Korean, and they turned and looked at me. It seemed that they were all tired and angry.

I was introduced in Korean as the teachers all pretended to pay attention. When Mr. Park clapped his hands, a reluctant applause rippled around the room. The only people that dared to ignore the introduction were standing in a far corner, loitering by an open window. One was a tall, overweight white man, and the other a skinny, short-haired black woman. They were the first foreigners I'd seen since Incheon airport.

I noticed a sour look on Mr. Park's face as he tried to ignore the two foreigners at the back of the room. It was hard to see them, actually, because the little room was so cluttered with teachers. Only their race and clothing made them detectable, and I realised just why the locals had stared at me so much on the street. The teachers' room was filled with nine young Korean women, and it was tough to tell them apart. They all had the same haircut, the same make-up, and wore the same ridiculous clothes. All of them wore baggy, pastel-coloured t-shirts adorned with bad English, and either hot-pants or mini-skirts.

Mr. Park ushered me back into his office as the bell rang – a strange little tune that sounded vaguely familiar; perhaps a piece of classical music. I was told to sit down again in the same chair as Mr. Park parked himself in his own, which was bigger and looked more expensive. He crossed his hands behind his head and kicked his feet up on the desk. A wicked grin once again snuck across his greasy, pock-marked face.

"Eh-leek-send-uh-ruh!" he began. "You are teacher now, huh? You are not to the travel or do the drinking. You are my teacher. You are act like the teacher and you very happy. And I am happy, too."

I smiled, nodded, and said, "Yes, alright." Another grin broke out and this time his eyes completely shut and his little pig nose wrinkled up so much that his glasses nearly fell off.

"You tired now, huh? So go home... take a rest. You can work tomorrow morning. I not such bad guy. You and me, we are make the good friends! You good employee, I good boss. Simple."

Again I nodded and said some sort of vague affirmative.

"Many other teacher is not good. They like the drinking and the travel and the having fun. You can have fun, but you come Korea to teach. Right?" I said yes, but I don't think he was expecting me to reply as he continued talking over me. "You teacher first and tourist second. You responsible person. I am sponsor you, and I want you be good teacher. If you are trouble, I look very bad boss. Right?"

I muttered "yes" as he took a deep breath.

"Okay, you understand. I think you will be the best teacher! Number one! You better, anyway. America teacher very bad. Always do the drinking. Do you do the drinking?"

I paused for a suspiciously long time, not sure how to reply. Was Korea a nation of drinkers, teetotallers, or somewhere in between? I was too tired even to think of an evasive response. "Er, no..." I said, unconvincingly.

Chapter Three

I was made to sit around for another hour, drinking overly sweet instant coffee from a thin paper cup. When the bell rang and the teachers reappeared, Mr. Park pounced and brought the two foreigners into his office. They didn't look particularly amused, but both said "hi" to me as I sat in the chair, still struggling to keep my eyes open.

"Thomas, Karen," he said, butchering their names by adding multiple syllables. "This the new teacher. His name Alexander."

Karen frowned and shook her head slightly. "Yeah," she said. "We heard." Her accent was definitely English, though I couldn't place exactly where.

Mr. Park unleashed the same grin he'd used on me several times, and I realised it really wasn't just an unfortunate facial quirk – he genuinely disliked us and was grinning in contempt.

"I know you are show Alexander to be the good teacher and to have the good time, huh? So you take him home now. Bring him to school tomorrow. Show him how to eat, use apartment. Right?"

Thomas grunted something affirmative and turned away, while Karen merely shook her head again and did the same. Mr. Park looked down at some papers on his desk, no longer grinning, and I realised that he was done with me for the day. I was being dumped on the sullen, disaffected foreigners who probably wanted nothing to do with me.

I found my suitcase sitting by the front door of the school and was amazed that no one had stolen it. Thomas, who still hadn't said a word to me as we marched out of the building, picked it up with his massive arms, and carried it down the stairs. Karen followed, silently. I wanted to say something – anything – but thought it best just to keep my mouth shut.

At the bottom of the stairs we walked back out into the heat of the city. The sun was way down in the sky, casting an orange glow through the smoggy haze. Even the pieces of trash on the street cast long shadows. The traffic had died down a little, and people weren't rushing and pushing as frantically as they had been. The warmth felt very pleasant and I was glad to be in Korea, in spite of everything. Even the smell wasn't as bad now that it was evening. Perhaps I had judged it too harshly because of my tiredness.

"Dude," Thomas said, stopping and turning to face me. "Do you drink?"

There was that question again. I contemplated my response. Coming to Korea had been an escape for me. An escape from many things, and one of those was alcohol. I wanted to travel around the world to leave my old self behind, but I suddenly realised I didn't want to build a new life on top of a foundation of lies.

"Aye," I said. "I'm Scottish. Of course I drink."

Thomas smiled at me. It was a warm smile –the first genuine smile I'd seen since arriving in Korea.

"Let's go get a beer," he said. "There's a place next door. We call it 'the Pajeon Place.'"

Thomas looked at Karen, who was swaying back and forth on the road. She obviously wanted to go home and wasn't enthralled by Thomas' suggestion. She looked at her wrist – on which there was no watch – and nodded once without smiling. "Alright," she said. "Just one."

Thomas carried my suitcase into a little restaurant next door to the school. Whereas the school was in a thoroughly modern building that was designed for the single purpose of looking more expensive than it actually was, this little restaurant seemed solid and ancient, yet covered in layers of grime. It looked like it had never once been cleaned and had served customers since humans first arrived on the peninsula.

The walls were a yellowy-brown colour, golden kettles hung from string both inside and out, and the roof was made of grey slate. The floor was covered in discarded food and dirt that had been tracked inside. The menu was written on the walls in old Chinese characters, and dust and cobwebs largely obscured the unappetising photos that illustrated some of the options. On one wall there was a big TV playing a Korean baseball game.

There were probably around twenty tables in the small room, and all of them were unoccupied. We were the first customers of the evening and were greeted dryly by a woman who might have been the proprietor. She was tall and thin, with permed hair, and – as Thomas pointed out when she was out of earshot – had an incredibly long torso. When she sat down – which she did as someone else prepared our food – she looked like she would be six feet tall, yet when she stood she was barely five feet.

"Glad to have drinker, man," Thomas said. "Last teacher was fuckin' teetotal. A backstabbing, bearded bible-freak, too. But, man, you gotta drink in Korea. This place gets to you."

I laughed a little. "Thanks, man. You're really making me feel great about being here."

"Sorry. It's probably best you find out now. I mean, it's not all bad or anything, but the school kinda sucks. If you're gonna stay sane, you gotta drink. Fuck, look at the Koreans – they're drunk seven nights a week!"

"Seriously?"

"Yeah, man, they drink more than you Irish!"

"I'm Scottish, actually."

"Oh, right. Well, they're both part of England, right?"

I began to say something, but I realised Thomas was smirking. He was just fucking with me. And from the bored look on Karen's face I could tell she'd been through the same routine, perhaps several times.

"Where are you guys from?" I asked. I noticed that Karen hadn't said a word. She had her arms crossed and was staring at the TV.

"Minnesota," Thomas said.

"That's in Canada, right?"

Thomas smirked. "Well played, *Lucky Charms*."

I looked at Karen. "What about you?"

"England," she said.

"Ah, what part?"

"Birmingham."

"Okay. I went there once."

"Oh yeah? It's a bit shite, like, isn't it?"

"Don't remember. I must have been about ten when I went."

"What part of Scotland you from?"

"Edinburgh," I said.

"Posh boy, eh?" I almost detected the first hints of a smile, but it died away before taking hold.

I snorted. "I guess so."

"You play golf?"

"No. You?"

"No."

I've never been much of a conversationalist without a few beers in me, and Karen was giving the distinct impression that she regretted coming to dinner.

"How long you been in Korea?" I asked, aiming the question at both of them. They didn't seem to like each other, and whenever one spoke, the other turned to look at the TV.

Karen answered first: "A year, pretty much."

"So you're almost done?"

"Yeah. Extended my contract for three months, though. Don't know why."

"Okay…" I said, before I caught her glancing towards Thomas. She seemed angry at him, and he at her, only in a different way. He was trying to act as though only she was angry.

When it was obvious Karen would say no more, I asked, "What about you, Thomas? How long you been in Korea?"

"Six months," he said. "Well, six and a half. Five and a half to go. And believe me, son, I'm countin' the days."

"Sounds like you really like the place."

"Oh yeah, what's not to like? The smells, the sounds, the delightful people… Korea's a barrel of laughs, Alexander. A wonderful place. And Charleston is even better. You met Mr. Park, right? This is a whole fuckin' country full of Mr. Parks. Literally *and* figuratively."

"Jesus," I said, imagining more than one of him. If I

even had to meet five or six Mr. Parks, I'd probably jump on a plane to another country.

"What did you think of him?" Thomas asked.

"Makes my skin crawl," I said. "His smile is one of the most repugnant things I've ever witnessed."

"And the great thing is that you've just met him. You met *nice* Parky. Once you get to know him, he'll do everything in his power to fuck you in the ass. Remember that contract you signed?" I said I did, of course. "Well, that ain't worth shit, Alexander. That ain't worth shit. And the stuff your recruiter told you before you signed the contract? The stuff you think they'll stick to, even if it's not in the contract... That ain't worth shit, either. And it's not just Parky, or Charleston – it's Korea. This is a country dragged ass-backward out of the third world. They've got money and fancy cars and shit, but they're still cavemen. They didn't develop the morals to deal with this shit."

I looked at him, shocked by what I'd heard. It didn't seem right to be talking so viciously about a country, or rather a group of people. If I'd heard this kind of talk back in Scotland, I'd have been disgusted.

Thomas took a big gulp of beer. He looked a little angry thinking about Mr. Park and the school, but at the same time I could tell he was happy to have someone listen to him. He obviously liked to talk and wasn't getting Karen's ear on a daily basis.

"You see, in Korea you're *owned*. I mean, Mr. Park legally *owns* you. He owns your soul. Like a fuckin' slave or something."

"Come on..." I prodded, laughing a little. I looked at Karen, expecting her to tell me Thomas was talking shit. "Karen?"

"Basically," she said. "Yeah."

"Alright, I mean, he's not gonna whip you and you're

not workin' in the fields or nothing, but you're owned nonetheless. You have to do pretty much anything he says, and if you say no: *boom*, deportation."

"Deportation? You're shitting me." Thomas closed his eyes and shook his head. "How?"

"I told you. He *owns* you. Under Korean law, he literally owns you. If he decides to let you go, you can't fight it. You're out of a job, and out of the country. He can tell your next employer not to employ you. He can blacklist you. He can call immigration and you'll have only a day or two to get your shit together and get the fuck out of this hole. The law is totally on his side. We have no fuckin' rights."

"And what if I'm a fantastic employee? What if I kiss ass and suck up to this greasy prick? What then?"

"Then you'll be fine. Do your year and move on to a better school. Or, if you're smart like me, you'll take your salary, your severance pay – which, by the way, you probably won't get; I'll come back to that later – and get the fuck out of Korea.

"But let me tell you, Alexander, you probably won't suck up to him. Maybe you did that back in Ireland..." He grinned again. "...but it ain't so easy here. Mr. Park is a scumbag. Simple as that. And he'll use you like he used me and Karen and Chuck and Scott. All of us. We all got lied to, brought halfway around the world, and cheated. Parky fucks us every day."

"How so?"

"How many hours did your recruiter tell you you'd be working?"

"Nine-to-five with breaks. Plus overtime for anything else"

"Bullshit. You'll be working nine-to-eight, at least, and one break a day. You never get overtime. They'll make up rules and fudge reports and do everything to stop you getting overtime. Besides, you'll be lucky if you even get your salary on time."

"Why?"

"They get interest for paying you late. They'll take bills and fees from your salary, too, and that shit don't add up. You're paying for health insurance and I guarantee that if you go to the hospital you'll find out the school never handed the money over. I got stuck with a two million Won bill two months back 'cause Parky never paid my insurance for me. Took the money and kept it."

"What? Sue him!"

"Ain't no litigation culture in Korea, Alexander. This ain't like America, or even Ireland." He smiled. "But seriously, you can't sue someone older than you, or richer than you. It just doesn't happen. Especially if you're a foreigner."

I shook my head and looked into my beer. This was an awful start to my adventure. I really didn't want to believe Thomas, and a part of me refused to take his words as absolute truth. He certainly liked talking and most of what he said sounded too over-the-top to be true. Maybe he'd had a bad experience, and it was likely that I would go through the same thing, but I wouldn't resign myself to it just yet. You can't travel so far and give up so readily.

We continued to talk about Korea for the rest of the evening. Thomas was extremely negative but appeared to let up a little when he realised how bad he was making me feel. I think he knew that I'd eventually come to see Korea the same way he did and that there was no point in forcing his views on me. Karen mostly kept quiet, but after a few beers she lightened up and laughed whenever we stopped talking about Korea. She seemed outgoing and enthusiastic when she talked about travelling through

South East Asia, which she was planning to do with the money she saved working at Charleston.

We ate for about three hours, going through dozens of little plates of side dishes and bigger plates of mixed vegetables and miscellaneous meat and seafood. It all tasted the same, but it wasn't bad. Everything was red and vaguely spicy, except for a big pancake-like dish that we tore apart with chopsticks. Thomas called it "pajeon" and explained that they referred to the restaurant as the "Pajeon Place" for that reason. There was plenty of kimchi – the food that I'd eaten on the plane, and whose smell had since haunted me. It really had a nice taste but stunk to high hell.

The booze was what I remembered most from that first night. The beer tasted like cat piss – worse even than the cheap Scottish or American brews that I'd consumed as an impoverished, alcoholic student. It wasn't undrinkable, but it was impossible to enjoy. The flavour was utterly artificial, and I suspected that nothing organic had ever come near a Korean brewery. Alongside our beer there was soju. Soju, I was informed, is a liquor that's made with rice. It really doesn't have much of a taste, which makes it far easier to drink than any other liquor. It was like drinking stale water, only with every shot my brain melted a little more.

I really didn't feel the effects of the alcohol for a while. It was only when I stood up and asked where the toilets were that I was suddenly hit by drunkenness. I looked around and realised that the restaurant was full. I'd been so engrossed in talking to Thomas and Karen that I hadn't even noticed. Now, though, there were dozens of businessmen in cheap, shiny suits, all drinking shots of soju and laughing loudly. There were a few women at the tables, all in short skirts and blouses – all looking desperate to impress, and all being grab-assed by the already red-faced, drunk businessmen.

When I stood up, Thomas pointed me in the direction of the toilet. It was past the kitchen and outside. I made my way between all the tables of drunk people and their hundreds of bottles of soju and stacks of dirty plates. They were all so loud that they had to shout across the room to order more food or drink.

I pushed open the heavy metal door and walked into a little dark alleyway, and then found the toilet. It was a hole in the wall with a urinal and one stall. The urinal was exposed not only to the toilet, but to the street, and, when the door was open, to the inside of the restaurant. I didn't fancy urinating in front of so many people, so I opened the door to the stall. Inside, there was a small trough in the ground – a device known as a "squatter." It was filthy, of course, and there was a small handle beside it for flushing. At the back of the stall there was a little yellow basket for depositing used tissue paper, and all over were puddles of urine. The whole place reeked of faeces. I spent a few seconds trying to figure out how one might use a squatter, and then gave up and decided on the urinal.

As I peed into the disgusting, decades-unwashed urinal, a girl walked into the toilet. I was embarrassed. I didn't like urinating in front of other people – especially women. She turned and looked into a broken mirror behind me, swaying back and forth and making strange wailing sounds. I could tell she was about to be sick, and I tried my best to finish and leave, but I'd drunk a lot beer and my bladder was full.

Before I could finish peeing, the girl stumbled towards me and put one arm around my waist, pressing me almost against the grimy wall. I struggled to keep going, not wanting to pee on the ground, which was already soaked. Then she swung around me and vomited into the urinal.

I moved to one side and tried to pee around her head, but it was too late.

I finished and backed away, looking for a sink to wash my hands. Of course, I didn't know then that washing one's hands is something that's rarely done in Korea. There was no sink, so I stared at the girl as she slumped back against the side of the stall, hair dripping piss and vomit onto her blouse, her legs splayed open, and one high heel hanging off. It was a sorry sight, but there was nothing to do, so I reeled away and went back inside.

CHAPTER FOUR

I woke up the following morning to the most awesome bright light. It was insufferably bright, in fact, and hurt my head tremendously. I could hear a terrible pounding and I wasn't sure if it was the headache or the light making me crazy, but after a minute of lying there, I realised it was my door.

"Dude!" Thomas said, laughing, when I opened the door. "Holy shit!"

"Fuck off," I told him. "What the fuck are you makin' that goddamn racket for? Banging on my door at this hour…"

I looked down at myself as I said this, and the strangest thing happened. It was almost as though I flew up and out of my body and looked down upon myself from a place by the ceiling. I could see Thomas at the door, wearing a polo shirt and slacks, laughing and looking away, and there was me – my hair was wild and bedheaded, I was stooped from the hangover, and I was naked except for my boxer shorts. Worse, I was partially covered in vomit, and there was red chilli paste smeared on my stomach. On the floor around my feet there were a dozen oranges, a few chilli peppers, and a giant carving knife.

"Er, I just woke up, Thomas. I'll come knock on your door in half an hour…"

"Dude, what the fuck?" He was still laughing. "We gotta work in fifteen minutes."

"Okay," I said. "I'll meet you there."

"Do you even know where we're at? Do you know where the school is?"

"I'll figure it out!" I shouted and slammed the door in his face.

What a goddamn mess, I thought. First day of work and I'm hungover and half-naked in front of a co-worker. If that had been Karen at the door she could have sued me for sexual assault. Now Thomas could go around telling everyone in town that I'm an alcoholic pervert who rubs himself with chilli peppers.

I got dressed, puked twice, and walked outside, assuming that I'd remember where I was. I had no recollection of coming back to the apartment or even leaving the restaurant. All I remembered was the scene immediately outside the school – a Baskin Robins and a Tous les Jour bakery. The problem was that there were thousands of them in Daegu. If I walked and found the wrong one, I'd probably never make it back to my apartment. I'd probably wander the streets of Daegu until I was old and had learned the language but forgotten my identity – an elderly white man, so immersed in Korean life that no one even stared at him or shouted "hello!" when he shuffled by, soju bottle in hand.

There was a giant road outside my door. One direction led east and the other west. I wasn't sure which way to go, but it was too hot to stand around and decide. The sun beat down ferociously as people stared at me. Several of them spat on the ground by my feet and I had to jump out of the way twice. I headed east and found myself outside Baskin Robins in fifteen minutes.

"Why you late?" Mr. Park asked me. He wasn't smiling.

"Jetlag," I said. It was an unconvincing lie. I hadn't showered, shaved, or brushed my teeth. Soju oozed through my skin and polluted the already filthy air around me. He knew I'd been drinking, and we were both beginning to realise that I was still a little drunk. "I'm still on Scottish time."

"Don't happen again!" he shouted, and walked away, shaking his head.

Then a short, fat woman of maybe thirty approached me, grinning dumbly. "Hello Alexander teacher!" she said in a voice that was far too loud. She wore a tasteless but probably expensive grey and pink suit. She was horribly ugly, but I didn't feel sorry for her. I felt the ugliness came from something inside her – an inner malice that manifested itself as puffy eyes and a shapeless jaw. Everything about her said she'd sucked dick to get the job, and that she was struggling to hold onto it. I couldn't look her in the eye because she embodied a hopelessness that frightened me.

"Morning."

"Come with me please teacher," she said. Her voice was chillingly cheerful. I realised that she was Debbie, the incompetent supervisor that Thomas and Karen had warned me about the night before.

I followed her through to a glass conference room in the little foyer and sat on an expensive black sofa.

There was a glass coffee table in front of us, covered with Charleston information packs for parents. Around the tiny room there were textbooks that I later discovered were only for display. Very little was taught at Charleston.

"How are you teacher?" Debbie asked me.

"My head's pounding," I said. "And I think I'm about to puke."

"What?"

"Nothing. Doesn't matter."

Debbie pulled out a giant ring-binder full of guides to teaching and spent the following two hours reading each page to me. She didn't add anything or ask me anything to check my comprehension. She just read loudly. I was in agony as the hangover tightened its grip, and I really did think I was going to vomit. The air conditioning in the foyer didn't quite make its way into the conference room, and the heat was sweltering. Debbie's hair was plastered across her forehead, but she didn't seem to notice. I kept sighing loudly to signal my displeasure with the situation, but she didn't pay any attention. After a while, I amused myself by correcting some of her mistakes. There were too many massive pronunciation errors to correct all of them, but I corrected enough to keep things interesting. After that I corrected things she'd gotten right, hoping that in future she'd say them incorrectly.

When she was done, I had to watch all the teachers teaching their classes. It was absurd. Everything was so stupid. The only good teachers were Thomas and Karen, and they spoke no Korean and made little effort. They just had fun with the kids, and the kids picked up language as they went along. The Korean teachers stood there and spoke Korean, and then had the kids repeat words over and over. Most of the time what they taught was actually wrong. A woman called Sonya was teaching shapes to one class and kept saying "ovar" instead of "oval."

Korean people generally have a lot of trouble with *r* sounds, but then when she wrote it on the white board for the kids to see, she spelled it "ovar," too. I didn't correct her. I didn't care enough. Besides, in another classroom one of the teachers was busy telling four-year olds to say, "I am name is…"

By lunchtime I had vomited once in the tiny stalls of the children's restroom and twice outside on the street, hidden behind one of the bright-coloured school buses. Despite all that, I was feeling much better when the bell went at twelve-fifteen. I had emptied my stomach and was ready for food again.

Thomas took me through to the school kitchen, where an old Korean woman – indistinguishable from any other old Korean woman with her permed hair, floral blouse, baggy pants, arm-warmers, and look of absolute contempt for the world around her – was filling metal trays with food. It was different from what I'd eaten at the Pajeon Place. It didn't look nearly as appetising.

I took my tray and metal chopsticks and trudged through to one of the classrooms, which at lunchtime became a canteen for the teachers. They looked ridiculous sitting on chairs that were too small even for the children. Thomas walked off in the other direction and I asked him where he was going.

"You'll find out tomorrow, dude," he said. "We gotta work through lunch, too."

I sat down among the Korean teachers, who ate without talking, yet still managed to be incredibly loud. They slapped their tongues around their mouths and slurped horrendously while I stared like an idiot at the tray in front of me. It was an entirely different concept to what I was accustomed. Obviously I'd come to Korea to experience different things, but when battling a hangover

I found it difficult to stare at a tray filled with squid tentacles and a soup that looked like it was made from piss, seaweed, and tiny little yellow vaginas.

In the middle of the afternoon, Thomas had a well-earned break from classes. He had an entire hour of leisure time although, strictly speaking, he was meant to stay in school and prepare. But free time was so rare and precious at Charleston that the foreign teachers took each and every opportunity to get outside and away from the children.

I was meant to be observing Liz's class as it said on my schedule, but Thomas was quite insistent upon my skipping class.

"It's my first day…" I protested.

"Man, I've been here six months!" Thomas argued. "I'll say I tricked you. It was my fault. And besides, they won't even notice… How many times have Debbie or Mr. Park come to make sure you were observing the right class?"

"None."

"Then come on, let's go get coffee."

We went outside into the heat, which was becoming oppressive with the passing of the afternoon, and turned right. The main road that led to our apartments was left onto the highway that stretched from one end of the Daegu to the other and was lined with big stores and banks. To the right it was smaller businesses – bars and convenience stores and restaurants. All the buildings were small and dilapidated. The road was dirty and crowded with parked cars and fast-moving motorcycles. Piles of cardboard were stacked by the edges of the road and there was no pavement.

We turned a corner and went onto an even smaller street with smaller buildings and fewer restaurants and bars, and there seemed to be some kind of dump behind a shoddily built fence. Old men and women were sifting through the trash for something.

One building was modern and shiny. A sign above the door – written in English, like all places with high prices – said "Fruu." It was a fancy, hip coffee bar in the middle of an old, poor neighbourhood. Cool jazz played and trees grew from the floor. Everything was green or white, and looked spotless. It was the exact opposite of what I'd seen outside.

We went through to a conservatory and sat on wicker chairs at a glass table. A tree grew through the floor here, too. Everything inside was so pretty, yet beyond the three glass walls lay Daegu – a squalid, ugly wreck of a city. Cheap Korean cars – all identical – jostled for parking spaces, and the dump just ran wild with old people and their carts. I kept expecting to see stray dogs join them, but there were seemingly no dogs in Korea. I hadn't seen one since arriving. The ground looked dirty, like if you fell you'd never get your hands clean. People spat on it indiscriminately. Old men occasionally stopped by to urinate against a wall or a tree, and once an old lady squatted behind a pile of tires.

Thomas opened the glass doors and let the air in. It was nasty polluted air, but air nonetheless, and it cooled us as we sat just out of the sun. We ordered two expensive caramel-loaded coffees. Thomas said we'd need these each day to see out the rest of our contracts.

"Do you come here every day?" I asked.

"No," Thomas said. "Only the days I get breaks." He looked over my shoulder. "And you're about to see why."

Seconds later the sliding door to the conservatory opened and a gorgeous barista walked in. She was cute as hell in her apron, with her short skirt and dumb English t-shirt, and her giant Nike trainers. She was curvier than the average Asian girl, and she was showing plenty of leg. The oversized trainers gave her an added cute-point.

Thomas looked her hard in the eyes when he said thank you in Korean and asked for an ashtray. "Jaeddeori," he said, softly, and I wondered who this guy was... He spoke like the smoothest ladies' man, but I wouldn't have guessed that from anything he'd said earlier. The smile didn't come off his face until well after she'd gone back to the other room and brought him an ashtray.

He passed me a cigarette and lit up, and we sat in the conservatory, listening to cool jazz, sipping our drinks and bonding over nothing in particular.

At the end of the day I taught one class. That was my training over. Two hours of listening to Debbie talk and seven hours of watching teachers teach. I'd really learned nothing except that appearance was all that mattered. The kids clearly weren't learning much, and most of the Korean teachers spoke almost no English. The whole thing was a joke. If I decided to jump about and spout gibberish I would have been considered a good teacher... as long as I smiled and wore a tie.

I was painfully unprepared but there was no backing out now. This was what I had travelled thousands of miles to do. It was my new job. Alexander, pathetic loser turned responsible teacher. I psyched myself up and tried to strut confidently into the classroom, but then found Mr. Park, Debbie, and three Korean teachers sitting at the back of a room of twelve ten-year olds. I froze. It was one thing to have kids watch me, but *adults*?

I stood in front of the class and tried to copy what I'd seen the others do and mix it with what I'd been told to teach. I had two pages of a textbook to teach for forty-five minutes, and after six or seven minutes, those pages were finished. I didn't know what to do, and the kids weren't happy. Mr. Park was shaking his head. He was red with fury. An important aspect of teaching in Korea is that the kids must look like they're learning. If it looks that way, fine. It doesn't matter whether they learn a thing. These kids weren't learning, and they looked bored. I tried playing games, but with the director, supervisor, and three Korean teachers in the class they were too scared to move. None of them would say a word.

I began to realise that the kids really didn't want to be there. It was early evening and they'd been in school since eight in the morning. After school they went to academy after academy, learning nothing and getting bored. I thought before coming to Korea that the kids would be eager to learn a language that would open realms of possibilities in their lives, but evidently I was had been absurdly naïve.

I looked at Debbie, pleading with my eyes for some help. This was my first class and I'd received no useful advice or specific instructions on how to teach. Most of what I knew came from the information Thomas and Karen had given me between classes. Debbie stared at me stupidly and then looked down at her notes. She didn't know what to do, either.

When they got bored enough, the children realised that they could act up. None of the Korean teachers attempted to control them, even when it became obvious that I didn't know what to do. One boy – whose name was Thunder – jumped up on the table and began running in circles, pretending to be an airplane, as the others laughed and screamed.

"Thunder!" I shouted, after spending twenty seconds staring in disbelief and struggling to remember his stupid name. "Get down! Stop it! Thunder! Sit down!" I threw every simple command I knew at him, but it did no good. I wanted to scream curse words at him and explain that he was ruining me in front of the people who now owned my soul, but he didn't know a word of English. I didn't speak his language and I wasn't physically threatening him, so he wasn't about to listen to me.

Another kid jumped on the table and began running with Thunder. This child's name was Rion, which was a misspelling of Lion. I shouted at both of them in futile despair. By the time Rion picked up the CD player that had been sitting on the table and held it above his head in a Godzilla-like grasp, I wasn't shouting. I was pleading with him to not cost me my job. Didn't he have any sense of decency? Wouldn't he listen to reason and spare me? I couldn't take it anymore.

The other kids laughed and screamed as Rion threw the CD player down upon the floor, spraying its brains across the linoleum. Only then, only after I was ruined and branded forever as a degenerate without the ability to even stop a small child from misbehaving, and thus destroying any potential respect or trust that might have developed between myself and anyone at the school, did Debbie and Mr. Park intervene. I swear those bastards were whispering encouragement to the students. I bet they made them misbehave and told them to ignore the foreigner, and to cause as much damage as possible. They wanted me to look like a damn fool, and they succeeded.

After school we all walked outside in the same sombre silence as we'd done the previous evening. I was exhausted even though I'd sat around all day doing nothing. Just being around children for that length of time was enough to leave me aching for bed. I could hardly imagine how Thomas and Karen felt, as they'd been working the entire time.

Thomas uttered one simple word as we moved out onto the street: "Beer?"

I didn't say anything, but veered right with him as Karen shook her head and walked off home. She didn't even say "good-bye."

Thomas and I walked silently into the same restaurant as we had the previous night and found it once again empty. I guessed that eight o'clock was probably the opening hour and that we were beating the crowds by a small margin.

As we sat on the small blue plastic chairs, Thomas let out a mighty groan. "God…" he sighed. "I *hate* that place!"

I didn't know what to say. He'd gone on and on the night before about how much he hated Charleston and Korea and Mr. Park and I didn't want to query him further on these subjects. Besides, he didn't seem like the sort of guy who needed prompting in order to spill his mind.

Before either of us had managed to start any sort of conversation, the long-torso'd woman was standing by our table and Thomas had a big smile on his face. It seemed sincere. I could tell he actually liked the restaurant, in spite of his hatred for everything else. He said a word in Korean that would later become very familiar to me: "Maekju," meaning "beer." Then he said a few other words – including "soju" - and the woman smiled at what seemed to be his crude grasp of Korean. She quickly rushed off to bark orders at someone in the kitchen and returned momentarily with two big bottles of Hite beer and a little green bottle of Charm soju.

Thomas poured the soju into each glass and topped it off with beer. "This is how I like it," he explained. "Everyone else does shots – and that's fine – but damn, if soju ain't the nastiest drink. Mix it with Hite, though, and it's alright. Here, try."

"I don't mind soju," I told him. "Just tastes like stale

water."

"Fucking Irish."

He handed me a drink and told me to say, "Geonbae," which means "cheers" in Korean. I told him how to say "cheers" in French, and he laughed. We were actually talking about something other than how much we hated our jobs.

"So, *Lucky Charms*, what's your deal?"

"Huh?"

"What d'you like to do?"

I laughed awkwardly. "I don't know. Drink?"

Thomas said, "Geonbae" and finished his soju-beer mix in one shot. "I can see that," he said. "What else? I figure you as the bookish type."

"Yeah," I said. "That's about right. I read quite a bit."

Thomas snorted and looked away. "I used to read when I was your age." He laughed a little and I knew he was just fucking around. Thomas seemed like a weird guy. I liked him, though. He had a strange sense of humour, as though he had once upon a time been a pretentious little kid and now looked back with some sort of good-humoured self-loathing. He was a cynic, but ironically so. A reformed hipster.

"How old *are* you?"

"Older than you by a bit, Lucky Charms."

I looked at him, unsatisfied. He wasn't old enough to be coy about his age.

"Twenty-seven."

"Twenty-seven? Jesus, that isn't old. Come back in ten years and I'll accept your attitude."

"Ha! Older than you. How old are you, anyway? Fifteen, sixteen?"

"Twenty-two," I said. It was true. I had not long turned twenty-two.

"Wow, a baby, huh? I remember when I was your

age…" Thomas looked off into space with a grin on his face. I could tell that he was both fucking with me and seriously looking back on his younger years. "Yeah, I used to *read* stuff. I bet you write or play guitar or something, too. You look like the type."

"Yeah, that's me. I play guitar, write a little bit."

"Figures."

"You didn't do anything creative back in the day?"

"Hells yeah, son! I *wrote* back in the day! I used to be into the whole punk thang!" He was adopting some faux-ghetto persona. I'd noticed it the previous evening – he occasionally slipped into what I assumed was a knowingly poor attempt at hip-hop talk, but without letting on that he was kidding. "We used to put out these underground magazines, writin' 'bout politics and shit… Damn, we thought we were all that."

"What about now? You're too old for reading and writing, huh?"

"When you get to my age…" he began, grinning stupidly, "you realise what it's all about."

"And what's that?"

"Money, I guess. Life's too short to care about stuff. Get laid, get paid…" He sounded like he was going somewhere but he trailed off mid-sentence, looking almost bored with the conversation. "Shit, man, what you wanna eat?"

"I don't know Korean food yet. You choose."

"Yeah, okay… They got some kinda spicy chicken shit. It's pretty good. It's hot, though. You got spicy food in Ireland?"

"That's fine with me."

Thomas called over the woman and ordered the allegedly spicy chicken. This time he did more pointing at the menu and less speaking. He laughed a lot, obviously embarrassed by his inability to speak adequate Korean.

When he was done and the woman had disappeared into the kitchen, I asked him what he did for a living – other than teaching – because he had previously become distracted and changed the subject. I didn't get the impression that he deliberately changed the subject. He seemed to be hyper-active and have trouble concentrating.

"I'm a computer systems analyst," he said. "A straight up geek, yo!" He looked genuinely proud of this fact.

"'Computer systems analyst'? How did you end up in Korea?"

Thomas let out a fake sigh. He seemed to enjoy talking and then pretending that anything he was asked was a burden to answer. "My mother was Korean. I was adopted as a baby and raised in America, thankfully. I guess I never spent more than a year in this shit-hole until I made the mistake of coming back." He stopped and took a sip of his beer/soju. "Yeah, I guess my dad was some GI who knocked up some Korean skank, and as soon as I was born she passed me off to an orphanage. It's for the best, really. I mean, imagine growing up here! How fucked up are these people?! You know this place has the highest suicide rate in the world? Seriously. Look it up. And look at me! Do I look Korean to you? Growing up here would've been mad difficult."

"You got lucky."

"Hells yeah, Lucky Charms. This place is the asshole of Asia. The *asseoul* of Asia!" He laughed at his own stupid joke. "To think, if I looked Korean I probably wouldn't have ended up being chucked in the orphanage. I'd probably have grown up here and turned into an asshole like the rest of them. But my momma looked at me and thought I was too white… Shit, imagine that…"

"So I take it you didn't come back to find her."

"Hells no, I never wanna see that woman again! I came

back because my *real* parents were naïve enough to think that Korea was some fucking paradise or something… Shit, they got the baby they could never have and decided Korea was heaven! They've never been, of course, or else they would've known.

"So shit, I grew up being told, 'You're Korean *and* American and you should be proud and shit,' and then I come here and find out that, a) Korea fucking sucks, and b) that Koreans *hate* white people. These fuckers look at me and spit on me - sometimes literally, sometimes figuratively - and if I try and explain that I'm one of them - which, incidentally, I now realise I'm *not*! - they don't believe me. Which is fine. I don't wanna be Korean. But damn, it's a shock to the system to come all the way around the world and find out you're not who you were told you were. I wish my parents just told me that I came outta my momma's vagina."

"You're a weird guy, Thomas."

"Geonbae!"

We finished off the first bottles of beer and soju and ordered more. Our food arrived soon after, and by the time we'd finished the various spicy dishes we had killed another two bottles of soju and four bottles of beer.

It was only when I staggered back into the bathroom to urinate that I recalled the girl from the night before. I laughed so hard I couldn't piss for a minute or two, and when I stumbled back into the restaurant – not realising how drunk I was – I told Thomas. I wasn't sure if he believed me or not, but he launched into another rant about Korea:

"These Ko-reans…" He extended the world contemptuously with each beer. "…can't drink for shit. They go out seven nights a week and get blind-fucking-drunk but they can't handle it. Man, it must be genetic or some shit. I don't know… I mean, you can't imagine how fucked these guys get. Well, actually, *you* can – you *saw* it… They get carried home night after night. Guys and girls, all wasted. It's a drinking culture and no one here can actually handle their booze. It's why they're all in bed by ten o'clock."

"Shit," I said, "Sounds like Scotland." Thomas sneered and held up another empty soju bottle. Then realising for the first time what had happened, I asked, "What time is it?" I looked at my own watch after asking the question and answered myself: "Ten o'clock." I had gone for one single beer to deal with the depressing end to my day, and now I was drunk. The time wasn't important – I could live with little sleep – but I'd been drinking for two hours without even thinking about it.

"You wanna head home, huh?" Thomas asked. "I thought you Irish could handle your liquor."

"I want to make a better impression tomorrow," I said. "I can't be hungover two days in a row. God, I actually have to *teach* tomorrow morning."

"You *think* you can't go in hungover two consecutive days, but in fact that's how Korea works. Everybody does it."

"Well, I don't function very well when I'm hungover. I'd rather get a decent night's sleep and do my drinking on the weekend."

"That's gay."

"Perhaps, but I think I'm done for tonight."

"Alright, alright… I thought you were cool, Lucky Charms, but I guess you're as bad as those rotten English."

We laughed and stood up. The restaurant was busy, but men and women in business suits were already being carried out into the street to vomit or trying desperately to shove their car keys into the door of their Hyundai.

At the counter – by the front door – the long-torso'd

woman told Thomas the price as I fumbled with my wallet. "How much?" I asked. "I don't think I paid anything last night. My money's still here."

"Don't worry, son. I got it last night and I'll get it tonight. Newbies don't pay."

"No, man, I'll pay. It's cool."

"Listen," he said, reeling away from the counter and out into the street. "I remember my first month. It's tough being here. Once you've got your first paycheque you can buy me a beer or some shit, but until then I've got you covered."

"Cheers," I said. "I appreciate it."

"No problem. Anyway, fuck it, Korean food is mad cheap. Only time you spend real money is when you want something Western, and you'll get the craving soon enough."

"I dunno, man. I quite like Korean food."

"Yeah, it's alright, but it all tastes the same. You'll get bored." We each lit up a cigarette and then Thomas began to laugh. "Just try and control yourself on the way home…"

"Huh?"

"You don't remember, right?"

"No…"

"You were hilarious last night, dude. Hilarious. You kept trying to buy oranges and chillies and shit. You kept throwing money at this old woman on the ground and she was all confused and telling you to go away."

"Jesus, that's embarrassing."

"Nah, it's cool. It's what Korea's all about – being drunk and acting like an asshole."

CHAPTER FIVE

I woke up the next day and lay in the blinding light for several minutes, terrified to move. I couldn't tell whether or not I was hungover. When I rolled over and looked at my little travel alarm clock, I realised that I was going to be late for work. It was fifteen minutes before I was meant to be in class. I jumped out of bed and grabbed the clothes I'd left on the floor the previous night, and then quickly ran out the door into the already sweaty heat of the day.

On my way to work I finally realised that I was hungover and cursed soju and Korean beer for their ability to get me hungover without even have gotten properly drunk. It wasn't the worst hangover in the world, but it was enough to make a difficult day even worse. As I walked my head sank downwards from the headache and the heat.

At the office I had a minute to sit down and rest. My seat was between Thomas' and Sonya's. Sonya was busy looking at herself in a mirror while Thomas had yet to arrive at school. I remembered him saying something the day before about it being the only day he'd actually arrived at work on time.

I had spoken to Sonya a few times on my first day and I liked her far more than the other teachers, although admittedly I didn't know them well. Liz seemed like a bitch, Lydia lazy, Sunny stupid, Jasmine and Lauren ditzy, and Debbie an irritating whore. Sonya was far older than the rest of them and seemed to spend more time preparing for her lessons, which was fortunate as she was my partner teacher for many of the morning classes. She enjoyed being bossy and told me exactly what to do in each lesson, which I needed because I was so grossly inexperienced and unqualified for the job.

The morning went better than I could have expected. The fear of failure scared me into action, and while the classes were dumb and amateur, they weren't bad enough to get me fired. Debbie sat through each of my first four classes, and although she had to discipline the kids for me at times, she didn't have too many complaints. She asked for me to be louder and more active, and I said I understood.

With each relatively successful class, my confidence grew and my hangover dissipated. By lunch I was doing much better, and by my afternoon break – which coincided with Thomas' – I was feeling strong enough to go for coffee.

We went to Fruu to ogle the waitress whose name was now Hot Coffee Girl. We talked about books and movies and politics for half an hour, and then went back to finish our day.

Afternoon classes were tougher because the kids were older and had already spent most of their day in school. For them, Charleston was extra schooling. It was one of the many hagwons to which their parents sent them and someplace they just didn't want to be. They viewed classes with the native English teacher as time in which they could goof around instead of being forced to learn. But they were a little easier because Debbie was no longer observing me.

Many of the afternoon kids were badly behaved and I sent them to Debbie. I really didn't want to because I wanted her to think I was capable of controlling a class by myself. Unfortunately, I didn't have a choice. The little bastards were killing me. Even with my hangover more or less vanquished I couldn't raise my voice loud enough to command their attention. They just ran around the class, and I couldn't bring myself to grab them and spank them like I'd seen the Korean teachers do. That sort of thing would get you arrested in Scotland.

In between classes, Karen asked me how "the little brats" were, and I told her I'd sent a bunch of them to Debbie. She frowned and told me to use that as a last resort. "She beats them. So does Mr Park. Send your kids to the office and they'll come back with bruises."

And she was right... I thought the kids were crying because they'd been shouted at. But instead, they were crying because they'd been beaten. I began to notice the bruises. I soon decided never to send another kid to the office again.

I asked Karen after another class if we should report Charleston for beating children. She laughed and told me, "Don't be silly. In Korea, everyone beats children. Mothers, fathers, aunts, uncles... I've seen old men on the street hit kids! In schools it's just as bad. The Korean teachers hit the kids and the directors hit the kids. The directors are worse, actually. They have sticks they use for it. We're lucky here that it's only Parky and Debs. In the public schools, I've heard it's just about all the teachers. Even some of the foreigners get away with it."

"You're coming downtown tonight," Thomas told me between our last classes. "I want you to meet some people. They're the only cool people you'll meet in Korea, so you've got no choice."

"Downtown? I don't know, man. I've got to work tomorrow."

"Come on, Lucky Charms. Work here don't mean shit. You didn't come to Korea to work, right? Hell no. You came to have fun."

I relented and said I'd come and Thomas looked happy. After school we went home and he told me to bang on his door in half an hour.

Always prompt, I banged on Thomas' door exactly thirty minutes later and he didn't answer for a long time, so I banged again. I could hear loud hip-hop music coming from inside. He came to the door several minutes later with a towel around his waist, having been in the shower.

"Damn man, you're fast."

"Sorry."

"Damn straight! Now come in."

I walked awkwardly into my new friend's apartment and took my shoes off. The place was basically the same as mine, except for a few items of foraged furniture, and a few plants that Thomas explained were given to him by "random Korean girls."

"Beer?" he asked, but before I could answer he'd already opened a bottle and was pouring two glasses of cheap Korean beer. He handed me one of the little glasses, which was obviously stolen from a bar because it had the same logo as the big bottle of beer – Cass.

Thomas went into the bathroom with his beer and some clothes and came out dressed. He was wearing much the same as he did at school – long shorts, a polo shirt, and a baseball cap. We pounded our drinks as Thomas frantically switched between songs – all of which sounded the same to me. I despise hip-hop, but Thomas seemed to be getting very animated just listening to it. We talked about work and drank some more beer and soju.

"We're waiting for Jonathon," Thomas said. "He's a good guy. He has a car and he's been living in Korea for five years. Mina - his girlfriend - is easily the hottest girl I've seen in this country, but she's a total slut."

"He's a soldier?"

"No, medic. Gets paid a ton for a few hours work, then gets drunk every night. He cheats on Mina all the time."

"Sounds like a nice guy…"

"Yeah, I guess he's a dick. I think he's been in Korea too long. We call him the White Korean."

Jonathon arrived after twenty minutes. He was a small and skinny white guy, like me, but he had blonde hair and a little beard. While I could have been pegged by a bystander as part of the indie scene in my skinny fit clothes, he could have as easily been pegged as hip-hop in his trendy baggy gear.

"What up?" he asked as he strutted into the room. He looked confident and maybe angry. Certainly, he was determined about something.

"You ready yet?" he barked at Thomas. When he spoke his voice was demanding. I began thinking that maybe Thomas was right. Jonathon had that air of superiority that so many Korean guys seemed to walk with.

"Slow down, man!" Thomas said, coolly.

"No! Let's *go!*" Jonathon's tone flitted now between demanding and whiny.

"I've got to get ready."

"You *are* ready! Look at you!"

"I need to get my game on," Thomas said. He jumped over to his computer and threw on some apparently great hip-hop song and began jumping around even more, hyping himself up for the evening. Pretty soon he was dancing, popping his shoulders and waving his massive arms shamelessly.

Jonathon shook his head and rolled his eyes theatrically. I got the impression this had happened dozens of times before. "Good lord!" he said. Then he looked at me and asked if I was "Alexander from Scotland."

"You like to drink?" he asked.

"Of course."

"Well, then we'll get along fine. Now help me get this bitch in the car and we can *go.*"

Jonathon's car looked pretty much the same as all the other cars on the road, except dirtier and it had an expensive sound system built into the back. Inside, it was filled with junk. There were two boxes of random assorted crap, pairs of rollerblades, clothes, letters with US Military stamps, empty food packages, shoes... There was barely room for me – a small guy – to sit. I ended up perching on top of the clean clothes, after pushing the dirty ones onto the floor, which was also covered in crap, and seemed to be growing some kind of mushroom.

Jonathon turned on the stereo and immediately the speakers exploded into the hardest bass I'd heard outside of a nightclub or concert. The vibrations rippled through my chest and skull as we reversed quickly onto the street and then raced into the night.

We passed beers back and forth. This time they were

cheap Korean stout, which tasted far better than nasty Cass or Hite. Jonathon drove fast and I got to see some of Daegu for the first time. It all looked exactly the same as the little part I had already seen – kalbi restaurants, Western bars, sporting goods retail stores, big ugly apartment buildings. There was so much construction – the city was growing fast enough to watch.

We drove for about twenty-five minutes through the city. Traffic was heavy. People drove aggressively and seemed to rely on their horns as much as their steering wheels. There were dozens of traffic lights, and so it was all very start-stop. We'd be driving at full speed for a minute and then stopped for three.

Eventually we pulled into a small, quiet street with businesses offering things for foreigners – American clothes, haircuts for black people, a travel agent that spoke English. The road was known as the Camp Walker Service Road, as it led to the main gate of the city's biggest American military base.

Jonathon parked the car outside the travel agent and made Thomas and I wait on the street. "Be quiet," he whispered. "I'm going to get ready."

He ran up a flight of stairs and into the upstairs apartment. I asked Thomas why we weren't invited.

"He doesn't want Mina to know we're drinking. She's crazy. Got the Kimchi Rage."

"Kimchi Rage?"

"All Korean girls are crazy. If you fuck with them, they'll go nuts. It's in their blood. We call it the Kimchi Rage."

"*All* Korean girls?"

"Yeah, they seem sweet at first, but then they just blow up in your face. Jonathon's ex – Crystal – found out he was cheating on her and smashed up his car. She wrecked all his stuff and kicked his ass. Kimchi Rage, son!"

"Damn."

"Yeah."

"Wait… She was called Crystal?"

"What can I say? Jonathon isn't exactly picky with the ladies."

Jonathon came down after ten minutes and looked pissed. He'd obviously fought with Mina but wouldn't give us the details. We walked down the road for a while as Thomas cracked jokes about Jonathon, then caught a taxi, which Jonathon directed to the downtown area by asking – in Korean, of course – for the Sam Deok fire station. For some reason I was surprised that he could speak the language even though he'd been living there for years.

In the cab we had more beer and listened to Korean radio. Thomas and Jonathon said horrible things about Korea and about taxi drivers, but the driver didn't seem to notice. He probably knew they were insulting him, but he didn't know what exactly they were saying. I felt sorry for him and refrained from saying anything negative.

"This is one ugly motherfucker!" Jonathon cried, looking right at the guy. "Mean-muggin' me like that!"

Indeed, Jonathon was right. The taxi driver had been staring at him the whole time. Or at least every time he stopped the car.

The taxi stopped outside the fire station and immediately we were standing right in the middle of downtown Daegu. There were more foreigners than I could've imagined. Restaurants were packed and the streets were crowded with people, crashing into one another and staggering drunkenly. I felt immediately claustrophobic. This was even worse than the area around my apartment.

Thomas led the way through the crowds, unashamedly

pushing people out of his way and all the time I followed in his wake, hoping not to get lost. I had no idea how to get home. I knew that with my propensity for getting blackout drunk there was a good chance I'd wake up on the streets of downtown with no idea how to get back.

We wandered down a few narrow streets that were no less busy than the main drag, and climbed a long flight of stairs into a smoke-filled bar at the top of what appeared to be an otherwise derelict building. Thomas led the way across the crowded room to a table against a mirrored wall and introduced me loudly to a small group of foreigners. I sat down and tried not to look nervous as he went to the bar to buy drinks.

Jonathon was the loudest of the group and introduced me to everyone. Much to my embarrassment, they seemed to know me as the guy who got wasted on his first night and puked at work. Thankfully, though, they all appeared to be alcoholics and assured me that getting drunk and going into work hungover was practically expected of foreign teachers.

Uncomfortable with being the centre of attention, I sat down next to Jonathon after the introductions and attempted to talk to him some more, telling myself I'd speak to the others later. He said he had been in Korea for five years, working on an American military base as a medic. He got paid a ridiculous wage to sit around watching TV all day, and at night he went downtown and cheated on Mina. Jonathon listened to hip-hop and dressed and spoke as though he was black. He was the sort of person I'd never have known in another country, but we immediately became close friends. He made me promise to drink with him a minimum of four nights a week.

I worried about Jonathon because he looked so depressed. He was hyper at times, but ultimately very angry at Korea and felt a lot of resentment about having wasted five years in a country he despised. When someone spoke to him he would put on a smile, pop his shoulders, and bounce about in his seat. But in between those moments he would brood silently, always sipping a Jack and coke.

"Why are you still here?" I asked him.

"Mina," he said. "And money." He laughed, then added, "But not necessarily in that order."

After a few drinks I worked up the courage to engage the rest of the group in conversation and learn a little about my new friends.

Annie was a Korean-Canadian girl. Like so many of the English teachers in Daegu she looked Korean but didn't speak Korean, think Korean, or act Korean. She grew up in Canada as a pot-smoking, tree-hugging, feminist vegan who listened to indie music and read books. She'd always dreamed of coming back to the country of her birth, and now she was here she was depressed. In Korea people torture animals before they eat them and women are second class citizens. She enjoyed being away from Canada's racist hicks but hated that she was utterly surrounded by yet more racist hicks in Korea, who treated her and her foreign-looking friends like scum. Annie also was at the disadvantage of being half-black. Her father was an American soldier and she had been put up for adoption because no one could stand looking at a half-black baby. Now she was back in Korea she found herself loathed even more than her white friends once again, and she yearned to get back to good old Canada.

I clicked with Annie more than I did with Jonathon, but Jonathon's pushiness meant I talked more with him. We had nothing in common but he didn't seem to mind. I got the feeling that he liked talking to people with whom he shared no real interests.

Beth was a big blonde girl from Virginia. She was almost a full head taller than me and was nearly double my weight. She was chirpy and seemed to enjoy Korea more than the rest, probably because she was the sort of foreigner Koreans liked – someone they could stare at and mock and have their insults bounce right off. I could tell she didn't like the place all that much but compared to the rest she was a breath of fresh air. She always laughed off the disparaging remarks and said things like, "Oh, come on… It's not all *that* bad." Beth always had a cocktail in her hand, just like the rest of them. We dealt with life the same way.

Jonathon explained to me that when Beth first arrived in Korea she was ditched at the airport by her prospective employers. They had made her pay her own airfare, but when she got to Incheon they saw that she wasn't exactly as slender as they had guessed from the photos she had sent and abandoned her there. Luckily she had a friend in Seoul who helped her survive those first tough days and get another job.

The last member of the tight group was Oliver. Oliver tried hard to be funny, and I sensed in him perhaps the greatest loneliness and the most distaste for Korea. He was half-Korean, although it was harder to tell than with Annie. Annie had Korean eyes along with her dark skin, but there was nothing in Oliver's appearance to say that his mother was another Korean woman knocked up by an American soldier. He – like Jonathon – was bouncy and outgoing at times, and quiet and brooding at others. He always made jokes and it was hard to get a real sense of who he was and what he meant.

We all sat around a filthy table in a hip-hop bar for American soldiers, listening to the worst music I could imagine, and sipping on the strongest drinks I could tolerate. The place was called Effort and that's exactly what it took to tolerate the atmosphere, but we were all drinking rum or Jack Daniels instead of soju, and it made a nice change. Korean booze made me feel like I was about to die.

It was nice being around a little diversity, too. There were dozens of foreigners and only a few Koreans in the bar. Mostly it was military personnel, but quite a few people looked like teachers. You could tell. If a person was black or Hispanic, there was a good chance they were in the military. Koreans could barely tolerate white people teaching their children. When they saw dark-skinned people, they assumed they couldn't speak English. Annie said that everywhere she went people would stare and shout, "African! African! African!" and that not many schools were willing to hire her. Karen had said the same thing.

The military guys were all big, too. They all wore hip-hop attire or military uniform, and at one o'clock they'd disappear as curfew passed and the military police would tour the bars and clubs and round up the ones who were too drunk to make it back to Camp Walker on their own. There were lots of them. It was cheap to drink, and there was evidently nothing to do on base that was better than coming downtown and trying to fuck the local girls.

The teachers were mostly white or Korean-American. They dressed with more diversity than the soldiers, and came from far-flung locations. Although Korean people would scream "American! American! American!" at any white person on the street, a lot of the teachers were from the United Kingdom, Australia, New Zealand, or South Africa.

We sat at the table and talked about Korea and about teaching. Everything was negative. I'd hoped to hear some positive stories. I'd hoped that maybe Thomas and Karen hated Korea just because they had bad jobs, but sadly it seemed that everyone was unhappy. They all had big salaries, but they spent it on booze most nights to get away from the realities of life in a country that didn't want them there. It felt good, though, to talk to these people. Venting to Thomas and Karen was becoming repetitive and it was nice to have another sympathetic ear to bend, or to hear new nightmarish stories from other schools – telling me that at least I wasn't in this on my own.

I ended up talking to Jonathon for most of the night. He didn't come across as particularly intelligent, but he was street-smart and down to earth, and more importantly he was easy to talk to. Aside from his hatred of anything intellectual and his disdain for anything I liked, we seemed to share many of the same views about life. In other words, he was another cynic.

"Everyone leaves, Alex," he told me. "They're all bitches. Man, I hate Korea but I stick it out, y'know? But it's the same old shit, every damn time. Someone comes, they hate it, they leave. I understand. I know. But damn, man, you make a friend, a drinking buddy, a good guy… Then they're gone. Every month I lose a friend. That's no damn way to live, Alex."

"But you make new friends, too. People come and they go."

"Who the fuck wants that? I want people in my life *to stay*. These guys," he gestured at the group, "are good guys. The best. I love them. But they're here for a year, Alex, and I'm probably gonna be here 'til I'm an old man. Shit, Thomas got five months left. Annie got four months. Beth got four. Oliver got six." He shook his head and finished his drink. "What the fuck am I doing in Korea, Alex?"

Jonathon got up and bought us more rum before I could answer his question. Things were getting blurry.

I could no longer hear the dumb rap lyrics and only the beat found its way into my head. Conversations came and went. My ears were struggling to focus on anything. How many times would I go to bed in Korea drunk? I was already sitting on a hundred percent record.

"I dunno why I'm so depressed," Jonathon said, sitting down. "I don't mean to bring you down when you're new here. Shit, it's nothing you don't know already."

"Don't worry. I'm starting to see this place for what it is, and I admire you for putting up with it for so long."

"Amen, brother."

"So why did you come here in the first place? I mean, you're not a teacher, right? You're not a soldier…"

"Same as everyone, man. I was bored, broke, and horny. I mean, I had me some ass in California, boy, yeah I had me some ass! But… I wanted to see the world, man. I wanted to see Asia. I wanted to fuck some fucking Asian pussy, y'know?"

"I know."

"And I *have!* I mean, damn, man! I've had a lotta pussy!" He looked up for a minute and I wasn't sure whether he was thanking some god or looking back through his vagina-filled memories. "I wanted to travel, too, y'know? And I've seen a lotta places… Thailand, Philippines, Japan, China, Vietnam, Taiwan… A lotta places."

"Doesn't sound like Korea's so bad," I said. His banter actually filled me briefly with a sense of hope that I hadn't felt since before arriving in Korea.

"I know, I know." He waved his drink in the air and made a weird face that told me he honestly didn't know why he was so unhappy. "I'm lucky, and I'm always glad I came here, but shit these people are *baaaaad*, man. I mean, you've been here a few days… What d'you think of Korean people? Are they nice? Are they friendly? Are they warm and welcoming?"

"No."

"No!" He spat the word into the air. "Exactly. Are they in any way civilised?"

"Well, there are cultural differences…"

"Bullshit. Culture nothin'! You've seen these people, Alex, you know how it works. They shit and piss on the street, beat you with umbrellas for bein' white! They stare, shout 'foreigner,' lie, cheat, steal…"

"People are fundamentally shit all over the world. In Scotland I'd get bottled or stabbed for walking home the wrong way at night. Seriously. It's not just Korea. This place seems crappy, but it's not exactly hell on earth."

Jonathon thought for a minute. "I hear ya, man. Korea's got its good points. No one's denying that." He sipped his drink. "And I know, I know, you've just come from the West so you're all filled with morals and shit… But let me tell you, man, this place will *change* you. It takes all those manners and values that people fill you with in the West – back in civilisation – and it takes them from you." He mimed the sentence, flailing around as some force robbed him of his humanity.

"I'm a good guy, Alex. I try. But there are times I look at myself and ask who I am. I mean, I would never, ever have said 'Koreans do this' or 'Koreans do that' back in California. Hell no!" He looked disgusted. "I was always so careful. My momma, she said to me, 'If I ever catch you speakin' 'bout another group a people like they's all the same, I'm gonna fuckin' beat yo' ass!' And you know what? She was right. But being in Korea changes you. You can't keep your morals and your common decency, Alex." He poked me in the chest. "It steals them. You're around the most racist people on the planet and they'll get to you. This is where hope came to die. This is the edge of civilisation.

"Hell, I don't even know what right and wrong are anymore!"

We both sat and stared into our drinks.

When we were finished drinking in Effort, the gang departed and staggered out onto the stinking streets. Even in my drunken state I was overwhelmed by the stench of human excrement exuded from the sewers. Downtown was infinitely worse than the area around Charleston, and I couldn't imagine being there when sober.

The streets were busy for one o'clock in the morning, I thought. I was surprised to see cars struggle between pedestrians, who wobbled towards bars, restaurants, or taxis in drunken stupors. It was weird, too, to see foreigners outside. During the day it was rare to see black or white people on the streets, but at night it seemed as though a quarter of the population was non-Korean. Everyone was united in intoxication. The Koreans held their liquor worse and struggled to stand. Many of the men pissed in the street while their girlfriends puked on the road. Their formerly immaculate cheap suits and imitation blouses were covered in spilt drinks and dropped pieces of food. Many of them were youngsters in their late teens and early twenties, dressed in faux hip-hop attire, strutting about embarrassingly. They looked terrified of the big black soldiers but imitated everything they did.

All of the shops were closed, but all along the main drag there were bars and kalbi restaurants waiting for drunks to fleece. Little carts sold cocktails in plastic bags, and people swaggered by with bottles of beer from the myriad convenience stores that remained open.

There was an unpleasantness that went above the stench of the air and the stifling heat. It was worse than the awkwardness of watching Korean people stagger about in t-shirts with poor English they didn't understand

61

or copying and mocking Western culture in the faces of real live Westerners. It wasn't just that Korean people were jumping out of the way of black people in the street, screaming in fear and running away. Something unpleasant existed in the night streets of Daegu – a contempt that ran thicker than that which blighted the city in the daylight.

Every time I saw a Korean-looking girl with a foreign-looking guy, I could feel tension in the atmosphere. Mixed-race couples drew a lot of hate. Street vendors spat at them and other people spoke loudly and hatefully. Groups of arrogant young males would circle the couples and pop their shoulders like they saw Americans do in old movies. Sometimes drunk Korean young men would crash into black guys and then back quickly away with their friends, terrified and proud at the same time. Tomorrow they'd tell their racist little buddies that they beat up some US soldier. The smell of potential violence lingered in the air. It felt as though one little slip could set the streets on fire for days.

When we came to the club street, though, the foreigners were treated as royalty. The hip-hop clubs tried desperately to lend some credibility to their shoddy little venues full of nerdy Korean kids in Fubu gear and dumb DJs in afros and wifebeaters, playing songs by Korean hip-hop artists that blatantly ripped off well-known American songs. It was all cheap and ignorant. I wondered why no one could see the ridiculousness of it. The Korean club scene was a sad parody of something these people saw on TV.

In the clubs everyone would avoid the foreigners but copy them shamelessly. There would be rings of space around any group of black guys, but the Koreans were watching intently, trying to steal their dance moves or drink the same drinks. Some guys upped their game and acted more gangsta than usual, in the hope that some black dude might see him and give his approval – the ultimate street-cred for a sad wannabe.

Outside one of the clubs was a huge sign, displaying house rules in Konglish for the benefit of foreigners:

No admittance on Minors
essentiality bringing identification
Committ no an illegal use of other is name
Committ nodangerous thing a possessor
be forbidden positively refundment
be not a missing lost responsibility
the outside food not carry
No admittance a drinken person
No trespassing and out service uniforum and full
uniforum

At the end of that first night downtown, Jonathon, Thomas, and I sat on the roof of a club called "Edge" and watched the sun rise over the bleak skyline. We were all drunk and I was slipping slowly into blackness. Our energy levels were fading and no one could say for sure what happened to the rest of the group. I was trying to remember faces from that night. I'd been introduced to so many people and had seen so many places that I was overwhelmed. I was also afraid of sobering up. I didn't want to face the reality of my situation: That in about four hours I would have to start work once again.

CHAPTER SIX

The next morning I was too tired to be hungover. I'd only stopped drinking a couple of hours before I had to work, and so when I arrived back at Charleston – reeking of booze and swaying a little – I was in a relatively good mood. I saw Thomas arrive from my classroom at about ten minutes after he was supposed to have started teaching. He stood at my door and pretended to shoot himself in the head, which the students found terribly amusing. They loved Thomas, like all the kids in the school.

My first class was Bell. There were ten kids and most of them were pretty well behaved, thanks to Sonya. They sat down and mostly stayed seated throughout class. Sonya had drilled them well and always provided me with enough material to keep them entertained for the duration of our lessons. After that I taught Watt, which was Sunny's class. Those little monsters made my life very difficult. There were three kids – Tony J, Tony B, and Tony C. They were a child mafia. They ran riot throughout the school, and then when class started they sat down for approximately a minute before tearing about the room. Tony J was the worst. He enjoyed stabbing the other students with pencils and then screaming, "Game over!" They were ferocious in their fighting but were best friends in between bouts of computer-game inspired skull-smashing and bloodshed.

At lunchtime I had to eat my squid and vagina soup in Edison class, along with eight little children who were about four years old. My job, according to Debbie, was to keep the children from misbehaving. Karen, though, told me that I was there to take the blame if one of the kids choked to death. I sat down and realised immediately that children are disgusting eaters. They coughed and spluttered – not unlike Korean adults – and choked repeatedly on their food. Every time one of them went red and their eyes bulged out as they gasped, I'd just sit and shake my head, hoping that eventually they'd get some air. The kids, of course, seemed entirely unfazed. They'd cough up the food, catch their breath, and then eat it again.

After twenty minutes Thomas came through to my room. "Dude, you gotta rush the kids. Tell them to eat faster. *Balli balli*!" he shouted, which means "faster" in Korean. The kids laughed and raced to finish their dinner. "See, I got my kids finished five minutes ago so I can get outta here and grab some *real* food."

Thomas helped me herd my students through to the kitchen, where they dumped their trays for the old woman. Then they charged through to the little library-playroom as we ran for the door. Downstairs we went into

the Tous les Jours bakery and Thomas bought a couple
of sandwiches. They weren't great as far as sandwiches
went but compared to squid and vagina soup they were
fantastic. We went down a little alley beside the store
and ate them as Thomas smoked. "I don't want the kids
to see me smoke," he explained. I said nothing about the
fact that the children saw him drunk or hungover almost
every day.

In the afternoon and evening I struggled through every
class, just waiting for the weekend. It was Friday and I
sorely needed my two days of rest. I expected to stumble
home and just sleep all weekend, but of course that was
never going to happen. At the end of the day, Thomas
said, "Hey, Jon called. You wanna head downtown
tonight?"
"I'm not sure, man. I'm tired…"
"Don't be a pussy. You down?"
"Okay. What about Karen?"
"She doesn't go downtown."
"Oh."
We walked home and got changed, and then I knocked
on Thomas' door again. He wasn't naked, thankfully, and
I came in and had some Cass as he bounced around to more
hip-hop. I resented the fact that hip-hop was becoming
the soundtrack to my entire Korean experience. That and
the ridiculous alphabet songs that we taught at school.
We took a taxi downtown, drinking in the back,
and got out at the fire station. Thomas pushed his way
through the crowds again, and I didn't recognise a thing.
The streets were so busy that it was hard to know where
I was. He guided us through the chaos to a little kalbi
restaurant off what appeared to be the main street.
We wandered into the little restaurant and sat on the
floor on opposite sides of a small table with a grill in the

middle. A woman brought ten little side dishes and a man brought a bucket of burning embers for underneath the grill. I'd never seen anything like it, although the bored look on Thomas' face said that he'd done it a million and one times.

He ordered some meat and soju and we talked about how much we hated our jobs until Annie, Beth, and Oliver arrived. They worked together for a big hagwon chain and seemed to go everywhere as a group. They'd just finished work and talked to us about how much they hated their jobs. We kept ordering more food and soju and after maybe an hour things became blurry. We left and met Jonathon at Effort. He was busy playing pool with a couple of guys from the military base.

It took about two rum and cokes and half an hour of sitting around in Effort before I stopped feeling like the new boy in town. I was just another drunk; another beaten down teacher on a Friday night, trying to get the sound of screaming kids out of my head with alcohol. We all bitched about our jobs and about Korea until the booze took over and we forgot it was just another day on the wrong side of the world.

Or at least they forgot. For me it was all new and exciting, and being drunk blurred it a little, but it didn't make me forget then that I was in Korea. It just made it easier to cope. I was still trying to be positive, but everyone around me had such negative things to say about the country. Beth defended it, but she always laughed and smiled and blushed, knowing she was wrong. She had to defend it, but she struggled. Thomas and Jonathon were the biggest cynics in the group. They were vicious in their attacks – Thomas was phenomenally well-read in all aspects of Korea, having grown up as a half-Korean. His attacks were barbed and undeniable. He had a head full of facts and figures that no one could argue against, and a memory full of unpleasant experiences that no one could take from him. Jonathon was less eloquent, less knowledgeable, but far more experienced. He'd been in Korea for five years and spoke perfect Korean. But he hated the place. He would bitch about it, and whilst he was right in many respects, I could see he was just getting it all out. Oliver and Beth were more reserved – both of them also half-Korean – but they still attacked the country. It seemed that everyone was simply out to get something off their chest.

As the night drew on, our group grew and shrank and merged with others. I was introduced to people and met others whom I'd already met but couldn't recall. We moved from one table to another, to the bar, to the dance floor, and all around Effort. With each drink, everything became a little blurrier. Every hour that passed made me ask myself if I should go home, just so I could make the most of Saturday. How would I ever enjoy Korea if I was too hungover to go anywhere?

Even though I kept forgetting names and faces, a little snuck into my head. I recognised Mike from the previous night. He was a half-Korean, half-Peruvian guy of around twenty-five or so. He was also a pool shark. Never once during the night did I see a smile drop from his face, and people kept buying him drink after drink. I saw him go to the bar once, and then he was given a drink for free.

There were three girls who always crowded the pool table and circled the room talking to nearly everyone. Their names were Jenny, Leah, and Liz, and they were loud and crude. Jenny and Leah were hot and Liz wasn't exactly ugly, but their brashness made me quieter than normal, and seemed to scare the most of the Korean people, too.

I got to the stage where I was staggering around the bar on my own, talking to random people. I can't remember any of the conversations I had, if indeed they could be called conversations. I seemed to bond pretty strongly with that little group from the start of the night – Thomas, Annie, Beth, Oliver, Jonathon – and kept getting very happy to see them later on.

Someone dragged me out of Effort, and soon I was on the street with that same group, plus a few others. Jonathon and I were staggering about with our arms around each other. He kept shouting about how much he loved Scottish people and we sang loudly into the night sky.

Then we were in Starz, and things weren't so fun. We stood at the bar, we danced, we drank, and we left. It was lame. None of us could stand the music. For some reason I assumed that people who liked hip-hop were completely indiscriminate in what they actually liked. It never occurred to me that hip-hop could be classified as either good or bad. To me, it was all shit.

The staff seemed to like us, though. Jonathon got free drinks as usual from a girl behind the bar called "Boss Mamma." Evidently, she was the owner of the club. All the bartenders were cute young girls in skimpy dresses, looking very much the same as the people on the other side of the bar, except that the people actually buying the drinks were all male. It seemed girls didn't buy their own drinks in Korea.

Outside, the door staff tried to stop us leaving. It was a joke, of course, and Jonathon got into a joke wrestling match with the doorman, a short and stalky man with a buzzcut and a handgun in his belt. It occurred to me that Annie and Beth were gone. It was just the guys now.

Soon we were in Edge, pushing to the bar on the second floor. It was busier than Starz, with more non-Koreans. Suddenly I was surrounded by big black and white guys, instead of Korean people. Space was limited. Getting to the bar was a challenge, and then shouting loud enough while there was even tougher. Trying to carry drinks anywhere else was almost impossible, so we went to the bar, took two shots of tequila and a rum-coke each, and downed them immediately.

We pushed onto the dance floor and sort of swayed back and forth. There was no room to dance. It was hot and sweaty, but I was drunk enough not to care. The music was terrible, but it was better than in Starz or Effort, and there was a better male-female ratio.

The main point of concern for me in Edge, however, was the soldiers – big dudes pushing about and always looking dangerous. The Koreans were clearly terrified of them. The guys would jump out of the way, and the girls would stand still in fear. Some of the women barely came up to nipple-height on these giant Westerners. On the dance floor they were worse. They would push up against the Korean girls and forcibly dry-hump the woman's hip or back.

Soon we were on a balcony on the second floor, overlooking the entrance and the convenience store opposite. We could see people queuing to get in. Koreans had to wait in line and pay, but foreigners more or less walked in without waiting and of course never paid. I noticed, though, that there seemed to be a hierarchy – the prettiest girls and the biggest black guys got in unaccosted, followed by the regulars, like Thomas and Jonathon. The quieter foreigners – little guys like me, if I wasn't with Thomas or Jonathon – waited in line, although they didn't pay, either.

Next we were on the roof and we had drinks. I didn't remember buying them or going there. I was time travelling, jumping through space. Confused, stupid, stumbling.

"I'm going to drop a glass!" I shouted.

Thomas, Jonathon, and Oliver burst into fits of childish laughter and lurched towards me as I suspended my drink over the street from four or five storeys up.

"You'll hit a soldier, dude!" Thomas shouted.

Jonathon just screamed, "No!"

They wrestled my drink onto a table and we all laughed about it.

"You'd have a better chance jumpin' off the roof than fighting some fucking soldiers, son!" Thomas explained. "Seriously!"

"You think?"

"Hell yeah," Jonathon said, still laughing harder than any of us.

"Those guys would *destroy* you," said Oliver.

I shrugged my shoulders. "Meh." I could take 'em.

"They're trained in unarmed combat," Jonathon said. "For wars! They'd *literally* kill you. If you jumped off the roof, *maybe* you'd live... With them... No chance!"

My last memories of the night are of staggering into a small underground bar called Trend, which stank of incense and was decorated like the set of an old movie about the Orient. There weren't many foreigners, but all the staff spoke English. The woman who claimed to own the bar was gorgeous and spoke English perfectly. Her name was Kelly and she had the most beautiful smile I thought I'd ever seen. I tried talking to her but faded too quickly into the dark of fatigue and drunkness.

CHAPTER SEVEN

The next morning, I woke at midday, having slept for four hours, and didn't feel nearly as bad as when I knew I had to work. My sleep pattern had been destroyed by jetlag and drunkenness, but I wasn't tired. Just waking up and knowing that I didn't have to go to Charleston was enough to put me in a relatively good mood. As I lay in bed I felt pretty good about being in Korea. I was on the other side of the world from my problems, settling into what I still hoped would be a new and more rewarding life. My job was terrible, but at least I *had* a job. And friends, too.

I wondered what to do… I hadn't really given much thought to free time before, but now I had some. I didn't have a phone to call Jonathon or Thomas, or any of the dozens of people I'd met downtown. I was on my own until Monday, and I had to find something other than alcohol to occupy my time in this new country. A part of me felt overwhelmed by choice even though I couldn't think of anything specific. I knew that I was on a whole new continent where everything was strange and different, and that doing anything alone would be an adventure. Yet I was a little afraid. Walking to school each day had been an unpleasant adventure because it meant walking among the most unfriendly people I had ever encountered. They just stared and pointed and said "waegookin" loudly. In the company of other foreigners they were easier to ignore, but on my own it was intimidating to be the only person of my race among the hostile locals.

I wanted to slap myself for being so timid. I had travelled across the world on my own in search of a new life and yet I was lying in bed, procrastinating. The thought process that had led me to fear going outside because of the nastiness of the people on the streets had taken more than an hour as I thought over and over about what to do.

Eventually, I got up and took a shower. It was the first shower I'd taken in Korea, which disgusted me when I thought about it. After that I put on some shorts and a t-shirt and wondered what the dress code was. At work, I'd been casually smart, although somewhat smelly. I had been watching what the girls were wearing, but not so much the guys. I wondered if it was acceptable to wear shorts and t-shirt in public. The country seemed very conservative, and I didn't know if it was alright for guys to show that much skin. All the males I could remember had been wearing trousers and long-sleeved shirts or jackets. But it was too hot outside for such nonsense, so I elected to wear what I found most comfortable. Besides, I figured that people would probably stare at me regardless of what I wore. I had my camera around my neck, just in case I saw something that wasn't ugly, and my backpack contained a notepad and a couple of pencils, in case I found somewhere peaceful to write.

My plan was to head west and keep walking as far as I could before I collapsed. There had to be something west... As long as I didn't get lost. I had no knowledge of how to get home. I couldn't even read the signs to tell me the name of the area where I lived, and I hadn't thought to ask anyone before being dumped on my own for the weekend. I didn't know how to get on a bus or take the subway, or even what to tell a taxi driver. I realised that a more experienced traveller would've probably taken a business card from the school, but these thoughts were slowing me down, making me fear going outside even more.

I walked the fifteen minutes to Charleston and then kept going. It was the same route that the taxi had taken on the way downtown, and so I planned on going there and finding somewhere to have lunch. But it was a longer walk than I had imagined. It took an hour and a half to reach downtown, and there I found myself intimidated by the madness. All the streets were packed and all the businesses looked identical. I couldn't find any of the places I'd seen at night, not that I expected them to be open during the day.

I've always been good with directions and exploration. Walk in straight lines, keeping landmarks in sight. Don't think too hard, but keep your eyes open. Those rules didn't apply here, though. Everything simply looked too similar to differentiate between places. I more or less walked the length of the city along a straight route.

Being with Thomas and Karen, dealing with the hangover and coping with work, I hadn't thought much about the reality of my situation – about being in Korea –

but when I was on my own my brain went into overdrive and I became paranoid. I was on the other side of the world, starting a new life. All my friends were back home in Scotland. If Thomas decided he didn't want to bring me along with his friends, I'd have no one. If something bad happened, I was screwed. I had no money and I didn't speak the language. My parents were thousands of miles away... Panic filled me as I stood in the busy street, sweating profusely while the city spun around.

I kept walking and calmed myself by thinking over a couple of escape plans, should things become insufferable. I told myself to enjoy the world around me. After all, it was new and exciting. I had travelled thousands of miles to start a new life and panic was natural, but I couldn't let it ruin everything.

The sun was beating down pretty hard and I hadn't seen anywhere I wanted to eat. I didn't know nearly enough of the language to go into any of the Korean places on my own, and the Western places just looked like terrible parodies of their counterparts in the West. I kept walking, hungry and hot, with blisters forming on my feet.

I walked for four hours across the city without seeing anything interesting. I meandered back and forth along side streets and followed English tourism signs to parks and temples, but everything was ugly and grey, and there were too many people. The sun made me feel good, though, and I knew it wasn't a wasted day. I felt I knew the city better, and that I had a whole year to do fun stuff. This was still my recuperation period from the flight; my settling-in period to Korean life.

When I got back home it was evening, and I'd walked for four hours across the city and four hours back. My feet hurt and my back hurt and I was tired from the heat.

I contemplated going to bed early, then waking up early and doing it all again, becoming a healthy and wholesome person. Tomorrow I would go east and find something else. My Korean adventure had gotten off to a rocky start with those nights of drunkenness, but I was going to be alright. I'd come to Korea to change my ways, to find Buddhism and experience culture on the other side of the world, becoming a noble and enlightened person. But instead I was back in nightclubs, waking up with a hangover every day.

I took my clothes off and jumped into bed at nine, then stared at the ceiling, waiting for sleep.

At quarter past nine, the phone in my living room rang. It startled me. I had never used it and assumed it didn't work. Who would have my number? Was it the school? I didn't want to have to explain to someone that they'd gotten the wrong number... or that I didn't speak Korean.

It was Thomas.

"Yo! Come down to my house in five minutes and we're gonna get our drink on!"

"Alright," I said.

I threw my clothes back on and ran downstairs.

"Damn, you're fast."

"I was bored," I said. "I almost fell asleep."

I took my shoes off and went inside. The place smelled like sleep.

"What did you do all day?"

"I walked across the city."

"Huh?"

"Yeah, all the way across. Took me four hours."

"That's crazy! Why d'you do that?"

"I was bored."

"Huh."

"What did *you* do?"

"Slept. I just woke up."

"All day?"

"More or less. I was on the internet talking to some friends. Watched a couple of movies."

Thomas handed me a beer and beckoned me through to the little room, which in my place was filled by a washing machine, but in Thomas' it was bigger, and had a desk. On the desk sat his laptop, which had been moved from the other room so he could smoke as he sat at his computer. The windows were wide open and the cigarette odour didn't last long, though he was a heavy smoker.

"What is there to do in Daegu?" I asked.

"Drink."

"That all?"

"Yup." I took a sip from my beer and decided to not believe Thomas. He was a cynical guy but I was determined to stay positive about Korea until I had reason to feel otherwise. I wouldn't take his bad experiences and make them my own. Even if Daegu was awful, Korea still had mountains and beaches. There would always be something out there that was worth seeing.

Thomas reclined in his chair and lit a cigarette. He waved his arm over his computer and his face filled with love. "Sweet or what?"

"It's a nice computer."

"'Nice' nothing! It's a demon machine."

"Mine sucks."

"Everything sucks in comparison to this." Thomas rambled into technical details about his computer that I didn't understand. I just stared at the screen and pretended to listen. He had a window open that contained recently downloaded files, including a dozen movies that weren't released yet and that I wanted to see.

"Fastest internet in the world," he said. "Daegu's good

for something."

"So you're a geek, then?"

"Hells yeah, son!" Thomas looked proud. He touched his heart. "Through and through. Half-white, half-Asian, and all geek!"

Thomas changed some songs on iTunes and I laughed at his eclectic taste in music. It was much the same as my library, except for all the hip-hop.

"Yo, I got more beer in the fridge we gotta finish before leaving," he said. "So hurry up."

We took a taxi downtown and stopped, as usual, opposite the fire station. It was busier, apparently, on weekends. Walking was difficult, but we still had our beers and it appeared that while foreigners were fair game for staring and pushing, we appeared more dangerous with an open drink in our hands. Girls would panic and jump out of our way, and guys would put their heads down in fear of making eye contact.

Ahead of us were four big black guys, walking down the middle of the street. They cleared a huge space around themselves simply because of their size and colour. The locals swerved maniacally to get out of the way. Girls squealed and jumped in fear. Some people even darted into stores to avoid them. Everyone stared and whispered.

"Koreans think they have guns," Thomas explained. "They see it on TV everyday, poor bastards. And not just soldiers – all black people. Even Annie."

As we watched them swagger along, obviously amused by their ability to clear such a path, Thomas began pointing at a group of fairly typical Korean girls. They were toddling along in their ludicrous high heels, pointing and laughing at the group of black men. They were making monkey noises and pushing the mockery further than any of the other people on the street.

Thomas knew what was coming. He'd seen it before. Before it even happened, he was covering his mouth and beginning to laugh. The soldiers – it might seem presumptuous, but groups of large black men in Daegu are invariably soldiers – suddenly broke step and jumped towards the young women, screaming and beating their chests. The girls, of course, fell to the ground in tears as everyone changed tack and pretended not to have noticed. Nobody looked at the men as they continued walking, laughing at their own little joke.

Thomas had tears streaming down his face, too. "Serves them bitches right," he said, and I had to agree. They were dusting themselves off and trying to fix their make-up, looking like true victims... but they were victims of nothing more than their own ignorance and prejudice.

In Effort we drank until the night became blurry and then slipped into morning. We cruised the clubs aimlessly and watched the sun rise from the roof of Edge.

CHAPTER EIGHT

I settled into the teaching life with reluctance. It wasn't easy to wake up with a hangover and know I had to spend ten hours feigning enthusiasm for something I despised. It wasn't so much teaching I disliked as the academy style of teaching. I didn't enjoy having to act like a monkey for Mr. Park and Debbie, making kids repeat things and teaching them from textbooks that were littered with idiotic mistakes. Half of what I taught them was irrelevant, and half was contradicted by Korean teachers who knew nothing of the language. None of the kids wanted to be there. They were too young.

The kids mostly just ran wild in my classes. They spoke no English and I spoke no Korean, and they were raised in a society where people of other races are to be mocked. Trying to impart any wisdom on them seemed an impossible task. Besides, I felt it was ridiculous that I was now a teacher. I had no training, and I didn't understand kids. Many of the children I taught clearly had severe learning or behavioural disabilities. It was obvious but their parents refused to accept the fact. Consequently, the kids suffered and I suffered. They deserved a real teacher.

But the kids were difficult to deal with. There were hundreds of them, crammed into small classrooms and made to sit in tiny chairs. They were restless, and some of them were outright violent. They beat each other constantly, quoting lines from popular computer games as they smashed chairs against skulls. Half of them would scream abuse at me – calling me "foreigner" and mocking my "big nose." It was all in jest, of course, but it still was troubling. The Korean teachers would simply laugh and agree with the kids. And why not? I do have a big nose.

Sonya was my co-teacher for most of my classes. As such, she was the one who made the schedule and decided what I had to teach the children. I was lucky in that respect because Lydia and Sunny – the other Korean teachers – were useless. They were incompetent and spoke almost no English. Thomas and Karen had gotten used to teaching what they felt was necessary, but I liked having someone like Sonya to help me.

Whenever I came in hungover, Sonya would laugh and joke about Thomas and I drinking too much. She kept a special box of medicine in her cupboard that was full of things to help me make it through the day. Sometimes she'd give me something to stop me from vomiting and other times she'd give me something to help my headaches. She even massaged my head, hands, and shoulders from time to time.

Sonya was open with the three foreigners and didn't feel afraid of us. She liked practising her English and sharing her views and opinions with us. She was the only Korean person I met who told me that she didn't approve of beating children. "I think it is cruel," she explained, quite rightly. Her English was far better than most English teachers in Korea, having lived in America for two years. She was overworked and constantly tired, but always smiled.

One day, she looked at me carefully. "You are Jewish, right?" she asked. Then she made a gesture with her hands that signalled I had a big nose. "You look like Jew."

"No," I said. "No, I'm not Jewish."

Thomas was standing right behind me and I could hear his breathing stop. I wondered whether he was about to laugh or to push me out of the way and attack Sonya.

"Oh good!" Sonya smiled from ear to ear and put her hand to her chest. She made a fake look of relief and bent over.

"What? Why?"

"I hate the Jew," she explained. Her face contorted. Again, it didn't look entirely real, but it was. Sonya always seemed fake. "I think they are only interested in money. They are always lie. Jews steal so much!"

I didn't know what to say, so I stood silently. To my surprise, Thomas remained silent behind me. *Had she actually said these words?*

"Can you teach page fifty-six, fifty-seven next class?"

"Yeah, sure."

My respect for Sonya dropped, but not as much as it should have done. According to Thomas and Karen, it was a regular occurrence to hear a Korean person make insane racist statements about Japanese and Chinese people, although I'd only heard a few questionable remarks. When I heard it, it sickened me, yet it didn't surprise me, and I knew that it wasn't just Sonya. She was a product of a fundamentally warped culture – a country with a philosophy that differed very little from Nazism in its ethnocentric one-blood proclamations and contempt for anything remotely different.

One day Karen and I were called into Mr. Park's office and told that our nationalities were no longer valuable to the school. We had to pretend to be American.

"I know it not good," Mr. Park explained, laughing and flashing his sickening grin. His forehead was extra oily because he probably knew Karen wouldn't stand for what he was demanding. But he was trying to be our friend. Sometimes he'd just act nice and do a terrible job. His voice became high and whiny and he'd move his arms and shoulders too much. "I hate American. You cannot trust them, right? They always do the drinking too much… But this is Korea, right? This is my country. This is my business. People want American teacher.

"You are United Kingdom people. That good, but now you need pretend be America people, right? Just in class. You go home and be United Kingdom people. You go drink with friend and be United Kingdom people. But this my school and you my teachers so you America people, right?"

We stared at him and then looked at each other. I didn't know what to say or do. A life of poverty and unemployment had left me unable to deal with crooked bosses. When I'd been temporarily employed it had been impossible for me to refuse the demands of a person responsible for my meagre wages. I simply didn't know how to talk sense to an out-of-line employer.

"So you speak more American now. No speak England or Scotland language, right? No speak what we don't want learn. In Korea we want learn America English…"

Karen suddenly exploded. "This is fucking ridiculous!" Mr. Park cowered, taken aback. "We come from the country that invented this stupid fucking language! You knew that when you hired us, so don't give us any of this shit!"

Her face had become a burning red colour and her hands were pointing like guns at Mr. Park's chest. He just sat there, staring at her in shock and horror, saying nothing. I could almost hear the heartbeats of everyone in the next room as silence fell upon us.

"This isn't the first time you've fucked us, Mr. Park. I went to the tax office last week and they said you'd only registered me as havin' earned three million. Three million! In a year!"

Mr. Park seethed with rage but didn't say a word.

"And when Thomas went to the hospital a few months back… Where was his health insurance? The money you take out of our paycheques… Nothing! You're fuckin' us, Parky, and it's not on. The jig's up."

Karen stood silently after her outburst. I could tell she had more, but she looked like she regretted saying this much. Those were her trump cards and she'd thrown them out there for no good reason. She needed to keep them for the end, when Mr. Park would inevitably try and fire her to avoid paying severance. Those were big bargaining chips and she hadn't want to throw them away so easily.

The silence was broken as Debbie burst into the room, ready to jump to the aid of her boss. She stood as though she were about to tackle us.

"What is going on?" Debbie yelled. Then she broke into a flurry of Korean and Mr. Park shouted back. I guess that he told her to stay there because she did. She braced herself for an attack.

"I'm leaving," Karen said. She spoke matter-of-factly, as though she'd been running through the situation in her head and had suddenly risen above all the emotion and hysteria and had somehow reached a platform of logic and sense. "I'm not going to put up with this shit anymore. This place is a fucking joke." Ironically, or perhaps she intended it on some level, her accent died down and she spoke in a flat and lifeless manner.

She turned to leave and Debbie planted herself in the doorway, her hands firmly gripping the frame. She shook her head and the motion wiggled her fat ass.

I wanted Karen to push her out of the way, or to punch her in the face, but of course she didn't. Through the silence in the other room I could almost feel the collective will of the other teachers urging her to smite Debbie, who was detested by everyone who had to work with her.

Mr. Park was fuming in his chair, obviously looking for the words required to put across whatever ridiculous thoughts were running through his oily head. Nothing came to him, though, and he just sat there scowling at us.

Karen shook her head and laughed to herself and I could see the fear in Debbie's puffy dead eyes. She looked about ready to crack. She knew Karen had been wronged and wasn't the sort of girl to accept that bullshit, and she wondered if she was about to lose any teeth over the matter. A girl of Debbie's swinish complexion couldn't afford to lose any teeth.

After a few seconds, she moved and Karen pushed roughly past her and walked out of the school, followed shortly by Thomas and me. We could hear Mr. Park cursing loudly at Debbie.

CHAPTER NINE

Every day after work Thomas and I would go to the Pajeon Place for dinner. There we'd drink beer and soju, and maybe four or five nights a week we'd end up taking a taxi downtown to meet the rest of the group. I always meant to stop because I felt guilty going into work hungover or even a little drunk. But at the end of a long day at Charleston I honestly felt so exhausted that no amount of rest or sleep could relieve me. The only thing that I knew would work was venting my frustrations at Thomas over a couple of bottles of soju or bitching about it all with numerous other teachers in Effort. Every night we went home drunk, and every morning we staggered into work, laughing at each other for looking so bad. In between classes we joked with each other. Sometimes we had to cover for each other after puking in the bathroom, and more than a few times Mr. Park would actually pretend to befriend one of us to get dirt on the other. "So you think Thomas is do the drinking many times?" It was only my contempt for Mr. Park that kept me from feeling completely and utterly ashamed of myself.

Karen wasn't fired after her outburst with Mr. Park. In fact, nothing was ever said of it again. She came to dinner from time to time, and Thomas knew enough to keep his mouth shut. Maybe once a week, when work got bad enough, she'd come and drown her sorrows. She wouldn't ask, and neither would Thomas, but on those nights when she was desperate and lonely and needing to know that she wasn't in this all by herself, she would just veer right at the front door of the building and invite herself along. I liked Karen and was always glad she came, but she never stayed long. She didn't get along with Thomas, and they both refused to say why. Thomas pretended he liked her, but I wasn't buying that, and he wouldn't elaborate, even when drunk.

On those few nights in that first month, Karen would sit quietly and stare at the baseball game on TV. She drank Thomas' beer and soju mix, ate a little of the increasingly tedious food, and would then leave after maybe an hour. Thomas and I would sit around longer, and as the weeks went by we found ourselves there until later and later.

Despite it all, though, we stuck with Charleston. Thomas told me about guys he knew who'd pulled the "Midnight Run" – which involved leaving the job without a word and disappearing from Korea altogether. The thought never actually crossed my mind, although I was surprised Thomas and Karen hadn't done it. I had nothing to go home to. I was terminally unemployed, alone, and no less of an alcoholic in Scotland than in Korea. Besides, I was always waiting for Sarah to appear. She'd said that she would come out in July, but once I arrived I found out that there had been no guaranteed job. It had just been an idea. An escape fantasy. She e-mailed me from time to time, saying that she had a job lined up, then that it fell through... then another job, but it fell through... I could tell, though, that she was losing interest. I couldn't bring myself to lie to her. When she asked about Korea I told her the truth, and she seemed decidedly put off. She had nothing better in Scotland, but she didn't want to move around the world to be just as miserable.

I never really saw Thomas on the weekends, except in the evenings. We were quickly becoming close friends and spending almost all our time together during the week, but come Saturday morning I was on my own. Thomas had a mobile phone but I didn't, and although we lived in the same building I rarely knocked on his door, nor he on mine. Our relationship existed, then, as some sort of support mechanism. We were stuck together at school and shared our woes in the evening.

On weekends I tried to rest and recover from the week. Although after work all I could do to get over the fatigue was drink and complain, on the weekends I just sat in my tiny little apartment, in front of my little desk fan, and stared at the walls. There really was nothing else I could do. Outside it was so hot and muggy, and my pores were so clogged with booze, that I'd sweat myself to death in an hour. The heat made the city stink worse than usual, too. With a killer hangover I could hardly stomach walking to the nearest 7-Eleven for a bottle of water. When I did venture outside people would treat me like dirt. I became a spectacle whenever I left my house and it made me uncomfortable. I began to dread trips to the store, and even the walk to school.

I had a list of things to do, should I ever gain the motivation to get out. From the internet I ascertained that there were several interesting locations in or around Daegu. I told myself that I'd climb Mount Palgong and take the bus to Haein Temple. Alas, in those first weeks I just didn't get around to anything. I sat and wondered about my predicament, telling myself that I'd go out and explore later. I asked myself why I was still an alcoholic, even when I'd come halfway around the world to escape that curse. Had I really been naïve enough to think that moving from one country to another would solve all my problems?

I was feeling pretty lonely, too. Thomas and Jonathon were great friends, as were Annie, Beth, and Oliver. Karen was decent company when she wanted to be, but I needed something more than just drinking buddies and people who shared my frustrations. In Scotland I'd almost gotten used to the loneliness. I'd become so accustomed to having friends and the occasional fling that I didn't dwell on it too much. I had fixated on Sarah, putting off the notion of actually finding someone and telling myself that she – as the only female in my life after university – was the right girl for me, and that we'd eventually end up as a couple.

In Korea, though, I found myself feeling desperate and pathetic. I had friends to drink and joke with but no one to go home with at the end of a night or to share my weekends travelling around the country and seeing what I hoped was the *real* Korea – a beautiful land that had thus far escaped my drunken gaze. It didn't help that Korean girls were rather attractive. They dressed like they had mental problems, but they were thin and took good care of themselves. They were very different from Scottish girls. But they were still just girls on the street, who stared at me because I was foreign and looked different, and were utterly unapproachable because they were of the one true bloodline…

I constantly told myself that a sober night or a hangover-free day was on the horizon. Although I enjoyed having a close group of friends to drink with, I also knew that I'd probably get more out of my time in Korea by seeing the country and doing things that I'd remember years later.

But from Monday to Friday I worked from nine in the morning until eight at night, and on Saturday and Sunday I was irredeemably hungover. No caffeine boost nor early night could fight the alcohol I'd consumed on Friday and Saturday, and I spent my weekends thoroughly depressed, at home in my shitty little apartment. I had maps and guidebooks and webpages open on my computer, and all of them told me that Korea was a fantastic country with innumerable quaint temples nestled among gorgeous mountains. I had trouble believing this because from what I'd seen Korea was an ugly, unfriendly place. But there appeared to be a few places that would genuinely enthral me if I got the energy to see them.

Instead, I sat at home, in front of my fan, thinking about the next week. I'd tell myself that it was just one wasted day; no big deal. I told myself that if Jonathon or Thomas asked me to go out, I'd tell them that I was having a sober night, and then I'd go to bed and wake up with the energy to face the following day.

However, when the time came for that inevitable phone call I would always cave. Thomas would usually ask me once and leave it, but then Jonathon would phone and ask me over and over. He was a needy guy. Every day he made me think he might shoot himself if I turned him down. No matter how much I wanted or needed to stay at home, I couldn't say "no" to Jonathon.

And so I'd sit there and stare at the walls until that call came. My apartment was comprised of one meagre, depressing room. It was about half the size of an ordinary living room back in Scotland. The walls were a dirty cream colour with scratches and tears in the paper, and the ceiling was much the same. The floor was linoleum and never clean. Even when I swept there was still dust and dirt. I realised after a while that Korea is just such a filthy place that things *can't* be clean. If I left the windows open over night, there would be a fine layer of pollution sitting on my desk and floor by morning. Dirt just filled the air of this rotten place. Of course, if I didn't leave the windows open I'd have melted. I lived on the top floor of a four-storey building, facing south, and the sun streamed in from five o'clock in the morning until well into the evening. Between that and the lack of air movement in the city, my room was always uncomfortably hot. I blacked out the windows with construction paper I stole from school, but the sun burned through, regardless.

I had a small bed by a window, a cupboard that was big enough to hold the two shirts and few other items of clothes that I'd purchased after realising I didn't bring anything practical with me from Scotland, a rusty metal desk, a cheap computer chair, and a fan that I pointed at wherever I sat. On the desk sat my trusty old laptop, which held a copy of every piece of crap story, poem, and essay I'd ever written, just waiting for me to find the inspiration to sit back down and start writing again. The kitchen was also part of the same room. There was literally no surface space. I had a sink for washing dishes, and a stove for cooking two pots at the same time. I had one knife, one spoon, one single chopstick, one pan, one plate, and nothing else. Fortunately, Thomas had bought me dinner almost every day during my first month in Korea.

The bathroom was a room *and* a shower. It was about the size of a large cupboard, and there was a hole in the middle of the floor for water for flow down. A shower head dangled near the toilet, which was thankfully *not* a squatter. Every time I showered I had to then tolerate a wet bathroom floor for the next twelve hours. That meant every time I puked I got wet knees, and every time I took a shit my trousers would get soaked.

There were cockroaches and mosquitoes that bothered me on the weekends, and cicadas that inhabited the trees outside, creating a screeching sound louder than any car, motorbike, or truck that I'd heard. Sometimes they'd try and chew through the bug netting on the window. For the most part, I was happy to spend my evenings anywhere but home.

I hated the thoughts that came with being trapped in that awful little place. My creativity and productivity had died upon arriving in Korea. I hadn't written a word since landing in Incheon and I couldn't even remember what it felt like to sit down and type. My head was full of loneliness and lust. At nights I spent my time with friends but, as Jonathon had pointed out, they wouldn't be around forever, and as much as I loved them there was always a sense of impermanence that kept me from becoming too attached. I missed my old friends from university, and the fact I was just sitting and stewing in my own lust.

The problem was that my drinking furthered my horniness but killed my charm. I'd always been the sort of drunk who talks to guys, falls asleep, or does stupid stuff. I was never a smooth talker and after more than three or four beers I just forgot about the women around me, at least in a romantic or sexual sense. In the morning I'd wake up and remember the girl who was eyeing me at the bar, or the one who'd approached me and given me the perfect opportunity to charm her pants off. But at the time those opportunities always passed me by.

It was frustrating to walk about the streets and see all the girls in their summer clothes, flaunting legs and smiling over coffees in shop windows. I can't say the manners of Korean girls did anything for me, but physically they were appealing. After my first month I still hadn't seen a grotesquely fat one. I hadn't seen any truly unattraction women. Sure, they all dressed the same – in baggy t-shirts with poor English scrawled on the front and back, showing no skin above the waist, with plenty of leg right up to the crotch – but they were thin and pretty. During the day they tottered about under umbrellas and parasols, looking irresistible... But of course I was just a foreign freak to them.

In the bars and clubs, Korean girls did sometimes swing towards foreign men, but I was warned away. Those girls, everyone knew, were riddled with diseases. They were hookers for language rather than money. They'd sit at the bar until a guy spoke to them, and they go home with him after a few drinks. The next night they'd sit there and go home with a different guy. Their English was good because they'd spoken to so many foreign men, and that helped them get good jobs. Thomas told me about three of his friends who'd gotten syphilis in Korea. One of them, naturally, was Jonathon. They told each other about it one night and it transpired that they'd all fucked at least six of the same bar skanks. Thomas was very coy about sex and wouldn't tell me if he'd had any luck in Korea. He just spoke about others and the things he'd apparently heard.

"Most of these girls are Christians," he said. "You think they put out, but they don't. They give head, but that's 'bout it. Anyway, the ones you *wanna* fuck don't want a foreign guy. The ones you *can* fuck have done every black or white guy in town. Man, you pick up some nasty shit from these hoes."

"What about the foreign girls?"

"Son, who the fuck comes to Asia to fuck some nasty-ass white girl?"

"True."

"I'm telling you, dude, you don't know what goes on 'round here just yet. This place is incestuous."

"I don't follow you…"

"You know Jonathon, right?"

"He's a man whore."

Thomas laughed. "Yeah. There aren't many girls in Daegu you *can* fuck that he *hasn't* fucked. Seriously. That boy would just about stick his dick in anything, I swear. Every Korean girl with white fever has been up in his pants. Half the foreign chicks, too. Anyone that puts out fucks Jonathon."

"Jesus, that's horrible."

"I get scared, son," he said. "I meet a girl and wanna take her home, and then I imagine stickin' it in… Her shit's probably stuffed with Jonathon's jizz."

I laughed, and then stopped midway through. Thomas was right. It was an appalling thought.

But the fact was these women, skanky or otherwise, were going home with other men, while I staggered into a taxi alone at the end of a night. I was a pathetic mess. No one wanted me and I could hardly blame them. I'd gained a little weight since coming to Korea, and no longer had the gaunt face of a sad drunk, but I was still no great catch. All those sad, horny dreams of bagging a gorgeous Asian girl were dying before me as I sat and watched bugs crawl over my dishes and listened to the whirl of an aging desk fan that just circulated warm air.

CHAPTER TEN

When my first paycheque came in after a month of living
in Korea, I felt like a king. I was a millionaire in Won,
and even in the equivalent Pound Sterling value I'd
never at one time possessed so much money. Mr. Park
had deducted numerous shady sums from the total, and
many of these I'd later come to realise were simply acts
of theft on his part, but I was still overjoyed. The first
month had been difficult. I was absolutely exhausted,
having worked for around ten hours a day, five days a
week. Charleston was not kind to me.

But a thousand pounds in any place is a big comfort. I
knew that my rent was taken care of, my food bills would
never amount to more than a fraction of my salary, and
that my only outgoings amounted to large quantities
of booze. I'd never be broke as long as I could stand

working at Charleston. For the first time in my life I had economic security. Moreover, I was thinking of all the things in the world that I could buy. I could feasibly piss away large sums of cash without worrying. I began counting the days until my next paycheque and knew that I only had to make this one last a month before the next – something I'd never really experienced before. I even began thinking about the possibility of going somewhere nice on holiday one day.

I also had job security, which, even though I hated my job, was a tremendous comfort:

"Dude, Parky paid for your flight," Thomas reminded me. "He ain't gonna fire you for anything! If he does, he loses the money he paid to bring you here."

He was right, as usual. Mr. Park was not about to fire me for anything less than punching him in the face or murdering a child. It didn't matter how often I came in hungover or how lacklustre my teaching was – the worst he could do was whine at me and tell me to improve. I didn't have to worry about losing my job, running out of cash, or any of the things that had previously blighted my working life. If I could bring myself to care as little about Charleston as Thomas, I'd probably cruise through the year without a hitch.

But I didn't like Charleston. It irked me to work for a cheap pimp like Mr. Park. Whenever I saw him I felt every bad thing in the world had collected itself inside his ill-fitting shiny suits. He slunk around the school watching his employees with a vicious eye – waiting for the chance to complain and make a crude racial generalisation. "Foreigner too lazy," he frequently remarked. "Foreigner don't understand."

Debbie was just as bad. The squat little bitch had barely taught a day in her life but waddled around the school looking for something to complain about. Her English was too poor to express her complaints, and frequently she chose to write them on little Post-its, surrounded by love hearts and smiley faces. Sometimes she'd write, "Teacher, please more energy thinking! Love, Debbie!" and there would be a dozen schoolgirl drawings scrawled over the remainder of the paper. Thomas and I both received dozens of these each week, and we collected them and stuck them on the corkboard wall behind our desks, competing to see who could get the most. The key was trying to make Debbie both unhappy and afraid to speak to us personally.

When I was made to do my first set of monthly evaluations, Debbie told me to be honest. I had to write about and grade over a hundred students, and there was only one computer for the staff to use. Thomas, Karen, and I had to stay behind for hours to write our evaluations, and when I was done I received a Post-it note on my desk, saying: "Teacher, more nicely evaluations please!" When I asked her what she meant, she told me, "Parent don't like pay for school when children are not doing good class, teacher. You need write good things, teacher! More nicely!"

Although it went against everything I stood for, I caved and wrote an entirely new set of evaluations. I had to stay behind until ten o'clock, at which point Mr. Park impatiently kicked me out of the school. He and Debbie were standing around doing nothing, but they seemed agitated. He said they wanted to leave, and I wondered why they had to leave together.

"You go home now," he told me. There was no grin this time.

"Alright," I said. "But I always try do my best for the kids…"

Two hours later, after Thomas and I had eaten dinner in the Pajeon Place and gotten good and drunk, we walked past the school and saw Mr. Park and Debbie leaving together. I had suspected what was going on, but that confirmed it – they were fucking in the office and wanted me gone. No wonder a dumb bitch like her was head teacher.

"Debbie teacher!" Thomas shouted from across the road. "I hope you guys didn't knock any of those Post-it notes off my desk!" She smiled stupidly as Mr. Park scowled and scurried off towards his Hyundai.

Although I came to care less and less about Charleston, I still worked hard for the kids. Mr. Park stopped taking such an interest in me as it became obvious that I was ignoring all of his advice. I think he also realised that the kids were starting to love me. Just like Thomas, I would walk out of class to the sound of "Goodbye, teacher! We love you!" and I'd be greeted in the foyer each day by a hundred screaming children. We were treated like rock stars by the students and lepers by the teachers and parents. Our classes were the only ones that made sense to them, and we didn't even speak their language. We didn't beat them or force them to memorise and repeat stupid phrases. We just had fun with them. We let them laugh and play - things that Korean kids are simply not allowed to do.

But it bored me. The kids were alright but teaching them for so many hours each day was slowly and surely driving me insane. Every class was virtually the same. I was teaching the same pages of the same books to kids with the same names. I'd make the same jokes and they'd give me the same responses. I realised that Thomas was a fun teacher for the same reason I was becoming a fun teacher – we were largely just trying to amuse ourselves. Instead of standing like we were meant to and chanting "cat cat cat" we would do magic tricks and let the kids listen to Bob Dylan on our iPods. I taught one of my classes to sing "Mr. Tambourine Man" and Thomas taught his to rap along with Lupe Fiasco. Karen cared a lot about teaching and took a more serious approach, but still her classes also revolved around the students having fun. I set myself the goal of making the children laugh in each class I taught. I thought that was an honest and decent thing to do. They weren't allowed fun, but by god I'd give it to them. I felt sorry for them, especially when I managed to teach them enough that they could describe their lives to me and I really came to understand just how much crappy education they received. From morning to night they were in school. They had no breakfast, tiny lunches, and no snacks. They weren't allowed outside. They couldn't run. At home they had computer games instead of time outside with their friends.

Nonetheless, I found myself mind-numbingly bored as I taught phonics and basic vocabulary. My throat was worn raw from chanting "a a a" and "dog dog dog" all day long. In the end, they learned better from playing bingo and running about the classroom finding letters. Using my imagination to make games they'd enjoy pretty much kept me sane.

But they weren't all little angels, and my sympathies for them and my efforts to help them learn and have fun were all frequently thrown aside as both my students and I were constantly aware of the ancient divide – teachers and children. No matter how fun my classes were, I would always have to stop them from having *too much* fun. Give those little bastards an inch and they'll take a fucking mile.

It was hard to think of them as children as I stood there each day, getting to know them. They were my job. They were little people and they were things. I could make them do what I wanted, with some effort. I could teach them and manipulate them. But ultimately they were kids with the desire to make trouble and have fun at any cost. Even the good ones could surprise me with a sudden deviation from their concentration.

Eric K, one of my youngest students, used to enjoy climbing out of the second-floor window, and I'd frequently have to pull him back in. He'd laugh and giggle, knowing that I always got him in time, and he seemed completely unaware of the possible consequences of his actions. I asked Mr. Park to secure the windows, but he refused, muttering something about money and time.

Another student, Tony J, junk-punched me four times. The problem was that he didn't always mean it, but that I didn't entirely mean for my response to be so aggressive. I hadn't realised before taking the job, but five-year olds are the same height as my crotch. They flail their limbs and can't control their rage. Sometimes it's anger and sometimes it's an accident, but every few weeks, you can expect a punch to the worst place a man can take a punch. If you don't see it coming, you can't really mete out an appropriate response, either. When Tony J first junk-punched me – by accident, I might add – I responded by swiftly back-handing him across the face. It was an accident on my part, too. The shock of a blow to the groin was so unexpected and sickening for me that I had no control over my response. My brain was running slower than my body. Tony J recoiled in fear and horror, expecting the beating of his life, and for the next half an hour that kid was better behaved than he'd ever been.

I was expecting a call from Mr. Park, asking why he'd watched me beat a child on CCTV, or that the kid's parents had phoned the school and wanted to know why a dirty foreigner had slapped their son. But nothing happened. Tony J was just too used to being beaten to register that one extra shot. He knew it at the time, but by the end of the day it was probably gone from his mind, like all the others. It never left me, though. I never forgot the day I hit a child in the face. That sort of thing stays with you for life.

But being another abusive teacher didn't exactly keep the little brats in line. They loved to beat each other, and to cheat and lie. Violence between students wasn't something I liked to see. I had no training in child behaviour, but I knew that some of the students were too young to have much self-control. Many of them had behavioural problems, and many of them showed signs of incredibly violent urges. Someone would borrow a pencil and then the next minute that pencil would be lodged in the arm of another child for no obvious reason. Blood would pour and everyone would scream, and I'd wonder what the hell I was doing there. I didn't even know first aid.

Cheating was a big problem, but the other teachers told me to ignore it. Korea is a brutal, competitive society. *Dog eat dog*, as they say. One big nasty dog farm where children are raised and beaten by strangers until they're ready to go out and make money for their uncaring parents. Every kid in my classes, from smartest to dumbest, would go out of his or her way to cheat on even the smallest task. I told Thomas and he explained that half the foreign teachers in Korea are paid to write entrance essays for Korean students to American universities. Any time a student gets a good grade from school it has nothing to do with studying or intelligence – it comes down to the money in white envelopes that are passed from parent to hagwon owner without questioning the morality of the deed.

Chapter Eleven

The heat became unbearable during July and August.
Even when I managed to get a moment at home to try and
write it was so hot that I couldn't. Sometimes I'd lie on
the bathroom floor with the cold water on my feet. I spent
my time in bars partly to abuse their air conditioning and
suck up the iced drinks. On my way downtown it felt
as though I might melt into the pavements or evaporate
on the subway. There wasn't a breath of air in the city.
Even at night the humidity was stifling, and I'd get drunk
enough to stop caring and then wake up in the morning
absolutely soaked in sweat and unable to do anything
about it. It's a wonder I never died of dehydration. The
fan in my room was pointed at my bed in a vain attempt
to cool me, but mostly it just kept the flies away. Any
Korean person will tell you this is dangerous because it

is a scientifically verified fact that a desk fan can split atoms and result in the immediate death of anyone in the vicinity. Fan Death. Look it up.

Thomas and I would get downtown and burst into a bar or club, then stand in front of the air conditioner for ten minutes before even buying a drink. We had to get cool enough to stay cool and to remove the sweat from our sodden clothes. Once we were settled, though, it wasn't so bad. The nights I stayed at home were tough, and the times I was at home and waiting for the call to go out were particularly uncomfortable. I began spending the minimum amount of time outside or at home that I could possibly manage.

Downtown was my home away from home. I spent most of my time at work, and much of the rest in Effort. We played cards there and talked shit. Thomas, Jonathon, and I were soon close friends, and everyone around us became closer as we spent each night in the same room. Even the people I didn't really know were becoming my brothers-in-arms. We were all united in the same battle for our sanity, lost in a society that simply didn't want us. We were all kept under lock and key during the day, and at night we gathered because we could, and because we had nothing else. There was a very strange and warped sense of community in these places. Sometimes it was unspoken, and at others overstated. Sometimes it split into the military and the teachers, and at other times the gap was bridged.

I had become a part of a scene again. It wasn't like being in Scotland, where I was part of something I cared about and knew. Here, I was lumped in with others according to race and nationality. We were all considered impure and degenerate. I had little in common with anyone except being an outsider, but that was often enough to force conversation. Even if nothing was said, something was shared. I'd buy people drinks and they'd return the favour, and we'd talk about absolutely nothing for five minutes.

The group made my desperation for female companionship worse. It heightened my awareness of Daegu's incestuousness and made me yearn for someone to fuck or love who wasn't already tainted by the jizz of a hundred other guys. It wasn't just Jonathon that was humping his way through the population. The girls I knew all seemed sweet and innocent at first, but later I realised that just wasn't the case. They were like everyone else – horny. At the end of the night they all went home with some guy, and at first I was too naïve to realise.

Thomas and Beth would always leave at the same time and come up with some excuse. Naturally, I believed them. Thomas would say "This is gay. I gotta bounce," and Beth would use that as her cue to have an early night, too. They'd leave under the guise of walking each other to the taxi and no one left behind would say a word. It was only one night, when I said to Thomas that I was also done with drinking and wanted to go home, that he told me to wait five minutes. "Dude, don't be cock-blockin' me from the peanut galleries," he said, in all sincerity.

"What the fuck does that mean? 'Peanuts'?"

"It means I got a thang goin'! Don't be cock-blockin' me, dude!"

"Alright, alright," I said. "Beth? Seriously?" I didn't mean to be nasty, but she wasn't exactly a looker. In fact, as a white chick she broke Thomas's rule about coming to Asia and only fucking the locals.

"Yeah, son, bitch screws like a pro."

"I wouldn't have thought it."

"Beth's all about the balls."

"Gross. Thanks for the image."

"You're welcome. Just wanted you to know. Girl's gonna have my balls all up in her mouth tonight."

"Okay… I won't 'cock-block' you. Just quit ghetto-talkin' me. I have no idea what you're saying."

Thomas laughed. "'Ghetto-talkin'? Seriously?" He laughed again. "Alright, catch you tomorrow."

Thomas and Beth had been fooling around for a while and no one had said a word. Maybe everyone knew, and maybe they didn't. People didn't talk about sex, and I thought at first that it was ignorance or decency. Maybe they respected privacy. Later, I realised that everyone was fucking everyone and talking about it made it all sound worse. They preferred not to think about where their temporary partner had been before.

Jonathon was also cheating on Mina – whom I'd never met after two months of knowing Jonathon – with dozens of others. I'd wander around downtown with him at four or five in the morning as he trawled for ass and only came up with girls he'd already fucked, and sometimes he'd make weird confessions, like: "I pumped that bitch in the toilet at Heart. Only took seven pumps and I was done," or "I fucked both of them and they ain't know it, haha!" I could barely fathom just how many girls he'd been with. They were all stunning, too. He had good taste.

One night we were sitting on the roof of Edge, watching the sun rise over the kimchi pot-littered roofs of brothels and love motels, when he told me that he was screwing Annie. I didn't know what to say. She was a smart chick and he was a dumb military guy. I loved him, but he wasn't really the sort of guy she'd normally go with. I think I realised then just how warped life was for expats in Korea, trapped together in pathetic little groups. Everyone fucked everyone in the orgiastic heat. It was only me who went home alone each night.

"Mina ain't know, but she thinks she knows!" he told

me. "Bitch is crazy. Got the Kimchi Rage."

"Ah yeah, the Kimchi Rage."

"Yeah, Alexander. You know what the Kimchi Rage is, right?"

I said I did.

"Every Korean girl got the Kimchi Rage, Alexander. They're crazy. I mean, you fuck another girl and they'll go fuckin' nuts! Datin' a Korean girl is trouble, man. Mina's cool and everything. I mean, she's hot. But damn, she's crazy." His face contorted as though he'd brought up some hideous memories, and he shook his head violently. "They all are! My ex, Crystal, fucked up my car. Got her brothers to jack my tires and shit! Fucked up."

"I heard about that," I said, but he wasn't listening.

I wondered why there hadn't been more problems created by this giant gangbang, but then reasoned that it was the time constraints of an E2 visa. In a year of teaching, you could only sleep with so many people… Many teachers didn't even reach that one-year mark and bailed early. Some switched cities, leaving a trail of broken condoms and tears from one end of the country to the other.

CHAPTER TWELVE

Daegu began to get intolerably boring for me, and I could hardly imagine what it felt like for Thomas or Jonathon. The heat, the smell, the sights, the people – there was nothing good about Daegu. Everything was unwelcoming. The streets were crowded with the nastiest people on Earth and the air hung around my head like a week-worn sock. I yearned to explore but lacked the motivation to do it by myself, and so months snuck by without my having done a goddamn thing worth remembering. I became furious with myself for having wasted so much time. I couldn't account for any of my weekends, and all my weekdays blurred together into drunken, hungover, sweaty days at work.

One typical drunken night Jonathon suggested that we – referring to the group of friends and casual acquaintances that drunk in Effort four, five, or six nights a week – take a trip to Busan at the weekend. That Friday evening after work I found myself being dragged to Dongdaegu train station and pushed onto the high-speed KTX train to Busan, a port city on the South East coast of the peninsula.

Jonathan, Thomas, Oliver, and I played poker and drank soju and beer around a table as I admired the train. It was more comfortable than any train I'd previously ridden, and cheaper, too. It was travelling at incredible speeds across Korea, rushing us towards a place I was promised surpassed Daegu in all respects. Outside the windows Korea flew by in a blur of green and brown, and I wondered what it was like to stand in the countryside. Annie, Beth, Jenny, Leah, Liz, Mike, Will, and Derek were all littered about the train, talking and scaring the shit of the Korean people, who expected us to start some kind of gunfight at any minute.

Soon we were in Busan and split between taxis, moving slowly across the giant industrial city towards Haeundae – the touristy beach area. Busan smelled so much better than Daegu that I wanted to roll the windows down in spite of the air conditioning. The salty sea breeze was a welcome change from Daegu's still and relentless humidity. The overall temperature, too, was several degrees lower. Even in the darkness I could see Busan was one sprawling ugly mess of a city, but it beat the hell out of Daegu's tame and mundane sequence of convenience stores and brothels.

When the taxi stopped outside a big expensive hotel, I could hear the sea just over a little park full of trees. I had an incredible urge to run towards it and dive in, but Jonathon – who had elected himself leader of our group – said that we needed to find a motel that was cheap and big enough for us to all sleep in one room.

We split and searched for a suitable place in groups of twos, and someone found one after maybe half an hour of wandering around winding little backstreets of neon hotel signs. The rest of us snuck up a fire escape and we all sat in a tiny room with no bed, huddled around a collection of liquor bottles and basking in the ailing air conditioning. Jonathon suggested we play a chaotic drinking game with a pack of cards he'd brought, and soon we were absolutely wasted drunk and falling all over the place. Mike produced three well-rolled but weak joints and about half of us smoked. It had been three months since my last joint, which was longer than I'd gone without a smoke in more than six years. The combined alcohol and pot had me reeling.

At about two in the morning we headed for the beach, stopping on the way to buy dozens of bottles of beer and soju. Will stole three bottles of whiskey from a convenience store and walked out shamelessly as the clerk stood there, too afraid to say a word. I felt a little guilty for a while, but I then forgot about it as we stood on the soft white sand, staring at a welcoming blackness and absence of land. Somewhere out there was Japan, and Jonathon wouldn't let anyone forget about it. It was, he said, the greatest place on Earth.

It was immediately quiet, with no walls off which sound could bounce, and only the lapping of the sea on the sand could be heard over our talking and laughing. Shadows flitted in the dark along the long stretch of empty beach. Apparently Haeundae was busy during the day, but it was impossible to tell.

We sat on the beach and watched the stars, laughing and drinking. No one seemed to want to go in the water, but I did, and I knew Jonathon did. Although we seemed to have little in common, I knew he usually shared my feelings. If I was angry, he was angry. If I was hungry, he was hungry. If I wanted to get naked and dive into the Sea of Japan, then so would he.

I stood up and walked down to the waterline, beckoning Jonathon behind me. I tore off all my clothes, except for my boxer shorts, and ran into the surprisingly warm water. Jonathon followed immediately, laughing like a child. He sometimes got that innocent stupidity of which I was also capable. It happened to us when we were drunk and reverted back to our juvenile selves – forgetting we were adults with bad jobs on the wrong side of the world. We laughed and ploughed through the waves. I began swimming about and wondering when I last swam, or indeed when I'd last felt so happy. I couldn't recall such a feeling of innocence. All the times I'd been drunk in Korea had felt so wrong because I was a foreigner in a country that didn't want me, getting drunk to forget a job I hated, and knowing that I'd go into work hungover. Now it was Friday and I felt unburdened. I was in a new place, doing something different. I felt free.

Some of the others came into the water, but Jonathon and I were much further out than they were. We were bobbing in the water double the distance of the buoys that dictated the furthest safest distance for swimming. We were far enough out to see the shoreline as a blur of orange lights, and to see the city curving around the coast. Even the giant hotels looked tiny and insignificant from our vantage point.

"Man, this was a great idea!" I shouted, treading water excitedly.

"Yeah, dude, I'm so glad we did this."

"I fucking love the sea."

"Me, too, man. Me, too. I'm from California, dude. We got the best beaches in the world!"

"I'll have to come visit you when you're back there one day."

"I'll be here for a long time, Alexander."

"Fuck it, man, you should get out of here. Fuck Korea."

He laughed. "I know. But it's comfortable. I got money, a girlfriend..."

"You're telling me Mina wouldn't come back to the States with you?"

"I guess, man. I mean, she came one time. I took her on vacation a few years back. She might. But shit, Korea's alright."

"I can't imagine myself sticking it out for five years..."

"You get trapped here, Alex. Korea just takes a hold of you. Everyone who opens up gets stuck. They don't like it, but they get stuck here."

"Well, shit," I said. "If I could do this every weekend then maybe I could stay in Korea a few years."

"Yeah, man, this is the shit! We need to do this more often."

We swam nearer to shore after our bodies became tired from the exertion of drunkenly treading water and paddled about with the others. Only Thomas, Oliver, and Beth sat on the beach. Everyone else was splashing about.

"Yo! Let's get naked!" Jonathon shouted, and everyone laughed. It seemed like a dumb drunken suggestion that would go nowhere, but by the time they had a chance to dismiss it, he'd whipped off his shorts and slapped me hard in the side of the face with them. I laughed and took off my own, and then Derek followed. Mike and Will laughed and shouted "fags!" and swam back to shore.

Annie swam around us, laughing, but she kept her bathing suit on. "Alexander, you're so fucking crazy when you're drunk!" she said. "You, too, Jonathon. But you're always kinda crazy..."

Jenny, Liz, and Leah all took their tops off and floated about on the water, as Annie swam off back to shore, looking embarrassed. Jonathon began whooping and hollering like a real military boy, and I quietened a little, suddenly feeling a little embarrassed. I hadn't expected to see my friends' breasts floating in the moonlight, or Jonathon's white ass glimmering like the moon in the water.

We laughed and splashed about for maybe three or four minutes as Jonathon tried to get the girls to take off their bikini bottoms, but they wouldn't. After a while, Liz and Leah put their tops back on and swam back to shore with Derek, calling Jonathon and I "super gay." Jenny stayed with us as we frolicked around where our feet could only barely touch the sand.

"So you guys are actually hardcore," she said. Jenny spoke strangely. She was Japanese-American and spoke in some weird ghetto accent that I couldn't place, and probably was unique only to her. She clenched her jaw a lot when she spoke and popped her shoulders like a lot of the military guys. She was attractive, but strangely macho in spite of her stunning tits and ass.

"Yeah, Jenny," I said. "Didn't you know? Us Scots and honorary Scots are super-fucking-hardcore."

"Jonathon's an honorary Scot?"

"Shit, yeah. I couldn't let him wallow in American citizenship forever. He drinks too much and too well to be a Yank."

"Didn't know you were the kinda guy to get naked in public, Alexander…" she said. "I mean, I know Jonathon's a perv and everything, so I kinda expected…"

"Fuck you, Jenny!" Jonathon shouted. "If you didn't have such big titties I'd drown yo ass out here!"

Jenny snorted. "They don't always float," she said, and disappeared under water to prove the fact. Jonathon turned and looked at me and raised his eyebrows as though to say, *Bitch is crazy!*

Soon, though, Jenny's head was back above the water and Jonathon was red-faced and grinning. She was jerking him off under water as I stood awkwardly, suddenly very aware of my nakedness. "Er…" I began to say something, searching for a witty remark or anything to alleviate the weirdness and to excuse myself, but nothing came to mind. I just started to swim away while sliding my boxers back on.

"Hold up, Alex," Jonathon shouted. "She's got you next."

I just laughed and swam away.

After five or so hours of drinking on the beach I blacked out and woke up in the motel. The group was spread out across the floor, lying like sardines from wall to wall. I was lying between Annie and Jenny, and I realised that what had woken me up wasn't the sun or the air conditioning. It was only nine o'clock and I'd slept for less than two hours. I didn't really want to be awake, and it didn't look like anyone else was up.

I realised that Jenny's hand was on my dick and she was rubbing it slowly as I lay on my back, feeling even more awkward than I had done in the sea. My shoulders and legs were touching Annie, and most of my friends were lying around the room. If any of them woke up they'd have an ugly view of my junk. I raised my head a little and looked over. Jenny looked as though she was asleep, but she was grinning, and I knew it was a ruse. That horny little bitch. I could see that she had Jonathon's dick in her other hand and was slowly waking him up. At least, I hoped she woke him up, or else someone was about to be woken by a faceful of jizz.

Jonathon woke and grabbed Jenny's thigh, and she sat up and swallowed his come. A minute later I did the same and she sat up and took that, too.

"Ain't so bad, Alexander," she said, laughing softly. "Jesus." Then she rolled over and went back to sleep, leaving Jonathon and I looking at each other in disbelief. His face was a picture of shock and delight, and he kept shaking his head like he couldn't believe his luck. Even a player like him didn't get that happening every day.

"Let's go," I said.

"Where?"

"Beach. Beer."

We stood up and dressed, and I realised that I'd lost various items of clothing, but I didn't care, and went outside half-naked. We walked onto the street, which was bright enough to burn my retinas, but pleasantly warm in the sea breeze and under the bluest of skies. There was neither stifling humidity nor rank stench of human excrement. We walked into a convenience store and picked up four beers each, and walked slowly towards the beach, laughing and smiling. It was the happiest I'd been in Korea.

CHAPTER THIRTEEN

"So d'you fuck Jenny or what?" Thomas asked me at school on Monday, having kept quiet about it all weekend. A sick part of me wondered if anyone knew what had happened in the motel, or even if they'd mistakenly thought I'd screwed Jenny in the sea. There was some definite street-cred to be gained from doing a thing like that, and after a few months of obvious patheticness demonstrated by the innate social dysfunction of not getting laid in such a sleazy city, it would have been very cool to have finally – and publicly – banged a chick in Korea.

"I'm not the kind of guy to kiss and tell," I said, turning my back and fumbling pointlessly with a stack of papers, hoping that Thomas would press the matter further.

"Kinda looked like you fucked her from where we

were standing," he said. "I'm surprised you guys didn't drown."

I laughed. "No, man, I didn't fuck her. I didn't want to catch anything that Jonathon gave her."

"You know she's only eighteen, right?"

"Huh?" I didn't know. I thought Jenny was my age or even older.

Thomas laughed hard and the feigned disappointment by shaking his head. "You youngsters... Can't stop screwin' each other. But damn, son, she's young enough to be in school!"

"Don't judge me. I'm about the only guy in this city not fucking some different bird each night of the week... Your cocks are all gonna drop off if you're not careful."

"Not me, son. I'm careful, and I don't really fuck as many girls as you think. In fact, I'm a pretty picky guy."

"That's what I thought, but what about Beth? How d'you know she's not riddled with the syph? I mean, she's fucking you, so she's probably fucked a bunch of other guys."

Thomas snorted. "Bitch probably got the syph, but I ain't care... I always wrap my shit. I'm careful, son."

"Even so..."

"'Even so' nothing. Don't gimme your spook stories 'cause I'm getting some legal pussy and you're stuck with high school girls who drift in from the sea."

"I'm just sayin', man, I don't wanna see you getting the syph from some hoe."

Thomas just laughed and waved me away.

Far from sating my appetite, that little incident with Jenny in Busan made me realise how long it had been since I had gotten laid, and how badly I wanted a meaningless fling. Moreover, I wanted something better than that. Sarah still occupied a big place in my mind, and I thought about her every single day. I thought about missed chances and lost love, and I wished for someone to hold. I needed something real, but in the meantime I would be happy to take whatever came my way.

Downtown at nights I spent more time on the dancefloor and less at the table talking to friends. I tried my luck with a bunch of Korean girls and kept either striking out with the clean-looking ones or bailing on the dirty girls when I had images flash through my mind of my rotting scrotum after their nasty diseases had their way with me.

I made out with a Japanese girl one night but was shut down and later she disappeared back to Japan. Jonathan and Thomas were disappointed because they wanted in on the Japan action. Both of them fantasised about Japan. Jonathon had been there and would tell me stories about the girls he fucked, and Thomas was obsessed with Japanese movies and always dreamed of hooking up with a real Japanese girl.

I found myself becoming repulsed by Western girls *and* Korean girls. The only girls that appealed to me were the ones that looked Korean and acted Western. I hated the fact that all the Korean girls were dumb, racist, and without manners, and that all the Western girls were fat and loud. I felt like I was surrounded by pigs wherever I went. Either they looked like pigs or they acted like pigs. Daegu was a city full of swine.

Annie and Beth helped me deal with the loneliness by telling me the right girl was around the corner. It was all clichéd bullshit but it actually helped. They both came on to me from time to time and I knew I could have slept with either of them, but I didn't want to. I didn't want to lose a friend, and I didn't want to catch anything. I figured if Jonathon had been in them, they'd probably have caught something.

"It's a shallow pool," Annie explained to me one night. "You take what you can get. All the guys here are fugly as hell – I mean *busted* fugly – so don't go whining about the girls. It sucks for us, too. You've either got loser teacher boys, dumb soldier bros, or Korean guys."

"Yeah, Alexander, you're in a place where most people don't speak English, and a lot of the ones who do are from a culture so far from yours that you'll never get along with them." I looked at Beth and her wise words made me want to fuck her immediately, regardless of what it would do to my relationship with Thomas. "There are, like, *no* good guys here. People in Korea are weird, and I don't just mean the Koreans. Foreign guys are *creepy...* Did Thomas tell you about Beardo? He used to work at your school before you did. That guy was straight up fucked."

"Yeah, man, and everyone's dated everyone. It's incestuous."

I didn't tell them that I knew about their flings with Thomas and Jonathon, although they probably knew I knew. I just took their strangely comforting words and tried to forget about love and hope. I'd gone from thinking that maybe I'd find love in Korea to thinking that maybe I'd just wait a year and find someone when I got back to civilisation.

That night, however, I struck lucky on the floor of Club Starz. Usually a place for young hip-hop wannabes and a few misguided foreigners, Starz lacked the space and street-cred of Edge. The door staff were nicer – always aiming to get the foreign crowd inside with compliments and drink offers. I'd gotten to know the owners on a first name basis – through Jonathon, the social butterfly – and I had at least one free drink every night.

Inside, Starz was nothing more than a giant dancefloor

and a bar. It was all on one level and was always sweaty in spite of the powerful air conditioning. I liked that it was less crowded that Edge, and I liked that the cute girls behind the bar knew my name and would serve me first, no matter how many other people were waiting for drinks.

Jonathon and Thomas had disappeared and I'd come to Starz with Oliver, who had then wandered off somewhere. It was about three in the morning and I didn't care that I was on my own. I was drunk, had another drink in my hand, and for some reason I was horny enough that I didn't simply black out and go home. I looked around the dancefloor, hoping to find one of the drunken skanks that loved white guys, but I couldn't find any of them. By three in the morning they'd all already been taken home.

I swayed stupidly in front of the DJ, drinking and just moving with the beats, trying to forget that I had to wake up in five hours and go to work. I looked around at all the girls and imagined fucking them all at once, just lying on the dancefloor and letting them crawl naked over me. Then I remembered that most of them were all probably the same age as Jenny and I told myself to stop. One girl, however, looked older. She looked about twenty-five and had bleached hair and giant breasts.

I stared at those huge, pert boobs and lost myself in filthy fantasies. Her tiny little gold cocktail dress covered only a fraction of those puppies, and I wanted her to turn because I suspected she was showing that much ass, too. She obviously read my mind because she immediately turned and showed that big, tight butt, the cheeks of which protruded slightly from below the golden hem of her tasteless but somehow gorgeous outfit.

I couldn't believe it but in between the words she spoke to her unattractive friends, the girl seemed to look at me and bite seductively on her straw. I assumed she was looking at some guy behind me, so I didn't get too excited, but I couldn't stop staring. She was perfect - an angel among the swine.

I stood and swayed like a moron, waiting for someone I knew to come find me and go grab some kalbi. I blacked out for a second as the booze gripped my tired mind and the monotonous beats lulled me half to sleep. When I came around again the girl was standing right in front of me. She sneered a little as though she were mocking my drunkenness. I guessed that she'd liked what she seen and come in for a closer look, only to be disappointed.

"Dance with me!" she said, in decent English. She sounded almost American, but I could tell she wasn't. Only a Korean would dress that badly.

"Sure," I mumbled, and stared at her tits. There was no point in being subtle. She didn't look like the subtle type, with her gold dress, bleached hair, face caked in make-up, and what I now suspected were fake breasts. She was, in spite of all that, absolutely stunning.

We shuffled badly for a few minutes. She moved more than I did and seemed to look away from me a whole lot. It was almost as though she didn't want to be with me. I didn't care because I was drunk and honoured to be dancing with the girl that I knew every guy the club was staring at. I just enjoyed the close-up view while I could, and moved closer and closer, wondering if I could just squeeze her ass.

I did. I grabbed her butt and squeezed it gently, just to make sure this angel was real. It felt almost too perfect. I rubbed the skin with my thumb and fingertips and told myself to remember this tomorrow.

"Like, don't get any ideas... I've, like, got a boyfriend..." She spoke like an idiot but I didn't care. I barely heard the word "boyfriend" because it seemed so irrelevant. Maybe Korean girls play stupid mind-games, too, I thought. Maybe she's telling me she has a boyfriend so I try and win her over.

"I don't care," I said.

"You should, he's a soldier."

"So am I."

She laughed. Damn, I thought, she isn't as dumb as she looks.

"I'm in the Scottish army. It's not a great army, but y'know... We've been independent for a while. We fought in Korea. Kicked ass. Saved you guys from yourselves."

She obviously wasn't listening. Her eyes were somewhere else, but her hands were on my chest, and working their way down, down, down... She stopped at my belt, which by this point was being pushed upwards by my dick as it stretched towards those giant tits.

"So are you gonna fuckin' kiss me or what?"

"What about the soldier?" I asked.

"It's three in the morning – he's already back on base. Fuckin' curfew and shit!"

I pulled her towards me and pushed indecently up against her. We made out sloppily like high school kids and I started rubbing my hands all over her, totally losing any control and decorum I might have had with a less attractive girl. I was a mess and she wasn't exactly composed, either. Her hands were rubbing my junk and her tits were almost falling out of that little cocktail dress.

"Let's go," I said. "My dick's about to explode."

She said nothing as I dragged her to the door and tried to get her onto the street. Then she complained that her jacket was in a locker and her friend had the key, so I gave the doorman five thousand Won to open the fucking thing immediately, just so I didn't have to wait an extra minute or risk a friend convincing her to ditch me.

We hopped in a taxi and I kept telling her to make the

driver go faster. I didn't care what she thought. I looked like a horny idiot and didn't care. Sitting next to me was the finest piece of ass I'd seen in Korea, and she was coming back to my apartment in the middle of the night. I hadn't played it cool at any stage, and now was no time for decency.

When we burst in the door, I immediately threw her on the bed and began fumbling with the cocktail dress. It was a hideous blight of a thing, threatening to ruin the perfection of her skin. It took impossible beauty to look good in such a monstrous outfit that I wondered what would happen when I ripped it off.

Her breasts didn't even look fake when I set them free. They looked like perfect mounds of real flesh, with perfect little real nipples. They were perfect as I flicked them, licked them, and buried my head between them.

Then I pulled down her red panties and caressed her warm, hot, and hair pussy. I could barely control myself as I looked down at her writhing naked body on my dirty bed. She was smiling now – a happy, naked, smiling, gorgeous little plaything for me to hump all night. I felt so much lust for her that I wondered if that was love. Had any girl's mind and being ever eclipsed that much physical beauty? What more could a man want than this perfect little body to lie on?

She dropped my pants and began fellating me in an awkward, toothy manner than didn't put me off her in the slightest. After thirty seconds I stopped her because I thought she might damage my dick and we wouldn't be able to fuck. I was glad she was no good at giving head, though, because that meant she had probably fucked fewer guys than any other girl in town.

I threw her back and lay on top, then pushed it inside. It wasn't easy. She was wet, but her pussy was tighter than any girl I'd ever known. I wondered for a second if

I'd stuck it in her asshole by mistake, but the look on her face said I'd hit the spot. She kept making these weird noises – like a dying animal with a sock in its mouth. "Uh-aaah! Oh-eeeh!" She was wailing loudly, and I wondered if the neighbours would be woken. But with every passing minute she seemed to take it better, and after a while I began to suspect the squealing was an act – a symbol of submission that was meant to turn a guy on. Hell, it *did* turn me on! I've always loved strong and sexual women, but this girl knew how to make a guy feel like a king. She lay there, squealing and wincing like it was her first time. The pangs of guilt I should have felt were allayed by the renewed feelings of lust I got as I looked down at her body and watched myself pound her little snatch. She was too hot... I couldn't take it... She didn't seem like she was going to come anytime soon, so I thrust hard a few more times and exploded inside her. Bless her heart, she pretended. She did a bad job of it, but she pretended just there at the end that she came.

I rolled off and smiled as I stared at the ceiling. We were both dripping sweat and struggling for breath. The rising morning sun was beginning to slip between the paper I'd stuck to the windows and it fell upon our naked bodies, but I could hardly look. I'd had an erection for such a long time that I was relieved to be temporarily rid of it. If I saw her lying there again I'd probably die from having too much blood in any one part of me. I just looked at the crusty ceiling and said silently to myself: "Well done, sir!" I laughed like an idiot, and she probably thought I was crazy, but I didn't care. I could retire from sex and know that nothing better was going to come along. That was it – the girl every guy aimed for. Anything else would be a step backwards.

I imagined waiting an hour or two and doing it again, and then showering and making breakfast and skipping work. We'd go to the beach and drink beer all day, and then sleep in a motel at night, and after that... Who knew? Anything was possible now. We'd probably get married and have kids and I'd spend the rest of my life lying on top of her, jackhammering away and never having to think about money or work or anything ever again.

I drifted into a dream for what couldn't have been more than twenty-minutes, but when I woke up and looked over, she was gone. My heart broke for a second, and then I told myself that no one plateaus like that. When you take a pill you always peak and fall back to Earth. If you're lucky you'll get up there again some day, but you never stay there. Life works in such ways. People would probably try harder if good things stuck.

Chapter Fourteen

Of course, when nine o'clock rolled around I wasn't at the beach with my beautiful nameless girl. I was at school, hungover, and wondering if it had really happened. It seemed so implausible. After months of going downtown and coming home alone, it seemed ludicrously unlikely that I would have gone home with the most beautiful girl in the city. I must have dreamed it, or else it was a drunken hallucination.

Either way I told Thomas as soon as I saw him. He seemed happy for me although I wasn't entirely sure if he believed me. I wondered if maybe he pretended he did to make me feel less pathetic. Maybe he believed I got laid, but that I fucked some poor unfortunate skank and was just exaggerating her looks. It didn't matter, anyway. I was beginning to realise I'd never see her again. She was now a memory and a story from my past.

When the bell rang there was no sign of Karen. Neither Thomas nor I noticed this fact at the time. We were busy talking disgustingly about Korean girls and walking to our classes. It was only after those first classes that we walked into the teachers' room again and were confronted by an irate Mr. Park.

"Where Karen?" he barked. "Where Karen go?"

I stood mute and afraid, wondering if Mr. Park was about to explode. He was angrier than I had ever seen him. His face was beet red. I wanted to say, "I don't know," but I couldn't even bring myself to do that. My head was pounding from the hangover and I was so tired and exhausted I could barely think, let alone speak.

Thomas, however, burst out laughing. When he laughed he made a scene. He didn't necessarily laugh as a natural reaction to something funny. Thomas usually laughed out loud as a way of drawing other people's attention to something funny. He slapped his giant thighs and bent over, bawling hysterically. "Dude…" he began. "She did the Midnight Run?" He laughed louder still. "That's freaking awesome!"

Mr. Park grew redder and redder until he began shouting again: "Why laugh? Why funny? This serious! Where Karen?"

I was trying not to laugh at the sight of Mr. Park throwing a tantrum. The fear had run out of me pretty quickly, and all I was concerned with was keeping myself respectable. Thomas obviously didn't care. He knew he was untouchable. If Karen had really quit in the night then we were both untouchable. Parky had no one else to take over. In a school that should really have been run with four or five foreign teachers, there were now only two. He couldn't fire Thomas for laughing. He probably wouldn't have fired him if Thomas decided to slap him right in the face.

Mr. Park looked at me and decided to ignore Thomas. He drew himself up and asked quietly, "Where... is... she? Where Karen?"

I cleared my throat and answered, "I honestly don't know. I haven't seen her since we left work yesterday."

Mr. Park looked satisfied to have gotten some kind of answer and turned away into his office. He slammed the door and all the other teachers began talking again. I didn't notice until he was gone, but they'd been silent as they watched us. Thomas was wiping tears from his eyes, and saying, "Dude... dude... dude..." as he tried to explain just how funny it was that Karen had bailed.

He managed to express his thoughts in between classes as the laughter subsided. "Dude, this is awesome. We all taught ten hours a day and now Karen's gone he can't even give us any more classes. This school needs *at least* three foreigners to operate. Damn, dude, this is hilarious. I love the idea of Parky having to explain to the parents why their kids ain't getting taught by a foreigner. They pay so much money to have one of us teaching them. It'll take weeks to get another teacher, too. He's gonna lose so many students! He's screwed!"

I said I agreed and that it was funny, but I didn't laugh. I hated Mr. Park and Charleston, but I didn't think that Karen's departure was anything to laugh about. Sure, it was funny that Parky was stressed and angry, but I didn't really care about vengeance. I was a little jealous, in fact, that Karen had the guts to turn and run.

After work we went next door to the Pajeon Place for dinner and soju. I wanted to go downtown but Thomas said he was too tired and I didn't have a phone to call Jonathon. My house phone evidently could only receive calls. Besides, I realised it was for the better if I went home early and got a good night's sleep. I'd only slept a couple of hours the night before, and if I went downtown I'd no doubt wander around the clubs until five or six in the morning, searching for the nameless girl.

"Can you believe Karen? That's shit's ballsy, son. I mean, she just upped and left like that."

"Can you blame her?"

"I'm not sayin' I *blame* her. Shit, she did the right thing. It's just... wow. Y'know? We were all in this thing together. She could've at least said 'goodbye' or something. She could've handed in her notice. Could've waited for a replacement teacher." He sipped his beer and soju mix and looked mournfully at the little bowls of spicy sides in front of us. "I know I said earlier it was funny – and it *is*, in a way – but it's also a little fucked when you think on it... I mean, I wouldn't just bail on you guys without a single word. I wouldn't run off in the night and leave you to clean up. It's great that Parky's upset – that's what I was laughing at – but she didn't need to do that shit."

"Ah, come on. Don't be sore. Like you said earlier, it's not like it can get worse for us. We're already at full schedule."

"Hey, man, you don't know. Karen and I were here long before you, Lucky Charms. We had a history. It was awful before you arrived. We stuck it out and when you came things got easier. Man, when Parky gets pissed things turn ugly. It's funny to an extent, but then again it's all gonna come crashin' down on us. Y'know, you don't think things here can get any worse, but they can and they will. Lemme tell you... Ah, shit. It ain't worth it."

"I understand, man. It sucks that she bailed on us, but I can't bring myself to be angry at her, and I wouldn't be totally angry at you if you did the same. It's hard living in Korea, and it's even harder when you have a shitty job. She couldn't take it any more and she snapped. So shit. We'll suffer a little for the next few weeks, but after that we're okay. A new teacher'll come along and pretty soon you're done here. Then I'm done. We're not here that long, man."

Thomas sighed. He looked serious and sincere for a change. Normally, even when he was angry he was theatrical and comedic. Now he looked depressed.

"What was the deal with you and her, anyway?" I asked, not really expecting an answer.

Thomas looked around, trying to avoid eye contact. He didn't want to answer me, but he knew it would help to get it out. "Shit, man. That girl... I liked her. We were friends back in the day. Things were different before you came, Alexander. That's not to say it was your fault, not at all. Just... when we were stuck in it together we were pretty close. Things started falling apart a few days before you arrived, and all of a sudden it was like she didn't want to be around me at all. She didn't want to get a beer after work or talk between classes. I don't know..."

"Did you fuck her?"

He snorted. "It was complicated, man. She... We were close. We hung out together at the apartments a lot, watchin' movies and shit. We'd share the same bed and tell each other everything. I didn't know what was goin' on, y'know? It was like we were datin' without the sex or something. Twice we got drunk and made out a bit, but we never spoke about it. Then, you came along."

"I see..."

"I didn't mean it like that. It's just, the dynamic changed. Two guys, one girl. Things are different. She became distant, I didn't make the effort... It was no one's fault."

"Shit happens, huh?"

"I think she started to get pretty lonely."

"Yeah, but that's not your fault, or mine, or hers. Like I said, shit happens."

"Yeah." He poured a half glass of beer and soju down his throat and immediately poured himself another. "Fuck it. Everyone leaves, right? Like Jonathon's always bitchin' on about: Everyone leaves. You make a friend one day, the next they're gone. Life in Korea, Alexander. That's how it goes."

CHAPTER FIFTEEN

Jonathon threw a barbeque on the roof of his apartment a week after my tryst with the hot Korean girl whose name I never knew. I'd made no secret of that night. In fact, in spite of my general distaste for boastfulness and macho nonsense, I was so proud of myself and so shocked by my luck that I told everyone I knew about a beautiful girl with a tiny snatch and giant breasts. The guys had all gotten a kick out of the story and most of them had bought me drinks as a form of congratulations. Annie and Beth seemed happy for me, too.

I was still riding that wave of euphoria as we approached the barbeque. People kept joking that I'd meet another gorgeous girl wherever we went, and I loved the attention. My confidence was rising higher than ever before and I began looking at every woman I saw as a potential fuck-buddy. Instead of seeing them and wondering what I'd have to do to get into their panties, I began asking myself whether I could do better. I had to be careful with my next step in the world of women – I couldn't take too great of a step down or else I might never climb back to the top.

I thought a lot about that nameless nymphet in the night. I could remember the contours of her body and the quiver of her tiny snatch any time I closed my eyes, and usually my memory of anything was pretty poor. Just like my seemingly hopeless faith prior to her entry into my life that I'd meet someone like her, I now hoped that she would return. There was every chance that she would. Daegu was a small city with a smaller club scene, and I was out almost every night. If she stepped back into a club, I'd probably see her again.

I thought about Sarah, too. In brutal, sad, comparative facts she was simply nowhere near the nameless girl in terms of looks. Sarah was pretty in a plain way, and I'd always liked her for her razor-sharp wit and her kindness towards her friends. When I thought about the two of them I thought how it would be surely impossible to blend those qualities without the world imploding. Wars would be waged and men would drop dead as blood rushed uselessly to their dicks. She would be the perfect woman. Hell, they were both near perfect, only in different ways. I knew I'd lost Sarah, and I didn't want to lose this nameless girl. But at the same time I wondered if she was the one for me. Would I look weird walking around with such a beauty on my arm? Did beauties like her even walk around? Or did they just come out at night and stay at home all day, making themselves look perfect? Did they even really exist? I wondered if maybe I'd gone crazy and imagined the whole thing… She was more like an airbrushed vision from a movie than a real, live human being.

Needless to say, I looked forward to the barbeque and the possibility that maybe I'd meet another girl and that my newfound confidence would let me walk away with her on my arm. Hell, maybe the nameless girl would be there! Jonathon lived near the military base and her supposed boyfriend was in the military. It was highly unlikely, but then so were the chances of a guy like me hooking up with a girl like her.

It was a particularly hot day and another sweaty night when the barbeque swung around. Thomas and I finished up work and each went home to shower, and then took a taxi towards Camp Walker. We found Jonathon's place and headed up to the roof, where we could hear hip-hop and laughing.

There were a dozen or so military-looking guys – big Americans with buzzed heads and confused looks on their angular cut faces. They stood around and spoke loudly, laughing and jeering about things I just couldn't make out. The rest of our little group sat around a picnic table, and a few groups of vaguely familiar people clustered elsewhere, everyone munching burgers as Jonathon flipped huge chunks of meat on the grill.

"Alexander! Thomas! Gimme some love!" Jonathon shouted as he saw us. Great, I thought; he was standing with the meathead soldiers. They were the only people on the roof I didn't want to talk to.

"What up, brother?" he addressed both of us. Then he turned to the soldiers and said, "Yo, this boy's new in town and is getting that mad pussy! Alex, tell 'em about the pussy you hit last week!"

I laughed and wondered how I could get away without saying a word. These guys were each about double my weight and didn't look impressed with me. They all wore sweatshirts from NFL franchises and I wore a t-shirt with a picture of a computer game character on it. I could hear them shouting "fag!" in their heads.

"Yeah, I… I banged some hot little thing. Got some Korean ass…" I didn't know what to say or how to say it, so I nodded and left it at that, instead turning and walking towards the people I knew, hoping that I wouldn't have to speak to them again.

I could see Thomas mingling with a group of three Korean girls in a dark corner. The smooth bastard was introducing himself before the party really got underway and they left with another guy. I wondered what Beth thought about it, but then realised I didn't care. I didn't want any part of any drama.

"Alexander, you sly bastard! Got anymore pussy?" Oliver was typically bereft of subtlety.

I laughed and said I hadn't, but the night was young, and that maybe the last one would swing by and he could see her with his own eyes. "I wish you'd been there, man," I said. "The only person who saw her was me. Where did you get to that night, anyway?"

Oliver offered some explanation as Beth talked over him: "You guys are fucked up," she snorted. "Nobody's as hot as Alexander says this girl was. No one."

The night dragged along in typical form and I began to wish that we were inside, in spite of the scenery. To the south was Apsan Mountain and all around us were the lights of the city. It didn't look so ugly from Jonathon's roof. The stars were invisible because of the pollution, but I could imagine them, and the clouds of smog looked pretty as they glimmered purple in the streetlights.

I began to slip into drunkenness and the night started blending together like all the others. Then she appeared. I was sitting with Annie and Beth on the white patio furniture when I saw someone new come up from the little stairway and onto the grey concrete of the roof. It was her – the nameless girl I'd spent a week dreaming about seeing again.

She wore a tiny little green cocktail dress. Just like the gold one it was ugly as hell, but barely detracted from her physical beauty. She teetered across the concrete on high heels, breasts pushed out against the world, her bleached hair sitting perfectly in the still air. She couldn't see me and I couldn't move. I wanted to shout her name but I didn't know it. I wanted to get up and run across and push her to the ground and fuck her right there and then, in front of everyone.

I contemplated telling Annie and Beth that she was there, but then I wondered if maybe she had been telling the truth about having a boyfriend. Maybe she really was dating a military guy and she had fucked me on the side. If that was the case, I would be happy to win her over, but I didn't want to get beaten senseless and thrown over the edge of the building. I sat there and watched her. She approached two other Korean girls and laughed and hugged them. There was something sad about how vacuous they looked – as though they were simply doing what they'd seen rich American girls doing on stupid reality TV shows. Nonetheless, it turned me on and I wondered what I'd have to do to get the three of them into bed…

I watched her teeter about unsteadily as she waved and flirted and seemed to go nowhere. Pretty soon, I knew, she'd see me. Then it would be her choice whether we spoke or not. If her boyfriend was here she'd probably ignore me, and if he wasn't then who knew? Maybe she'd straddle me right here and now and that would be it.

I shook my head. I'd fucked a beautiful girl but I was getting carried away by my horniness. Had she given me syphilis and now I was going crazy? I didn't care.

She wobbled over to the grill and I saw Jonathon turn and look at her. He didn't look happy. How could a guy not look happy to see that sexy little body move towards him? He turned back to his grill and shook his head, muttering something to himself as the girl kept talking. Her shoulders dropped a little and her head bobbed from side to side and I knew she wasn't happy, either. What the hell? Did they know each other?

Suddenly I felt violently sick. I thought I was about to vomit as I realised that the girl was Mina. Jonathon's girlfriend of four years. She was the girl he hated and loved and cheated on but said that he'd probably end up marrying. She was the most important girl in his life. This was their roof. I was sitting on their house, drinking their beer and telling people about fucking her and no one knew except me. And any damn minute she was going to turn around and see me and she'd know. And then somehow Jonathon would find out and he'd know, and I'd lose the best friend I had in this rotten country!

How did fate spring such a cruel trick? How could the best thing in my life become the worst? How did I become such an arsehole without knowing it? The feeling of sickness in my gut was split into the fear that Jonathon would find out, bring his soldier buddies across, and beat the shit of me, and the self-hatred that came from having wronged a friend.

Looking over at them left me stunned into silence. I completely withdrew from the people around me as I studied their body language and hoped to determine what was said. If she told him now I might just have enough time to run away. Hell, if he got his soldier buddies to jump me I'd probably stand a better chance just jumping over the edge and breaking my legs on the street.

But why would she tell him? She hadn't seen me. Not

yet, anyway. She couldn't tell him.

I had to escape. I needed to get off the roof and go home and somehow avoid ever meeting the two of them. I stood up and pushed towards the steps, knowing that if I slipped away no one would be particularly surprised. I was known for getting drunk all of a sudden and disappearing into the night. There would be nothing suspicious about it if I could just get to the steps without being seen…

"Alexander!" I tried to ignore it but the voice rang out again: "Alexander!" It was Jonathon. He didn't sound angry, but I didn't want to speak to him.

I stopped, turned, and walked slowly towards him. Mina still had her back to me. She was playing with her phone and I knew that if she looked up and saw me too late, she'd probably give it away. She had to turn now and see me and get the surprise over with before something awful happened.

"Where you going, man? You ain't bailing, right?"

"Er… Just, er… I was going downstairs. To the bathroom. I gotta piss."

"Charming. Well what d'you want, man? Burger? Hot dog? Ribs?"

He turned back to the grill and flipped a few random pieces of meat. At that point Mina turned and looked at me and her face lost some of its beauty. She aged ten years in an instant and lost any innocence she previously seemed to hold. Fear gripped her, but she stayed quiet. Her eyes penetrated mine and she gestured without subtlety that she wanted to know what the fuck I was doing there.

"Er… Burger. Yeah, I'll take a burger. Just hold up a minute," I said, turning and walking sharply for the steps. I climbed down, half intending to bail on the whole party. I wanted to run home, grab my passport and head for the airport. I felt like a total dick and I couldn't cope with the guilt.

I rushed down into the house and through the mess. The living room was huge and crowded with unnecessary furniture, covered in items of clothing and discarded boxes. There was a kitty litter box under a table that looked like it had never been emptied, and the place stank of cat piss and shit. The kitchen was big, too, but covered in bottles and dirty dishes, and trash bags lay ripped open. It looked like nobody had cleaned the house in years. I wondered how Mina had ever managed to make herself so beautiful in such a dump.

I ran into the nasty, mildew covered bathroom and puked into the blackened toilet. I flushed it and stood up. In the mirror I saw that I was whiter than usual. My hair was plastered to my face. I looked guilty. People would know something was wrong. What could I do? I had to go back up, even if it was for five minutes. I also had to speak to Mina, but I couldn't do it now because it would be too obvious. The thought of even looking at her again made me sick with shame and remorse.

Someone tapped on the door. I stayed quiet. Was it Jonathon coming to kill me? No, that was ridiculous. Was it just someone needing to piss? "I'm pissing," I shouted, angling for a response.

"Open the fucking door!" Mina hissed.

I ran and opened it and she barged in. "Oh shit, you can't come in," I cried. "We're trapped!"

"Fuck you, Alexander, this is my fucking house!"

"I'm sorry," I said. "I didn't know. I didn't even know your name. How could I have known?"

"Jesus, we're in trouble."

"I know, I know. I can't believe this."

"Listen, Alexander, we gotta keep this fucking quiet. Like, real fucking quiet. Jon and I got problems but he's my guy and I'm not losing him."

"Good, good." Her words soothed me a little. I could feel my heartbeat slowing to a healthier rhythm. "We can't say a word…"

"You're not gonna get all honest on me?"

"No, absolutely not. I'm keeping my mouth shut."

"Good," she said, turning towards the door. "Seriously, Alexander, if you say a word I'll kill you."

"Likewise," I said, although I didn't mean it. I'd rather run than kill an angel like her. Even now, with all the goddamn heat and tension and trouble I couldn't stop staring at her breasts. They were barely covered by that slip of shimmering green wrapped around her fragile little body.

She turned and put her hands to her temples in despair. It didn't quite look like real despair but I believed it. I think she just didn't want to ruin her makeup. "Alright, alright, once more," she said. "Quick. Jon's cooking. He'll be busy for ages."

"No… We can't…" Even as I said those words my fingertips were sinking into the flesh on her ass cheeks and my dick was rising quickly. She was fumbling with my zipper, trying to get my shorts off and pull my dick out.

"Quick, quick, quick," she kept saying. She pulled her panties to one side and I pushed it inside her again, feeling that amazingly tight, hot pussy squeezing my dick. I pounded her as hard as I could, as fast as I could, wanting it to be over in seconds. With a fuck like this it didn't matter how long it took.

"Uh-aah! Oh-eeh!" Shit! She was making those noises again! "Uh-aah! Oh-eeh!" Like a little animal being castrated she kept squealing and I knew the jig was up if anyone was anywhere inside the house.

"Shut up!" I cried. "Shut the fuck up!" I was in blind

panic and for some reason that just made me fuck her harder, which made her squeal louder!

"Uh-aah! Oh-eeh! Uh-aah! Oh-eeh!"

I put my hand over her mouth and she promptly bit the flesh as hard as she could, so I screamed and pounded her harder. She kept squealing. "Don't stop!" she said, the first real words she'd actually used.

"I'll stop if you don't cease that infernal squealing!"

"Wait, wait, wait! Aaaah!" Her pussy began convulsing hard around my dick and she squealed almost at the top of her lungs. I knew I was fucked and I was so damn close. She began backing away but I was seconds from finishing.

"Wait!" I whispered. "Just…"

It was too late. She pulled away from me just as I came, and it shot all over the front of her dress. She looked down and screamed, "Alexander!" She slapped me hard in the face as I scrambled for a tissue. I wanted to clean up and run out of the house. What had I done? My lust had beaten me. The first time was an accident, pure and simple. This was just a goddamn shitty thing to do, and now we were most likely trapped in the bathroom. Mina was wiping at the mess on her dress, and I knew there was nothing could be done. It was over.

When Mina stepped out of the bathroom she instantly ran through to her bedroom and I hoped that it was so she could change dresses. That would be as suspicious as hell, but it might just work. But when I went to the door I realised that she'd run in fear. Jonathon was standing at the front door, staring at me.

"It's not what it looks like… She spilt something on her dress, man, I swear… I was helping her wipe it off…"

It was an admirable attempt at covering the situation, but I knew it was too late. He'd probably heard everything. I could see shadows through the window behind him and

I knew his soldier buddies were out there, waiting for me. I was about to die, and I was almost certainly going to hell.

The beating wasn't too bad. Jonathon hit me once and told me to get the fuck out of his house. I think he knew even through his anger that Mina was a cheap slut. He loved her and he knew he'd wronged her, and he probably suspected she'd fucked other guys in the past because they'd fought constantly for the past four years. He was angry, but if he hadn't known she was that type of girl, I probably would have been killed.

When I went down he walked into the bedroom and the shouting and crying began. The door slammed and both voices screamed about cheating. Accusations were thrown back and forth, but pretty soon I was being dragged out onto the street. A big black guy picked me up and hit me hard in the jaw. I fell to the ground again and another guy picked me up and hit me in the stomach. They all fell on me as I lay there and took what I knew I deserved. After probably no more than thirty seconds my friends ran down and stopped the fight. I was pretty fucked up after thirty seconds of beating, but I remember Oliver, Annie, and Beth breaking up the melee and making sure I was alive. They didn't say much to me but helped me down the street to a taxi and sent me on my way home.

CHAPTER SIXTEEN

I didn't sleep much that night. I lay in bed, sweating and staring at the ceiling, thinking about Mina. I thought about how we'd shared that bed, about how we'd sweated so profusely together, and laid there staring at the ceiling as the sun rose and broke through the cracks between the sheets of black paper over the windows. I had destroyed my life for her; she had destroyed my life. My lust had killed so many friendships and I didn't even feel the sense of shame and regret that I should have felt. For so long I had been a pathetic lonely wreck, saddled with friends and never in love. Then Mina had slunk into my life, ruined everything, and changed me. I loathed her and loved her and lay there thinking only of her. Some little voice at the back of my head asked, "Why don't you think about your friends? Why don't you think about how much you've ruined your life?" but I didn't think about those things. Only Mina occupied my thoughts.

When morning came blazing through those same sacred cracks and cast its hideous glare upon the filthy bedsheets I got up and made myself a cup of green tea. It wasn't the first teabag from the pack, but it was close. I'd used my kitchen so rarely that it took me a good long time to actually get the water boiled, and afterwards I just sat on my bed staring at the room. I knew it was the last time I'd sit there. I was done with Korea.

When I arrived at school the others looked at me in shock and disgust. I'd staggered drunken and hungover into that place so many times I honestly didn't think my co-workers could think less of me, but there and then I proved that wrong. With my right eye swollen, my lip burst, and bruises everywhere else I was beyond a mess. I looked like I'd gone a few rounds with a professional boxer.

I wondered, as I stood stupidly at the doorway to the teacher's room, whether these girls knew what had happened. It was just a momentary lapse of logic, but I wondered for a second if perhaps I had become notorious. The way they looked at me made me feel for the first time like a monster, and I had gotten used to being stared at. Perhaps the Korean papers had picked up my story. Maybe Mina got things straightened out with Jonathon by saying I raped her.

Or maybe I'd just gone too far for even Korea's liberal attitude towards getting fucked up. As I slowly moved across the door to my chair between Sonya and Thomas, across from Karen's now empty desk at the window, I pondered my situation and was filled with a hideous sense of shame. Here I was at work, ready to spend the day teaching children, and I was stinking of booze, reeling from a fight, and living a life of depravity. I was unfit to be a teacher; a real fucking disgrace of a human being for even entertaining the idea of acting as an educator.

I slumped into my chair and rested my swollen head in my hands. Sonya appeared silently and handed me a small paper cup of sweetened coffee and two large brown pills. I said thanks and she walked over to the other side of the room to talk about me with some other teachers. I could hear the words "foreigner" and "soju" being said repeatedly, and I just felt worse. Up until then I didn't mind being the drunken teacher.

When Thomas showed up just before the bell he looked at me and laughed. "Shit, Lucky Charms, you look like hell! What d'you do? Get in a fight with US military or some shit? Haha! You look like an Iraqi! You spend last night in Abu Ghraib?"

I didn't even crack a smile. I looked up at him and shook my head. He knew, as I did, that it was my last day. I was never cut out to be a teacher, and now that I'd essentially proved myself as a scumbag to my friends I was finished.

"What's the plan, man?" he asked, sitting down. The bell rang just as he sat, but he made no movement.

"I dunno," I lied. I didn't want to bail on him. It didn't seem fair to leave the poor guy as the only foreign teacher in the school. "What can I do?"

"I don't know what you can do or what you should do, but I think I know what you have planned. You're thinking about the Midnight Run, right?"

"Not exactly. If I go I'm at least telling Parky. I hate the bastard but I owe him that much."

Thomas thought about this for a moment. "I wouldn't say you owe him, but it's the decent thing to do, I suppose. Not that you care about doing the decent thing…"

Thomas grinned and slapped me on the shoulder. "Shit, man, I don't care what you do. Why not stay here another little while? Ain't no need to go downtown, son. Just chill out around here and bail after the next paycheque."

"Yeah, that's a plan. I just feel like I need to get out of Korea. I don't even know where I'm going next, but I've got to go. This place is bad for me."

"No kiddin'. You drank like this in Scotland?"

"Pretty much, if I could afford it."

"Damn."

"At least I stayed out of trouble back home, though."

"Yeah."

He scratched his head and made a sound that implied he was trying to think of a plan. "Well, shit, Lucky Charms, I'm not sticking around here if you're leavin'. Fuck that shit. Where you wanna go?"

"I hadn't thought that far ahead," I said, which was true. I really hadn't put much thought into this. All I'd done was feel sorry for myself.

"Japan?"

"Japan?"

"Yeah, son, Jonathon says Japan's badass! Them girls is mad hot!"

"I might take a little break from women…"

Thomas laughed. "Whatever, faggot. I wasn't talkin' about you, anyway. If we go to Japan I'm makin' sure *you* stay at home. You're trouble, son. Fuckin' mad bitches and fightin' soldiers. You're straight up fuckin' crazy. But I'm gonna get me some Jap ass."

"Yeah?"

"Sure, we can get us some jobs in Japan. Beats the shit outta Korea, right?"

I thought about it. "Yeah, man, everything beats the shit out of Korea. Fuck this place."

"Fuck this place!"

I stood up and braced against the headspins and nausea. "When are we doing this?"

"No time like the present, I guess. Better do it before I think better of it and stick around here."

"Serious?"

"Hells yeah."

PART TWO

CHAPTER ONE

We were in Fukuoka a week before Thomas quit looking for a job and flew back to America, leaving me alone in a motel. He paid for several days in advance and then fled in the night. He said he might come back, but that after Korea he needed "a bigger dose of freedom" than even Japan could offer. I didn't hold it against him. Thomas had skills and abilities that would serve him well in America and had only come to Korea to search for his heritage, unlike the rest of us, who'd come out of desperation.

We had discovered as soon as we began looking that jobs in Japan weren't as easy to come by as those in Korea and didn't pay nearly as well. Everything was expensive and wages were poor, and simply looking like an American wasn't good enough to guarantee a job. The people were certainly nicer and the city was a lot cleaner, but without a job I knew I couldn't last more than two or three weeks. I kept myself happy by walking around and breathing the kimchi-free air, looking at pleasant parks, and basking in the fact that no one around me acted like a socially-dysfunctional Neanderthal.

I'd earned a lot of money in Korea and even the drinking hadn't diminished my earnings too badly. Booze was cheap, my wages were astronomical, I didn't pay rent or bills, and hardly even spent money on food. When I decided to leave I'd cleaned out my bank account and felt like a king. Yet after twenty-four hours in Japan I realised that I was in trouble. Korean money meant nothing in a place like this. Drinks were far more expensive and the motel would have bankrupted me if Thomas hadn't insisted upon footing most of the bill.

I looked around for academies but they weren't as common as in Korea. When I asked foreign-looking people about jobs, they all said they knew of nothing. Most of the foreigners seemed to be in the US Navy or owned businesses. Unlike the single twenty-somethings working in Korea, these people were middle-aged, qualified, married, and spoke the native language fluently. I began to worry. If I couldn't find something quickly I'd have to return to Scotland and plunge back into a life of drinking and poverty, or return to Korea and sell my soul for huge paycheques as fifty million people shat on me.

A young black man from France told me about a restaurant where I could wait on tables for enough money to cover my motel bill. His name was Fred and he worked there without a visa and knew his boss would hire me for a few days, so I went along and did the job. Teaching had been tough, but at least there had been a modicum of dignity to it. Now I was back to being everyone's bitch – from the chefs to the managers to the customers. I was sweating and my feet hurt and I hated it, but it was money in my pocket. I told myself it was worth it to live in a cool city.

It was a French restaurant and the food was good. I worked all day so I got lunch and dinner and didn't have to worry about food bills. The manager – whose name I never remembered – gave Fred and I a bottle of wine every couple of days, and Fred said it was because we earned so little and worked so hard that he felt guilty. I asked why he didn't pay us more and Fred laughed, not realising that I was serious.

After three days I was living on a sofa at the apartment of a friend of Fred's – waking, working, sleeping. I kept getting paid and I wasn't really spending anything, but I didn't have the time or energy to look for a better job. Waiting tables wore me out and soon I wasn't even able to enjoy the city around me. I went from the restaurant to the apartment and back – a ten minute walk – each day. I spent most of my time thinking about what my life had come to and where it was going. This was alright for the time being, but it wouldn't suffice for more than another few weeks. I needed a real job in a place that didn't make me sick.

Fred liked to drink but we didn't really make enough money to go out like I'd done in Korea. Even a quiet night on the town cost a small fortune. One Friday night, though, he took me out. "We haven't spent a penny in five days," he told me. "So now we celebrate."

We found a little bar above an orange-fronted fast food joint and bought a few drinks. It was ferociously expensive and I hurt every time I bought some rum, but it felt good to have the alcohol in my veins and to be amongst people. I felt like I was undoing days of suffering, in spite of having no real purpose for the money I'd saved. I knew that in the morning I'd be too hungover to look for a job, but Fred seemed excited and so I kept up, hoping for a fast buzz to come on and then maybe I'd stop opening my wallet.

A big South African man of maybe forty stopped by for a drink. He seemed to be a friend of Fred's and they talked quickly in French, largely ignoring me. I was annoyed, but after half an hour he left and Fred pushed a chalky pill into my right palm. "Here," he said. "You owe me eighty dollars."

After the bar we went to a club that Fred promised was a "meat market" and we each paid a heavy entrance fee. "Don't worry!" he told me. "We get some drinks, some pussy... It's fine!" Indeed, one drink was covered by the extortionate entrance fee, but that was a typically weak Jack and Coke.

Fred immediately began blending into the crowd. There were black guys, white guys, and lots of hot Japanese girls. They were all dressed far better than any Korean girl. I began to think of Mina, but I stopped myself before I got depressed and ruined the night.

I stood at the bar and tried to get drunk for cheap. I hoped maybe if I drank while standing still for a long time, that when I finally moved it would all hit me and I'd be drunk enough to go try my luck with some Japanese chick. I was buzzing from the pill – whatever it was – but too alert and hyper to feel drunk.

"You from Korea?" a big American asked me very loudly as I stood, nursing a glass of rum. He was tall and looked like he was in the military, but I didn't want to make that assumption. I hadn't been the type of person to make assumptions before I went to Korea, and now I was out I had to stop.

"How could you tell?"

"All y'all look the same," he said, laughing and looking me up and down. "Skinny-ass white boys in fancy clothes... Y'all's over-educated, over-paid pussies. Am I right?"

"You're not far off the mark," I admitted, and laughed. I wanted to buy him a drink but I couldn't afford it.

"You on a visa run?"

"Nah, I'm fleeing Korea. That place is insufferable. I heard Japan was better, so I pulled the old 'Midnight Run.'"

"Well, you's made the smart choice comin' here... These Jap bitches love skinny white boys with too much money."

"Actually," I said. "I'm pretty much broke."

The guy laughed. He put a giant hand to his barrel chest. "Well, shit! They ain't know that! I'm tellin' you, brother, these bitches will fuck anyone they think is American. Black, white, Hispanic... It don't matter. It ain't even about money, either, but don't say you're broke! They just love the big dicks. Got a big dick, don't ya?"

"Gets the job done."

"Well, brother, even if you's got the tiniest dick a white man ever had it's bigger than any she'll see on a local, so you's in luck. Hell, I figure that's why half these motherfuckers is in this damn part of the world." He gestured around the club full of Westerners seducing Japanese women. "They's all got tiny dicks that these Asian bitches just love to ride! They ain't never seen a big dick so they ain't know these guys' handicap!"

I snorted and shook my head in disbelief. The guy was making me a little uncomfortable, but the pill was making the hairs on my neck stand on end and I didn't feel like standing on my own and sulking.

"Ain't a place in the world with bitches hornier than Japan, brother, and Fukuoka's hotter than the rest of this country. You go home alone in this town and you's either too drunk to fuck or you's a fag. You ain't a fag, is ya?"

"Nope," I said.

"Well, you sure look like a fag, and you kinda talk like a fag, but I believe you."

"I'm from Scotland," I explained.

"I see. Good luck wit' that."

"Thanks."

"You play golf?"

"Nope."

He finished his drink and slammed the glass down on the bar. I was surprised the bar didn't break in half. His arms were thicker than my waist.

"Well, brother, what ya waitin' for? Get out there and tap some ass!"

I returned to the dancefloor and met Fred, and he introduced me to a gorgeous girl in a little red dress with red lipstick and high heels. Her breasts were big but not too big and didn't look fake. Her ass was lifted by the dress and looked like no more than a perfect handful. She was amazing.

"Cheers, buddy," I said.

"She doesn't speak English! Or Japanese..." he shouted, laughing his head off. "Neither does she!" he gestured at his girl, who was just as cute and wore a little black dress. "I don't think they're whores, though."

"That's good," I said. I'd never fucked a whore before.

Fred laughed. "I think they're Chinese," he said. "You ever fucked a Communist?"

"No," I replied. "How do Commies fuck?"

"We're going to find out, Alexander. This is our lucky night."

As Fred made out with his girl, I took mine onto the dancefloor. The pill was making me eager to move, and together we made odd, spastic shapes. It was loud and I talked at her for a while but she just looked down at her feet, glancing up and smiling from time to time. I figured that Fred had dumped me with the conservative friend, but after a few minutes we were kissing and rubbing up against each other. I didn't know her name; didn't think to ask. We hadn't shared as much as a word but her body was all I needed. I'd come out to get laid and it was going to happen.

The booze washed over me as we dry humped, and after a while I felt a sharp jab in the ribs. It was Fred. "Let's go get a hotel," he said. I muttered something about money, and he glared at me and said, "This is serious, Alexander. I haven't had pussy in a long time and neither have you. We can afford one fucking night in a hotel!"

We stumbled outside and into a taxi, which Fred instructed to take us to the nearest hotel. After an extortionate ten-minute ride, we were dumped back on the street and Fred was telling me to stay outside with the girls while he negotiated the price. The fresh air had turned the alcohol in my system into something infinitely more potent and I was reeling, struggling to keep my eyes open. Minutes later he was back outside, ushering us into the hotel. "I'll be back in five, Alexander," he said, and ran off. We had to be silent and sneak in, because apparently he'd booked a single room and no visitors were allowed.

Upstairs the girls and I found our room and went inside. I had no idea what to do or say. I didn't speak Chinese and was struggling with balance too much to attempt any rudimentary English. I flailed about and waved my arms at the bed, trying to say, "Make yourself at home," but just looked like an idiot instead.

Five minutes later Fred arrived with a few bottles of beer and a pack of condoms. "You owe me ten dollars," he said, opening two bottles and handing them to the girls. "But I'm cheaper than a pimp, no?"

Soon we were lying on the bed, Fred making out with his girl, me with mine. I was too drunk to really be uncomfortable, so I watched Fred and copied him. I didn't want to go too far and spoil everything. Soon, though, he was pulling off her shirt and I was doing the same. Then we were going down on them, then fucking them, then falling asleep.

CHAPTER TWO

In the morning I was woken by Fred's rough grip on my shoulder. I jolted awake and looked around. The girls were gone. The room was a mess, and I wasn't even sure it was us that had trashed the place. Presumably it was one of the cheapest hotels in the city.

"Where'd they go?" I asked.

"They're showering," Fred replied. "And I'm going to join them, Alexander. I thought I'd do the selfless thing and ask if you wanted to join. I'm a nice guy, no? I wouldn't fuck your one without offering you the chance. Just like last night – that could've been a three-way for Fred! But I thought, 'I'll help my buddy, Alexander.'"

"You're a good man, Fred."

"Fucking right. So you coming?"

I thought about it. It seemed a little awkward stepping naked into a shower as a group of four, but then again I hadn't had sober sex in many, many months. It would be nice to adequately remember such a thing.

By the time I got out of bed Fred was naked and knocking quietly on the bathroom door. I knew he didn't want them to hear. If they heard him knock they might tell him to go away, but if he walked straight in then he had a chance. Probably. Maybe they were whores, after all. I made a note to check my wallet.

I climbed out of bed and found myself already naked, so I walked in after Fred. The smooth bastard was already in the big shower, the two girls looking embarrassed but not entirely put off. I couldn't remember which one was mine, but thankfully Fred put his arms around one and began rubbing his big dick against the inside of her thighs. The other looked awkwardly around, not wanting to seem left out, and not wanting to seem too eager with me. I moved in, though, and put my hand on the small of her back, which she seemed very much to enjoy.

We washed and rubbed in a weird silence. Fred was talking to his girl in French and she kept giggling back at him, saying nothing. I didn't know what to say to mine, so I just lathered her back, and then let my erection push against her. After only a couple of minutes I slipped it inside and fucked her as she tried not to squeal. It occurred to me then just how good sex could feel.

I was about to come inside her when I realised I wasn't wearing a condom, so I pulled out and shot on her back. I hurriedly washed it off, but she didn't seem to mind. She turned and hugged me and kissed me, smiling and looking at me with her cute dark eyes.

Then she spoke. She said a word I knew, meaning, "It's okay."

It was Korean.

"Jinjja?" I replied, meaning "really". She stepped back, bumping into the naked, still-thrusting Fred, and her mouth dropped open.

She asked me, in Korean, if I spoke Korean. I said yes, a little.

Then she spoke in English: "You speak Korean? Why?"

"I lived in Korea," I said.

She slapped me gently on the chest and laughed. "You speak English?"

"Yes."

"Last night…" She stumbled for the words. Her English, evidently, was not great, but far better than my primitive grasp of Korean. "… I not understand. I think you speak France-speaking or something. Maybe Russia-speaking."

I explained, in Korean, that I was from the United Kingdom.

"England!" she blurted.

"Not exactly. Scotland."

She looked confused, but smiled and said, "Okay."

After speaking to the girl I suddenly felt awful for having fucked her twice, thinking maybe she was a whore. I didn't know her name and had only just found out where she was from. The thrill of screwing a random chick had totally subsided, and I was embarrassed because I was actually communicating with an attractive woman on some basic, adult level. I found myself immensely attracted to her, and not just because she was beautiful.

Looking at her, I felt she thought the same, and she looked embarrassed, too. She turned red and looked down, which of course was at our naked bodies, so she turned and looked at the faucet. Our silence was broken by the grunting Fred and his squealing girl as they neared the end of their humping.

I took her hand and led her out of the shower, then wrapped her in a big white towel. We retreated to the bedroom and sat awkwardly on the bed. I didn't know what to do or say.

"You live in Korea?" she asked.

I thought about it for a second. Should I tell the truth or correct her? "Yes," I said.

"Where?"

"Daegu."

"I live in Busan."

"Oh wow, I love Busan! I went to Haeundae beach in the summer."

She made an exaggerated face of disgust, following by a double thumbs-down gesture. "Bleh! I think it's dirty!"

"Yeah, but it's okay. I like it."

"Do you like Korea?"

"Yes," I lied. "Do you?"

"No."

"Why?"

"It's boring. It's dirty. It's small."

"What about Japan? Why are you here?"

"My friend," she gestured through to the bathroom, from where we could hear Fred and the other girl climaxing loudly, "is live here. She is…" She searched for the right word. "…boyfriend the Japanese man? Sorry, my English…"

"No, your English is fine. It's good."

"No, it's not. I want learn the English. I like travel, but it's difficult. English is help me to travel."

"Well I can understand you perfectly," I said, and I could. Her English was far from perfect but I knew exactly what she was trying to say.

"My friend," she gestured to the bathroom again, "is live in Japan."

"She's Korean?"

"Yes."

"I couldn't hear you speaking last night," I explained.

"I'm sorry. If I knew you were Korean I would have tried to speak a little."

She laughed. "It's okay. Foreigner don't speak Korean. It's difficult."

I shrugged. "Not really. We just don't try very hard to learn it. Anyway, I'm sorry we didn't speak last night. I feel terrible."

She cocked her head and looked confused. I'd spoken fast and none too clearly.

"What's your name?" I asked.

"Min Jung," she said. "Or 'MJ.' I think 'MJ' is easy to speaking. Foreigner can't say Korean name."

"I like Min Jung," I said.

She blushed and asked my name.

"Alexander."

"Alexander." She said it without dragging it out forever.

"Yeah," I said. "So when are you going back to Korea?"

"Next week. And you?"

I thought about it. Did I want to give Korea another chance? After only a short time away I was beginning to feel that pull so many expats get when they leave Korea. The harsh realities of life were reminding me of the positives I'd previously overlooked. A steady paycheque and job security made life a lot easier. I'd been broke all my life except those few months, and I began wondering what would happen if I went back and struck a different balance. With so many schools in Korea I would have no trouble finding a job that was more tolerable than Charleston. If I had a girlfriend to keep me company on weekends and found friends who didn't bring out my alcoholism, then maybe I'd find happiness. I began thinking about that one night in Busan, and how beautiful

Korea looked from the beach. Swimming at night with Min Jung sounded like heaven.

"Next week."

CHAPTER THREE

I ended up back in Korea only four weeks after arriving in Fukuoka. I'd made no money, spent everything I'd saved, and decided that the real world could wait for a while. Poverty was harder than it used to be. Living on sofas and not eating back in Scotland had never bothered me much, but after only a few months of big money in Korea I was converted. I didn't like that this was what I'd become, but there was no arguing with the fact. I now needed the stability of a job and the luxury of being able to eat every day.

Of course, Min Jung played her part in bringing me back. I didn't want to admit it, but she was the main reason I went. We met for coffee once in the week and then went out drinking the following weekend. She took me to her friend's house and we fucked. I realised for the first time that fucking was so much better with a girl I cared about. I decided I never wanted to leave her.

She seemed to like me, too, and told me to come back to Korea. All her friends spoke English, she said, and they worked as teachers in schools and universities and they'd all be able to get me jobs. I could pick the best one and live with her until I got my own place, which would only be for a few weeks. We'd live in Busan, where she was getting her own apartment and would have a relatively high paying job as a secretary of some description. She'd even lend me some money to take care of myself and pay for my ferry ticket home.

When we arrived back in Korea I had to enter on a tourist visa because my working one had been cancelled when I quit Charleston. That limited me to ninety days in the country, but Min Jung said not to worry because I would have a job within two weeks. I believed her but I still felt nervous walking through customs and immigration.

The sun was shining and the breeze blew salty air in off the Sea of Japan and Korea really didn't seem so bad. I had a beautiful girl holding my hand and I was coming back for round two. This time had to be better than the first. I'd make sure to do things right this time – no more excessive drinking, no more staying at home. I'd learn the language, make some Korean friends, and get out and explore the good parts of the country. No more dwelling on the negatives.

Min Jung's apartment was a twenty-minute taxi ride from the ferry terminal and we stayed silent the whole way, both thinking about the changes we'd made to our lives by randomly deciding to live together after meeting in a club and falling quickly in love. I was paranoid I'd do something to offend her, or maybe she'd speak to some Korean person and they'd tell her to stay away from dirty foreigners. Indeed, the taxi driver kept shouting at her in Korean about me. He said lots of things that Min Jung wouldn't translate but that sounded nasty. He kept flicking his teeth off his gums and hissing at me like a cat. I didn't care, though. I just sat quietly and watched the city go by under the afternoon sunlight.

Her apartment was no bigger than my one in Daegu had been. It was tiny and ugly and reminded me of a prison cell. The walls were bare and there was a mattress on the floor. A desk held a big TV and there was a little bathroom and a washing room, just like my old place. The kitchen was just a stove, a sink, and nothing else. But it was our place. Or rather, it was her place. I would be sleeping in the bed and so it wouldn't feel like I was entirely homeless.

"It's your home!" she said, as I dumped my laptop and a bag of clothes onto the floor and she hauled her suitcase through the door. I helped her with the second one, which I'd carried up the stairs and then ditched in the hall, and then we closed the door, fell on the bed and fucked. When she moaned and groaned they were the sounds of pleasure, rather than the forced sounds of a violated girl. Her pussy was tight like Mina's, but she got wetter and it was easier to slide in. I knew she enjoyed sex more and I hoped it was for the same reasons I enjoyed it more with her than Mina.

After screwing we went shopping for food. We took a taxi to HomePlus and I told her that when I got a new job I'd buy everything she needed for the next year, just to pay for her kindness in bringing me back and looking after me. "It's okay," she laughed. "I want help you. I love you." We kissed and the taxi driver looked as though he was about to plough the car into a wall.

For three days we sat at home, bored. I didn't need to go out to look for a job because Min Jung said her friends would find something for me. It turned out that she didn't have much money and that her job didn't start for a week. She had money to buy food and soju, but not enough to take us out to bars and clubs, or to go on trips. I didn't care too much because I was happy just to be with her. I also wanted to see what Korea was like in relative sobriety. The soju made sure I never actually stayed sober, but we always went to sleep early and when we woke up she'd cook a traditional Korean breakfast that ensured our hangovers dissipated by midday.

Sitting at home together was strange. I'd sat at home in Scotland when I lived with girls and had no job, but we didn't fuck. We just smoked weed and played guitar. With Min Jung it was just a case of waiting until we were ready to go again. There was nothing else to do. I had no books, no friends, and nowhere to go. I sat on the internet and read the news from time to time, but the Korean news made me hate Korea again and the international news made me depressed about the future of the whole world. We just sat there and talked, but there wasn't a whole lot to say because as soon as we got into a subject on anymore than a superficial level the language barrier presented itself. I felt terrible because she tried so hard to understand me and I tried so hard to explain, but often we just couldn't communicate. It was great that she was learning from me. She seemed to pick up words quickly and looked happy when she remembered something. I learned a little Korean, but it turned out I was far less adept at learning languages than her. It was fun but after a while teaching me became pointless because I reached the maximum information intake for one day. I felt like my head was about to explode. "Don't worry, babe," I said. "One day soon we'll both be fluent."

It was on the fourth day that I finally succumbed to cabin fever and said I wanted to go for a walk. "Where we go?" she asked. I told her I wanted to go alone. "Why?" She looked very hurt.

"I just need time alone."

"You don't love me?" I could see the tears coming straight away. I couldn't believe it because this didn't seem to be a situation that warranted any tears at all. Nothing big had happened. I had visions of losing her. I panicked. It became hard to breathe and I couldn't stop the thoughts racing through my mind – loneliness, homelessness.

"I'm sorry, babe," I said. "I need to be with me. Just me. Just for an hour. Then we can be together."

"You see other girl?" She looked angry all of a sudden.

"No, of course not."

"You see other girl?"

"No, Min Jung. I promise. Just you."

"Why you go alone?" The tears were coming thick and fast and I had no experience dealing with such a thing, so I completely backtracked. It wasn't a wise thing to do and it broke all my principles and morals, but I didn't care. I loved her too much to see her cry, even for a minute.

"Okay, babe, let's go together."

We spent time on the beach to get away from the apartment, but it was far away and so we had to choose between the subway and a taxi. She didn't like taking the subway because it was always crowded but she couldn't really afford a taxi, either. I really loved the beach, but I couldn't go on my own because she'd start crying, and we couldn't compromise on the money-taxi-subway situation. It was getting chilly out, too. Summer had suddenly disappeared and although it was still warm, it was also cold when the breeze swept in or the sun hid behind a cloud. The water was now far too cold for naked night swimming.

On the fifth day back, Min Jung got a phone call saying that her new job was cancelled. They didn't need her anymore.

"Oh my god," I said. "I'm sorry!" I hugged her tightly, expecting the waterworks to begin, and braced myself for hours of comforting her. I was thinking of all the words she'd taught me in Korean that might come in useful at a time like this.

"It's okay," she said.

"Huh? Really?"

"Yeah, I didn't want job! I don't need job!"

"I thought it was meant to be a good job, babe."

She shrugged.

I was confused. She'd seemed happy about having a real job that might gain her some respect and that seemed offer her independence.

"It's not matter. We go somewhere else. My family give me money."

"Really? I thought you were working so you didn't *need* their money."

"It easy not work."

"Okay, babe, whatever makes you happy." I hugged her again and we rolled back on the bed and fucked for a while as I wondered where we went from here. If she didn't get her job then she'd be sitting here with me all day, every day until I got one. That might get to be a little much…

CHAPTER FOUR

We moved back to Daegu after a week and a half in Busan and I wasn't particularly happy about it, to say the least. After Min Jung's job fell through she had to move to Daegu to be near her family, which was the only way they'd agree to pay her living expenses. She didn't have a rich family, and they didn't know about me, but they wanted their daughter to live well until she found a husband to take care of her. Strangely, Min Jung seemed to like this situation. She disliked her family and loved taking their money under the guise of finding a husband.

That meant that when we were back in Daegu we could afford to go and get drunk. That was good because in Daegu there just isn't really anything else to do. Busan has a few beaches and sights to see, but Daegu has nothing. Drinking is the only pastime.

Her new apartment was a small place very close to

downtown. It's a busy place, but the apartment was on a little side street on the opposite side of the road and so it could've been worse. Like all side streets in Daegu it was littered with bags of trash and the pavements were dirty and uneven.

The apartment itself was similar to her one in Busan – a "one room" with a mattress on the floor and no space to move. I mentally prepared myself for an indefinite period of time spent sitting around with her, hoping that a job came along to claim my sanity. A job would give me somewhere to go and, more importantly, a place of my own.

I still loved Min Jung but things were becoming difficult. Petty fights and misunderstandings did absolutely nothing to diminish how I felt about her, but I really didn't want to spend twenty-four hours a day in her company. It was too much. It would have been too much time to spend with anyone.

In the beginning we had screwed once or twice a day. We were bored and the fucking was fun. After a while Min Jung kept trying to screw me more and more and I just physically wasn't up to the challenge. We'd fuck in the morning and then at night. That was fine. I could stand that, although my balls began to ache and it took longer to get hard. Beyond that, though, I found myself pushing my limits. She'd giggle and smile and take off her top and start playing with the hairs on my stomach. I'd be thinking to myself, "Oh shit, not again," and she'd be moving her hands down and down and I knew there was no way I could say to her that I didn't want to, and so I found myself stalling for time. Instead of fucking, I'd try fingering her different ways, or eating her out for as long as she could stand it.

One time she was licking my dick and I decided to give her a lesson in fellatio. She gave what Thomas

once called "typical Korean head." Girls brought up in
a country where sex isn't discussed generally don't give
good head, he said, and she seemed to think that the faster
she bobbed up and down, the better it felt. I instructed
her slowly and bought some time before penetration.

Another time I convinced her to get rid of the muff.
The idea of trimming and maintaining evidently does
not exist in Asia, and she had a giant forest of pubes
covering everything. I told her I wanted to see her pussy
and she said "okay" and giggled, but insisted that I do
the shaving. I did it slowly and she seemed to consider it
foreplay, which worked for me. Afterwards we admired
her beautiful little snatch and how sexy it looked without
all that damned hair crawling over it.

But that wasn't enough. Now and then she'd demand
I fuck her and although I always gave her my best,
sometimes I'd be standing there and my erection would
wither away. It would be standing tall and proud, ready
for action… and then – flop – it was gone! She always
looked so sad then, as though I'd called her an awful
name. I'd tell her I was sorry and she'd spend the next
half an hour trying to revive it. I'd just shrug and say
"tired" in Korean until she left me alone.

With her family's money we managed to go out and eat
and drink. We went to the same restaurants downtown that
I'd been to with my old friends, but we went at normal
eating times instead of going after the clubs closed at
five in the morning. We went to different bars, too, and
so I didn't see any of my old friends. I was glad not to
see Jonathon because I didn't know if I could apologise
enough to him. I was ashamed of myself for wanting to
forget the whole thing instead of trying to make it better.
I knew that if Mina and Jonathon had split, then maybe
there would be a chance of making up with him, but

otherwise it wouldn't happen. I thought about everyone else. If I ventured into Effort for a few minutes I could catch up and find out whether or not I was welcome back on the scene... if indeed I wanted to be back on the scene. Spending every minute of the day with Min Jung was exhausting and stressful, but I wasn't sure that going back into rampant alcoholism and negativity was really a wise move. It would ease my boredom to some extent, but it might just ruin me.

"You have Korean friends?" she asked me one day.

"No," I told her. "Well, I used to know some people, but I don't talk to them now."

"Why?"

"I don't speak to my old friends."

"Do they live Daegu?"

"I don't know."

"Are they girls?"

"Some of them."

"Are they sexy?"

I thought for a minute and then decided upon the right answer: "No."

"Why you not talk to you friends?"

"We fell out."

She looked at me and cocked her head like she did when she didn't understand a word or phrase.

"Fighting," I said.

"Oh. Why?"

"Nothing. Just people being stupid."

"Stupid? Why?"

"Just... It's complicated."

"Why? You don't want tell me?"

"It's complicated." She looked like she was about to cry or kill me or both, so I added: "I wish I spoke Korean better so I could say more to you."

The Dog Farm

***

Communication was difficult and culture soon became a hindrance. When she was annoyed with me she couldn't express herself and so I couldn't make things better. Some days she'd just wake up annoyed and I'd ask her over and over what was wrong, but she'd say nothing. Likewise, when I was annoyed by her or by our situation, or when I felt trapped and helpless by being penniless and homeless in a country where I didn't even speak the language, there was no real way to get these feelings across. We talked and talked, but little real communication was done. We were just different people.

Although Min Jung was smart enough to see Korea as it was, and think differently from the other fifty million drones, she was still Korean and still loved her country to some extent. She still did Korean things and thought like a Korean, even though she pretended not to. I began to fear that she might one day show the famed Kimchi Rage.

She got frustrated when we would be out walking and someone would stare at us, shout at us, or spit at us. She'd curse them quietly and say, "I'm sorry," but would get angry whenever I agreed with her. It was as though only she could say bad things about her country.

She began to notice my smirks when something would happen that we'd talked about and she'd tried to justify it. Although she knew all about Korea's bad points, she didn't want me to hate the place, and so she tried to gloss over everything whenever I brought it up. But then if she caught me silently mocking something, she'd get upset and ask: "Why you hate Korea? It's my country!"

Sometimes we'd be walking along the street and someone would clear their throat loudly and then spit at the feet of someone else. Sometimes they'd cough in someone's face without thinking. Sometimes we'd see an old man pissing in the street, or an old woman squatting to shit. Everyone around us stared and pointed and said nasty things. Every time we saw something like that Min Jung would look at me and monitor my reaction. I realised that I had to get good at ignoring unpleasant things if I was to live in Korea much longer – for her sake and mine.

Min Jung was a good cook but she would only eat Korean food. Just like everyone else in the country, she'd eat kimchi three meals a day and wouldn't hear a bad word said against it. Nor could she accept the fact that some people simply can't stomach the same dish three times a day, every day of the year. In spite of her apparent intelligence and awareness of the outside world, and the fact that she'd lived in Japan for a while, she still said, "Oh, well, foreigner don't like kimchi," as though she were explaining how the genetic inferiority of all non-Koreans precluded them from enjoying cabbage that had spent months underground.

"The thing is, babe, I used to like it. I ate kimchi when I first came to Korea and I liked it. It's just that I need *diversity*!"

"What?"

"Diversity… It means, when everything's not the same."

"I don't understand."

"It's the opposite of Korea."

"Okay"

"I like to eat Chinese food, Japanese food, Korean food, Mexican, Italian, French, American… I like different things. I don't think it's healthy or even enjoyable to eat the same thing three meals a day, every damn day of the year."

"But it our food."

"And haggis is my food, but we only eat it once a year in Scotland. We're kinda like Korea… A small country with crappy, bland cuisine. The difference is that we can admit it and diversify our diets."

"You don't like kimchi…"

"Now and then, it's fine… but not for every meal."

"Why?"

"It's just not that great, babe. It's alright, but it's not amazing."

"I don't understand."

"You're Korean, of course you don't understand."

"I like pizza."

"And that's great, but all I'm saying is that you don't need to eat pizza with kimchi as a side. Hell, I'm not even saying that… I'm not saying anything! Just don't give me shit for not liking it as much as you, or for holding my nose when you open that refrigerator and the room fills with kimchi-stink for the next eight hours!"

"So you don't like it."

"That's not the point."

She walked over and opened the refrigerator and within a heartbeat the room was filled with the pungent odour of fermenting cabbage. It smelled like one of us had farted, but the smell of a fart dissipates. The kimchi stink would linger in the air and burn my nostrils for hours.

One dark, grey and thoroughly depressing Sunday afternoon, after a heavy bout of soju-swilling in the tight confines of the apartment, Min Jung suggested we go out for lunch. I could tell she wanted to dress up and point her tits at other people. She liked flaunting her beauty, particularly at people she hated, and she hated most Korean people – especially the ones that reminded her of her parents. Sometimes she got a look in her eye that said that for whatever reason she wasn't entirely happy but that she *was* feeling confident in herself, and just wanted to dress up nice and let people know that she was hot. Also, I think she liked showing people that she had a foreigner for a boyfriend – not because she was proud, necessarily, but because she liked to rebel. Probably there was not great difference in her mind between wearing a skirt that barely covered her snatch and holding my hand in public.

"What you want eat?" she asked.

"You," I replied with a stupid grin, but she didn't get it.

"Do you know boshintang?" She thought for a while, trying to gather the English words. "… Dog meat soup?"

I laughed, then stopped. She was serious. "Huh?"

"Dog meat soup. Do you know?"

"Really? Yeah, I guess. I've heard of it…" I thought of all the times Thomas and Jonathon had referred to Koreans as "dog-eaters" and had just assumed that they were making it up.

"Did you eat?"

"No, I've not tried it."

"It famous Korean food. Very tradition."

"So I've heard…"

"You want eat?"

I thought about it. On the surface, it really didn't seem like the worst idea. Why was it worse to eat dog than, say, pig or cow? Just because my Western heritage caused me some affinity for dogs didn't make them any more valuable an animal than those we considered food in the West. Perhaps I was being ethnocentric and close-minded in my unreasonable championing of one sentient being over another. Hell, there were vegetarians and vegans around the globe who'd call me a savage just for eating beef.

"Sure," I said. "I'll try it."

The Dog Farm

***

We took a taxi from outside the fire station and travelled through the city for a while until we were in an area of countryside. The land was flat, with few trees around and only the mountains and grey, identical tower blocks in the distance. Farmland stretched out in every direction – fields of yellow and green, growing mostly rice. Every now and then a little road would split a field, and old people in conical hats on bikes would cycle back and forth. Strangely, it didn't feel that far from the city. Daegu always felt like a village that had grown too big too fast – a ramshackle cluster of giant, ugly buildings that had sprung from the dung heaps of a farm, with its inhabitants maintaining the exact same mountainfolk behaviour they had before 7-Eleven and Starbucks invaded and shaped their streets.

We stopped outside a little building with a grey slate roof and yellow mud walls. There were expensive cars stopped all along the road, a few bushes and trees separating them from the fields. Min Jung paid the driver and we stepped out.

As soon as I put my foot onto the dusty road, I wanted to get back in the car. The hairs on the back of my neck rose and shivers shot up and down my spine as I was assaulted by the most repugnant of sounds and smells.

The sound of a dog slowly dying is something that should never be heard. It is a sound far worse than any midnight howl or terrified yelp – a high-pitched screech that strikes some primal nerve, uniting human and beast in a shared memory; the realisation that we are all living beings and should never be subject to such barbaric savagery. These wretched creatures were being dragged slowly to their demise.

I felt like my ear drums were about to burst and start

bleeding. The jarring screech rose and fell but remained in the air. There were three dogs, I think, dying. I couldn't tell what was happening but they were in unspeakable agony. That was the sound I imagine hearing if a person were tied down and tortured mercilessly for hours – a helpless, hopeless, and utterly sorrowful expression of pain – like something from a horror movie, only all the more disturbing because it was real, regardless of whether the origin of the sound was a human.

What struck me aside from the sound was the smell of death and pain lingering in the air. The stench of dog faeces and some strange odour I could only describe as that of departing life mixed with the ever-present reek of kimchi and the human-dung fertiliser that swept in off the fields.

What kind of depraved savage could eat in a place like this? What monster could listen to their dinner die the worst kind of death, talking with their kin, swilling soju, and waiting for a good old family meal? I felt sick imagining the scum inside. I was at the gates of hell, and hell was a dog farm.

"Babe, I'm not okay with this…" I said sheepishly.

She laughed and walked inside as the taxi pulled a U-turn and sped off back towards the city, leaving us in this place of death. "Come on."

I slowly followed, looking around in disgust. I didn't know what to expect… Human corpses rotting on the ground, blood spilling from cracked kimchi pots made of dried dog shit, old men and women cannibalising each other, babies being raped to death… Nothing would have surprised me. The sounds and smells were a fair warning for any horror.

All I could see was chicken wire everywhere to keep the dogs from escaping, were they ever to get out of their cages. The dogs were thankfully around back, out of sight. I don't think I could have stood to see their suffering in addition to hearing and smelling it.

Inside, the place was no different from any other Korean restaurant. Families sat around tiny tables, cross-legged on the floor – the men with their cheap suit jackets to the side, revealing sweaty pit-stains and potbellies protruding from between the buttons on their tacky shirts, ties swung over their shoulders and looks of gross satisfaction on their stuffed faces as they listened to the sounds of the dogs dying as the meat already began to rot in their gut; women covering their snatches with cheap knock-off handbags as their skirts rose over their hips, trying to maintain their dignity while coughing and spluttering bits of food back onto the table without noticing, never mind trying to cover their mouths; their children running amuck amid the sounds and smells of death, ignorant of the suffering of anything but themselves as they played their violent games.

They all turned and stared at me, of course, as I stood awkwardly behind Min Jung, who was asking the proprietor for a table. I looked at my feet and tried to block out the sound, which had not diminished since we entered the building. I was wondering how to back out and go somewhere else. I didn't want these primitives to have my money, or rather Min Jung's money.

Min Jung took off her shoes and walked over to a table in one corner of the room and carefully sat down, placing her handbag over her snatch, which was otherwise left utterly exposed by the combination of short skirt and sitting cross-legged. I walked around and sat with my back to the wall, which I hated because it meant I had to sit and be stared at by the natives. Also, it meant I had to look back in their direction and watch their foul table manners as they spat and coughed at each other, and fingered their food with their dirty, disease-ridden hands. After many, many months in Korea, I still hadn't seen any of them washing their hands after using the toilet.

"I so hungry!" Min Jung cried, then giggled and clapped her hands inanely. "Boshintang! Dogmeatsoup!"

"Babe, seriously?"

"Why you always sad? Just eat."

"You can't hear that?" I asked.

"What?"

"That!" I shouted. "Dogs being killed!"

She stopped and listened, smiling the whole time – unaware of any suffering. "You eat pig, right?"

"Not when I can hear them die."

"They are not die. They are make ready to die. They die quiet."

I said I didn't understand.

"They make dog ready to eat many time. Dog is…" She stopped and searched for the right word. "Hanging. They hanging the dog to eat."

"You don't see anything wrong with that?"

"It make dog taste good. And it give the man so energy! Make him last for the long time."

"But they're torturing an innocent animal. They're hanging it to make it taste better and give guys erections. That's stupid."

"You stupid." Min Jung looked annoyed for the first time since she first suggested dog meat soup. "Why you never want do Korean culture? It better than England culture."

"I'm not from England!"

"In Korea England and Scotland same. We don't say different."

"That's because you're all fucking idiots."

"Shut up!"

"At least we don't eat dogs like a bunch of primitive

degenerate pigfuckers!"

"Korea food number one food!"

I stopped and stared at her. Jesus, she was stupid. Was this the same girl I'd met in Japan? The girl who'd known Korea's flaws? She was no different than the rest of the drones – an ignorant nationalist savage.

"I'm not eating any goddamn dog meat," I said.

"Fine, you don't eating any. I eat all dog meat soup!"

"I hope you choke."

"What?"

"I said, 'Give me the keys, I'm going home.'"

Min Jung laughed and tossed the apartment keys at me. "I know you no have money. No taxi! Nice time walking!"

She made a scrunched up face of childish contempt at me as I stood up and walked towards the door. Naturally, every person in the building turned and stared at me as I left, either too mentally degenerate to realise that staring isn't even polite their own culture or too vicious to care.

As I looked back at Min Jung I realised that she hadn't expected me to actually leave. Eating alone in Korea is a terribly shameful thing. She was probably hoping I'd come back. She didn't think I was stubborn enough to walk all the way back into the city, but she was wrong.

CHAPTER FIVE

When I went back to find my friends I did it to get away from Min Jung. By this point I was thinking that if I did something to annoy her and we split up, I'd mostly be bummed by my homelessness, and not by losing my girlfriend. I wasn't even sure I loved her anymore, or if I ever had. I figured that a split was inevitable and I needed someone else to stay with when she conjured up some new problem, blew it out of proportion, and let the Kimchi Rage come crashing down.

But I had no time away from her. We spent every moment of the day together, and so I had to convince her to come out at night with me, and of course pay for the whole thing, and plan on running into a friend by accident. It might happen, it might not. No big deal.

Rather than walking into Effort and being surrounded by everyone I used to know, I told Min Jung we were going to a place nearby, called Trend. I figured that we could have a few drinks and then maybe I would see someone I knew and enquire about my friends.

It was a cool night when we went out and there was a fine rain. I wore a t-shirt and shorts, as always, and Min Jung dressed up in some fancy dress and make-up I didn't care about, taking hours to get herself ready. I felt a little nervous, as I always did in going outside. I didn't know if everyone had turned and decided to hate me or not. I didn't know whether random soldiers would start beating me. I felt ashamed and weak. Hell, I'd felt weak ever since getting beaten. I'd gotten quieter and lost a lot of confidence. The beating had humbled me, the embarrassment silenced me, the poverty of life in Japan had kept me down, and then Min Jung had made me happy for a while, before eventually wearing me down to the point where I felt like I meant as much to her as a comfortable bra.

We walked quickly towards Trend, which was on the same street as Effort and thus prime territory for being recognised. It was also a smelly and uneven street, and I used those as motivators in our speed-walking. I didn't want to spend forever walking along that nasty little stretch of brick. Weirdly, in spite of there being a constant and unpleasant funk in the air, this was the street that held Daegu's most expensive restaurants. People sat and ate poor attempts at Western dishes from overpriced menus full of spelling mistakes, listening to sappy love songs from the eighties and nineties.

Trend was downstairs and away from the street, with little signage outside. I remembered it growing in popularity as a foreigner bar but thought it probably wouldn't be popular enough to risk a meeting with someone I knew well. We walked down the stairs, past rows of mirrors and burning incense, and into the dark interior, where only the bar and the pool table were lit, and everything else sat in shadow. It looked like a good drug den.

I walked towards the bar, proudly holding Min Jung's hand. I realised that I'd never before walked into a Daegu foreigner bar with a hot Korean girl on my arm and even though the place looked empty, the bar staff would see me and later others would, too. I was so used to being the loner and loser that it was a nice feeling. Even though she'd been pissing me off, she looked good. She looked *real* good, all dressed up and cute.

Then I heard my name.

"Alexander!"

Oh shit.

"Alexander."

No mistaking the voice.

I turned and looked at the pool table and saw Jonathon and a couple of little Korean guys ranging in age from thirty to fifty, shooting pool. The rest of the bar was empty. Was I about to die? They didn't look tough. I thought about running. Of all the people...

"Alex, what up?"

He didn't look pissed, but I probably looked scared stupid. I felt like I was about to crap myself in shock. My skin instantly soaked itself with sweat and I let go of Min Jung's hand. I don't know why. Maybe I wanted to free myself up for the escape that might prove necessary. Maybe I didn't want her to get beaten along with me. I couldn't say a word.

Jonathon walked towards me and he didn't look too upset. He didn't even look that surprised. Hell, he looked a little happy...

"I missed you, man!" he said, and hugged me hard. "Come play pool."

I couldn't believe it. Jonathon wasn't the sort to play

a trick, so I wasn't worried about going over and getting jumped by his friends, but I was conflicted. It didn't feel right. The last time I saw him he knocked me to the floor and stormed off. I wasn't aware of anything having changed. Was he that drunk? How much time had passed?

I considered Min Jung for a second. I'd brought her out and now the obvious and important thing seemed to be talking to Jonathon. If there was any way of smoothing things over, it had to be done. He was a good friend and I'd betrayed him. I wanted to clear my conscience and make things right.

"Come on, babe," I said to Min Jung and dragged her towards the pool table. She looked angry, but I didn't care. I was bringing her along. I could understand her being pissed if I ditched her and went to talk to Jonathon, but I was including her.

We stood by the pool table and made the introductions. The guys were called Mr. Sa, Mr. Kim, and Mr. Yoo. They all spoke great English and worked with Jonathon on the base. They all said Min Jung was beautiful, while she fumed silently in response.

"Wanna drink?" Jonathon offered.

"Sure," I said. "But maybe I should buy…"

He didn't laugh or answer my remark and we walked to the bar. I felt awkward but there didn't seem to be anything to feel that way about… Had he forgotten the whole thing? Had Mina convinced him nothing happened?

We parked ourselves on the barstools and I looked briefly over at Min Jung, who was ready to explode with rage. She sat on the dirty seat nearest the table and seethed. She was playing with her phone, probably texting her friends nasty things about me. I didn't care. As long as those elusive friends found me a job, she could say what she wanted. All I cared about now was my freedom.

An extremely cute bargirl took our orders. She looked familiar, and I knew that I must have met her on some drunken night back before I'd left for Japan. The good old days. Jonathon told me her name was Kelly and that she was awesome, and then asked for free drinks, which she declined, laughing. Jonathon looked pissed. He always had a weird sense of entitlement and held quick grudges that died after a short time.

"You weren't the first," he said, not looking at me, "and you wouldn't have been the last. It's over and that's it. Fuck it. We don't talk about it again."

"I am so, so sorry…"

"I said we don't talk about it."

"Well, for what it's worth…"

"Shut up. No more."

Jonathon stared dead ahead when he spoke. He seemed embarrassed and I knew he was forgiving me because of his own guilt and shame. He knew Mina was a skank and ditching me as a friend for sleeping with her would mean he'd have to ditch a lot of guys in Daegu. Most of all he was just embarrassed. Being cheated on is a terrible thing. You feel like the lowest of the low, especially when you really loved the person and they fucked someone you trusted. It doesn't matter whether you suspected they were doing it in the first place. Worse than that is when you're made to realise that you've done that same thing to other people. Not only are you being treated like shit but you're faced with all the shitty stuff you did to people you pretended to love and care for. Jonathon had been brought down from his wild ways for a while.

I didn't know what to say so I shut up and watched Kelly pour our drinks – rum and Coke for everyone. She looked cute as she poured. She carried herself a little better than most Korean girls. She dressed subtly but sexily and avoided baggy clothes, poor English, and pastel colours. She just looked normal. Hot but normal.

"So where you been?" he asked.

"Japan. Fled the country."

"Fukuoka?"

"Yeah."

"Nice. You hit the clubs?"

"Of course."

"Better than Korea, right?"

"Yeah, Japan's beautiful, but I had no money."

"Ah, I see."

"Yeah, it's not the best place to be poor." He nodded. "I worked as a waiter for a bit and then met a girl who convinced me to come back."

"Well, believe it or not but I'm glad to have you back, Alexander. I missed you. I mean, comin' back to Korea's retarded as hell – this place sucks – but I'm glad you did."

"Yeah, I missed you, too."

Another silence. Our drinks came and I paid, but we just stood at the bar with them. I didn't look back at Min Jung because I knew she'd be burning holes in the side of my head with her devil gaze.

"So who's the chick? She the one that brought you back?"

"Min Jung. Yeah, I met her in Fukuoka."

"Cool. She's hot, man. Well done."

"Yeah, she's crazy, though."

"Yeah? I mean, she is Korean… What d'you expect?"

"Well, no. No, I take it back. She's not crazy. It's just… we've been spending twenty-four hours a day together for a long time and I'm starting to go nuts. I've got no money, no apartment, no job, no nothing. I rely on her for everything."

"That sucks."

"Tell me about it. She's driving me crazy. It's not her fault, I guess. I mean, she's a little weird but I could've done worse."

"Fuck it, man. A hole's a hole."

I laughed and shook my head.

"And an apartment's an apartment. If this bitch got money, fuckin' take it. Man, they all do that shit to us. Tell me you never had a bitch wouldn't take you for every penny you had? Shit, they all like that. Mina was always bustin' my ass for cash, man. Fuck it. Take her for whatever you can..." He looked as though morality swept across his mind, which happened from time to time. Jonathon spoke like an idiot but he wasn't entirely remiss. "Y'know. If you like her don't fuck her over... just take what's right."

"Well, once she gets me a job I'll get my own place, my own money, and I won't even have to think about it."

"Shit's easier when you don't live together."

"Yeah, man, I'm starting to see that."

More silence. We sat and drank our drinks without looking at the others. I wasn't even sure if Min Jung was still there. She'd probably walked home.

"So what happened when I was gone?" I asked. I had no idea what had gone on in my absence. "Where are you staying now?"

"Well, Mina moved out... *obviously*." The words hung in the air as he tried not to look at me and searched for the next sentence. That was a painfully slow process and I almost tried to change the subject. "She fuckin' killed the cat! Can you believe that?"

"Huh? What?"

"Yeah, man, remember that lil cat we got? She fuckin' killed it! Crazy bitches, man... Korean chicks is nuts. Killed it and moved out. I had to go toss the poor thing out on the street for some old Korean bitch to make soup with or something." He was laughing and miming the process of carrying a dead cat to the kerb.

"Jesus," I said. "That's horrible." I paused for a moment, then for some reason I said, "Min Jung eats dog..."

"Mina ate dog, too. They all eat it. She even tricked me into eating it once. Told me it was chicken. Tasted pretty good actually, but I wouldn't do it again."

"They all eat it? I thought that was an urban legend."

"No, they're dog eaters. Hang these poor bastards up 'til they croak, then eat them with kimchi."

I just shuddered at the thought and kept quiet.

"So..." he continued, "I got kicked out 'cause I couldn't afford the rent without her. So now I got another place. Fuckin' sucks, man."

"I'm sorry."

"Shit, man, shit sucks now! Everyone's bein' bitches. You and Thomas left, then Oliver went to Seoul..."

"What?"

"Yeah, man, he was all, like, 'Fuck this, everyone's leavin'!' and he just went and left. Guess you and Thomas meant more to him than me... Switched his contract to the same company in Seoul. Gonna be gone from Korea soon. Goin' back to school, last I heard. Not that I hear much from him anymore."

"Aw, man... It used to be you, me, Thomas and Oliver! Now it's just us... What about the girls? Tell me they didn't leave..."

"Beth's in Busan for some other school and Annie's back in Canada. Never hear from them anymore."

"Everyone's gone? Why the hell am I back in Daegu?"

"Mike's still about but doesn't drink so much... Jenny's workin' all the time and shit... Leah and Liz are studyin' for exams... Hell, everyone's stayin' at home. Now it's all these little teacher bitches. I swear, man, you got lucky when you came here. Ninety percent of teachers in Korea are fuckin' little pussies. Can't drink for shit and don't wanna have any fun. We had a tight group, man, and it's gone. Best group I had in this country, I swear it. Friends come and go but you guys were the shit."

I shook my head. I'd gone from not wanting to see anyone to being depressed that I wouldn't be able to see anyone. This was a lot of bad news to take. I needed some denial to help the situation: "It's cool, man, we'll get a new group."

"Yeah," he said, but I knew he didn't really believe it.

When eventually I turned back to the pool table, Min Jung was gone. Jonathan's friends were still there, playing pool, but she had unsurprisingly chosen to leave. I walked back to her apartment and spent about half an hour pleading with her to let me in as she sobbed and screamed. Eventually I apologised for ignoring her and by three in the morning I was forgiven.

CHAPTER SIX

My first proper fight with Min Jung occurred a week after meeting Jonathon. I knew it was coming, so it didn't cut me up too much and I prepared a few arguments to help her see why she was in the wrong and why she shouldn't ditch me. I basically figured out how to explain how lost I felt in simple enough English that she'd understand. None of that mattered, though. An angry woman is hard to reason with.

It started when I told her I wanted to go and meet Jonathon.

"You are seeing many girl!"

"No, I told you, it's just Jonathon and me – a guy's night."

"You are manhole!"

"We're just playing cards and pool. I'll be back early, babe. Why don't you go out with a friend and have fun?"

191

"Manhole!"

"What?"

"Manhole!"

"What the fuck does that mean?"

"You sleep many sexy girl!"

"No, you're fucking crazy. Shut up."

She began crying, and I realised she was trying to call me a "man whore," but I said nothing.

"Listen, Min Jung, we spend so much time together and I love it because I love *you*. If I didn't love you I wouldn't be around you so much. You know that." She whimpered. "I can't fuck other girls because I'm with you all the time, but when I'm not with you you need to trust me or else we're in trouble. Babe, I'd trust you if you went out with a friend."

"Fine!" she shouted. "Go with friend! I don't care!"

Jesus, there was no reasoning with this girl. I'd realised at Charleston that the concept of debate or argument doesn't really exist in Korea. People take their ideas and opinions into a "debate" and they stick with them to the end. All that matters is age, race, gender, and wealth. If you've got these over the other person then you've basically won. Of course, I didn't think Min Jung was holding her race or age over me, but she wasn't exactly skilled in reasoning like someone from a place where people reach civilised agreements.

I went out and met Jonathon and we shot some pool, played a little poker with Kelly in Trend, and then went home at one. I thought one was early and that the night had been civilised, but Min Jung thought differently. Her friends told her they'd followed me downtown and seen me dancing in Heart and Pride with other Korean girls, and apparently I'd kissed a few of them. Then I'd gotten into a taxi and gone home.

I tried to explain to her that this was all bullshit. I had witnesses that could prove I was in Trend all night, and she couldn't find anyone else who'd said I was in Heart or Pride. The doormen all knew me and would've recognised me, even after my long absence from the scene. Also, why the hell would I take a taxi home when Min Jung's place was less than five minutes walk from Trend, and less than two minutes from the taxi rank?

"You are manhole! Manhole!" she kept screaming. She wouldn't open the door for me and I didn't know what to say.

"Your fucking friends followed the wrong guy!" I shouted. "I swear, let me in and I'll explain."

"You are not explain! You are manhole! Manhole!" She began swearing in Korean. She used almost every bad word I knew, including many I'd never even heard but only read about on the internet. I was impressed by her craziness.

There was a thud on the street behind me and I suddenly felt sick. All noise inside ceased for a moment and I wondered if she'd jumped out the window. I'd be screwed if she had. The racist Korean police and media would paint me as the killer even though I was locked out. They'd hang me or torture me.

I turned and went out to the pavement and was relieved to see a carrier bag of my clothes lying on the street. How had I mistaken that for a corpse? It was split open and the few items of clothing I had kept at hers were now spilled onto the street – a sorry collection of t-shirts and underwear that probably wouldn't get any dirtier from lying on the ground.

"Fuck you!" she screamed and I looked up in horror as the crazy bitch leaned out the window with my laptop in her hand.

"Oh no! Babe, NO! SweetmercifulChrist-

Iloveyoudontthrowmylaptop!"
CRACK!

It was the worst of sounds. It was the sound of a lifetime crashing on the concrete, spilling what may as well have been my brains across the gritty, dirty, and clothes-strewn night street. My stomach twisted, my heart wrenched, and my eyes watered to see that shitty old computer explode on the ground, damaged beyond any imaginable salvation.

I'd always considered myself a writer in spite of my failures. All my life I'd noted down my thoughts, written poems and essays, stories, shitty novel attempts... I'd started and forgotten so many things but they were all saved for the future, for the time I got around to writing it all. It was all there – years and years of writing, of ideas, of notes and beginnings and possibilities. When it smashed I knew I was no longer a writer. I'd always been a bad one and I just hoped that one day I'd be able to paste it all together into something useable. But now it was hopeless. I'd have felt less depressed if she'd thrown herself out the window. It would have been better if she'd thrown a brick and it landed on my head and impaired the creative part of my brain because then at least I'd have something left in my laptop... Oh, that poor wretched machine. Dead. The only fucking thing I brought to Korea.

I slumped to my knees a few feet from the wreck and let my chin sink to my chest. I didn't shout or argue or acknowledge any of her madness. I didn't want to look at her. I wasn't angry. She'd broken me. I was half a man. Defeated.

When I looked up the window was closed. I didn't bother trying the door again. There was nothing for me in there. Min Jung had killed a part of me and I wouldn't forgive her. I'd rather die on the streets than go crawling back to someone who'd smash my beloved shitheap of a computer.

I walked back to Trend so I could ask Kelly if she knew Jonathon's phone number. There was no one else in the bar and it looked like she should have already closed up, but instead she was pounding vodka by herself, watching Korean dramas on TV, and listening to loud hip-hop music. She looked like she'd been dumped. I couldn't remember having ever seen a person look so lonely.

When I walked in she turned and smiled at me, and it looked like she'd been crying, or at least thinking about crying. "Are you alright?" I asked.

"Me?" She laughed unconvincingly. "I'm fine."

I looked at her and something in her eyes told me not to press any further. I didn't know her well enough. I liked her and I cared about her and I wanted her to be happy, but I didn't know enough to go asking personal questions.

"Do you know Jonathon's phone number?"

She shook her head, pursed her lips, and puffed out her cheeks. It was cute – something I'd seen many Korean girls do, but which had never looked cute until now.

"Well, what about… Shit, I don't know anyone in Daegu anymore. Well, do you know where he lives?"

"Somewhere near Camp Walker," she said, pouring me a rum and Coke.

I took the drink and sat down. She wouldn't take any money for it. "Near his old house?"

"I dunno. I never been."

Kelly shrugged and made a cute face that said she knew nothing. Her smile was adorable, but it contained too much sadness. I could tell she was hiding a lot of pain. I tried to figure out how old she was. My initial guess had been around twenty-one, but now I thought it could have been much, much older. She was beautiful in a womanly way, unlike so many others who tried too hard to seem young. Her eyes said she was closer to thirty, or maybe even older. She had a soft face, neither fat nor thin.

"What's the problem?" she asked.

"Remember that girl I was here with the other night?"

"Last week?"

"Yeah."

"Yeah, I remember. She was pretty." She smiled and we clinked glasses.

"She's crazy," I said. Kelly laughed and learned on the bar with her elbows like she'd done when we were playing poker. I tried my best not to look at her breasts. Now wasn't the time for that kind of thing. "She kicked me out of her apartment, broke my computer, and threw out all my clothes."

"Oh my god!"

"Yeah."

"What're you gonna do?"

"I'm not sure. I was going to call Jonathon and see if I could crash somewhere with him. I mean, I've got about five dollars to my name, no clothes, no computer, and no damn roof over my head. If it were winter I'd probably die!"

"Oh my god..."

"Even if I knew where Jonathon lived, I don't even have the taxi money to get out to his place, unless he lived ten minutes away. I don't have money to eat tomorrow, and that's if I live through the night."

"You shoulda got some money off her before she went nuts."

"I'm not really the thieving kind of guy... But damn, I'm in this country because of her and now I've got nothing. I'm ruined."

"Listen, Alexander, you can stay with me tonight.

I live nearby. You can take my sofa and I'll make you breakfast... or lunch. I don't really get up in the morning."

"Kelly, I hardly know you. I feel terrible being such a burden..."

She smiled and waved her arms drunkenly. I realised for the first time just how wasted she was. "It's okay. Just help me clean up and it'll be like I'm paying you. We'll find Jonathon tomorrow and after that you're his problem."

"Thanks, Kelly."

"You're welcome."

"By the way, what's your Korean name?"

"Yoon Seo," she said, very slowly.

CHAPTER SEVEN

I didn't sleep with Kelly, but I was sure I could have. She kept making advances and I told myself that I'd maybe come back later after the dust had settled with Min Jung. It was too soon and, even though I highly doubted it, maybe there would be a reconciliation. Kelly's apartment was like Min Jung's, which was very much like most other apartments in Korea – small, with minimal furniture and a big kimchi fridge. The only big apartment I'd seen was the one Jonathon had shared with Mina. At least Kelly had a tiny sofa that looked like it had been dragged up from the street and ditched in her room, then used as a basket for dirty laundry.

I woke up and Kelly was sleeping on the mattress on the floor. I felt awkward because I didn't know how to go about getting dressed and waiting for her to wake up. I didn't want to get dressed in front of her even if she was sleeping. That might seem weird. Then, if she woke up how would she get dressed? Oh fuck, I thought, it would have been easier to sleep with her...

I ended up lying on the uncomfortable little sofa until midday, when Kelly woke and made me breakfast. Nothing was awkward except that she seemed pretty dazed and confused from the previous night. I could see her wondering what exactly had happened. Had we fucked, kissed, or said anything embarrassing? She decided that nothing had happened and got showered and changed in the bathroom, barely saying a word to me. She looked very, very tired.

When she was done, she made me breakfast – kimchi and rice, with some kind of fish soup. It was the sort of meal that filled you, energised you, and held you over until the next one. The sort of meal I never made for myself but would probably lust for during the period of homelessness and joblessness that was sure to follow.

"So what do you gotta do today?" she asked, looking much better after her shower and application of make-up. Her smile helped, too.

"I have to see Jonathon, but I don't know how to contact him."

"How d'you do it last time?"

"Internet."

"You can use the computer at the bar, or go to a PC room."

"Good idea."

"You don't got his phone number?"

"No, I don't even have a phone."

"Shit."

"And I have to find a job immediately. I mean, someone who'll employ me and pay me really fast. Hell, even if it's just a day job. I need enough for something to eat and a place to sleep."

"You're in the right place, Alexander. I'm surprised you don't have something already."

I thought about it and she was right. It shouldn't take more than a day or two to find a job, but I hadn't even looked. Min Jung's friends had supposedly been looking for me.

"Just dress up nice and walk around a few schools. Shouldn't be a problem."

"How can I dress up nice?" I asked. "This is all I have!" I gestured at my white t-shirt and black shorts. It wasn't a terrible outfit, but it didn't exactly say *professional.*

"You shoulda picked up the things Min Jung threw out. I coulda washed them for you."

I smiled, embarrassed by her hospitality. She was far too nice – the sort of person everyone likes to take advantage of. "Thanks," I said. "I really should have but I was so fucking depressed I just walked away."

"Well, I can lend you some money…"

"No," I said, sternly. "Thanks, but no thanks. I'd feel terrible. You've already given me a place to sleep and a damn fine breakfast. That's more than enough. I already feel guilty taking this much."

"It's my pleasure, Alexander," she said. "You seem like the sort of guy who'd do the same for someone else."

"I'm not," I lied.

I asked Kelly if she could e-mail Jonathon for me and she said she would. Unless I caught him online it would be a waste of a day to sit by a computer and wait for his response. Instead, I went out job hunting for the first time in Korea. I knew the Korean characters for "academy" and so it was easy to find places. I soon realised that my attire wasn't particularly off-putting because all that really mattered was my race. The shorts and t-shirt just showed more of my white skin.

I didn't have a phone, so that was a negative factor. Everyone I spoke to said they wanted to call me later and I had to tell them I'd recently lost my phone. I didn't have any résumés or cover letters or business cards, either. I had to tell secretaries my e-mail address and ask them to write me back if interested. In any other country I would have been laughed out the door but in Korea they just saw someone they thought was American – someone they could show off to parents. I was pretty honest about myself. I didn't make up any fake degrees or qualifications. I just said I was looking for a job and very few places said they weren't interested.

I soon learned to avoid the big companies – huge chains of hagwons that hired through specific channels and sent their employees to do training in Seoul. These places would have been great to know about before coming to Korea, but they wanted official documents and lots of time to mull it over. Instead, I hit the little places – tiny businesses I knew would hire me illegally for a day or two just to handle some small classes. I didn't particularly want to work as an illegal immigrant in a country where there were posters everywhere that said: "Foreigner! We are watching you!" and had a zero-tolerance policy on illegal teachers, but I needed the money badly. I've never been a particularly lawful person, but I do generally like to avoid getting caught.

Ideally, I wanted a job that would hire me legally and for a set period of time. I needed a little security. If the job turned out anything like Charleston then I could switch and get another. It didn't matter. What was important was that I got something to see me through the next few days and weeks.

After four hours of walking around Suseong-gu – the rich part of town with too many hagwons and snotty little kids with bad parents, where Charleston had been and where all the big chain companies had at least one branch – I found a little park and sat down for a while. Trend wouldn't be open for another five hours and I didn't want to go to Kelly's place and bother her. She seemed too polite for her own good and I knew if I was annoying her she'd just put up with it. If I could find a computer I could try to get in touch with Jonathon, but that wasn't guaranteed and I didn't want to spend my last few dollars on a PC room unless I was certain I could speak to him.

I sat without a book to read or even a newspaper, just watching the trees and wishing it was even a degree warmer. How the weather had changed. It seemed as though autumn had fallen overnight, or over a few nights. The sweaty heat had been lifted by a cool breeze and my body wasn't used to that. Twenty-something years in Scotland apparently meant nothing. With barely any meat on my bones I couldn't weather the chill. Under the trees there was no sun, but it was pleasant enough. I could only smell sap and dirt, and it kept the pollution at bay. I watched a long-eared squirrel bounce about between thin branches and wondered if I'd seen any more impressive wildlife in Korea. Having barely been out of the city I hadn't, and even if I had travelled I probably wouldn't have seen a damn thing. Anything with a pulse ends up on someone's plate, blood still pumping.

There weren't many people, but the ones who did traipse by all came back and walked by a second time, swinging in close to my bench for a better look at the foreigner. Some people would stop right in front of me and stare, turning to talk to their friends – again there were those words: "foreigner," "big nose," "I don't like." I just sat there and let them stare, trying not to look as depressed as they were making me feel. I couldn't imagine going back to Scotland and trying to make other people feel as terrible as these people were trying to make me feel. One time I stared back and a whole family just shook their heads at me and turned away in disgust. Jesus, I thought, what a shitty country. Why did I come back?

I'd been sitting for about two hours when an old man came and sat beside me. He turned and stared directly into the side of my face. I felt about as uncomfortable as I could possibly have felt. I turned to look at him but he just kept staring, and I didn't have the courage to tell him to fuck off. I tried turning away but I could still feel his stare burning into the back of my head. A few people walked by and they all stared at me, and not at the old guy. I wondered what I'd have done in another country if I'd seen someone do that to a foreigner. I'd probably have gone over and punched the guy. But I'm better at defending others than I am at defending myself.

After fifteen minutes of staring I stood up and walked back to the main road, and then headed into town. It was a forty-minute walk, and I was feeling weak. I needed food. I contemplated the idea of going into a restaurant, eating a big meal, and then just running out on the bill. It seemed like a pretty flawless plan, but I wasn't hungry enough to get over the guilt. I knew I'd get away with it, but the owners would always treat foreigners like shit. I recalled stories of rare incidents of foreigner crime in Korea, and they were often followed by random, reciprocal attacks on other foreigners on the street. The sad thing is that Korea's a country where people overreact so strongly that I'd probably end up getting some innocent guy arrested, beaten, or having white people's dinners spat in for the next ten years. I didn't need that on my mind.

I went back into town and didn't know what to do. I tried sitting on a few more benches in parks, but I couldn't take the stares and the nasty comments. I got tired of adults pointing and whispering about me, and children screaming "foreigner foreigner foreigner" and then having a big group gather to gawk at me while I just sat not knowing where to look.

I was glad it wasn't raining. That would have made it the perfect day.

I went to Min Jung's house because I couldn't take the boredom of standing or sitting around all day on my own and being stared at by thousands of morons. It was too much to take, and I decided that even fighting with Min Jung for a few hours was better than staying outside. Besides, it was getting dark soon and although it wasn't properly cold, it would be too chilly for sitting in one place.

When she opened the door she was crying and I knew she'd been crying all day because her eyes were puffy. She looked ugly and old and I was glad because otherwise her looks might have made me break.

"Why you didn't come back?" she wailed as I pushed inside. "I am crying!"

"I see that," I said. "But it's hardly my fault."

"You don't love me!" she howled.

"I used to love you, until your cursed paranoia became a factor. I can't deal with ludicrous accusations."

"I don't understand. I can't understand you!"

"You. Are. Crazy."

"I not crazy!"

"Yes, yes you are."

She screamed and threw a plate at my head, which clipped my forehead and smashed against a wall. Blood immediately began to drip from a small cut. I put my finger up and examined the damage. It wasn't bad, but it might make it harder for me to get another job.

"Jesus! You fucking psycho bitch! Fuck you!"

"Fuck you! You sleep many sexy girl!"

"I've never cheated on you, Min Jung, and I never will. That's not me. That's not who I am."

"My friend see you with sexy girl..."

"Shut the fuck up you fucking idiot bitch!"

She began crying again, harder this time, as the rage seemed to die down a little. "I'm sorry," I said. "You're not an idiot. But you *are* crazy! Why can't you trust me? Why did you have me followed? And why do you believe your fucking dumbass bitchwhore friends over me? I thought you loved me... Lovers don't take the words of idiots over their significant others. Those bitches probably think all white guys look alike."

"They see you with sexy girls..."

"No, they didn't."

"Why you not back?"

"You fucking threw out all my stuff! You broke my computer, Min Jung, and I'll never forgive you for that. Never. That's like my brain. It has everything on it."

"I'm sorry."

"Damn right, you're sorry! You scare the hell of me, babe. How do I know you're not going to wake up in the night and decide I've cheated on you, then fucking kill me or something?"

"I don't! I don't!"

"Well, that's hard to believe, Min Jung, because it seems you always just assume the worst. You always just think I'm with some other girl. Shit, we've spent one night apart the whole time we've known each other and you instantly assume I've been cheating on you. I can't deal with that."

"I'm sorry!" She was falling against me now, crying her eyes out, and although I hated myself for it, I knew I was starting to forgive her. I've never been able to handle tears. No matter what the situation, they always make me cave.

"You have to change, Min Jung. You have to let me have friends. You have to be able to turn your back and know I'm staying faithful to you."

"I'm sorry!" she wailed again.

I hugged her and then lay her down on the bed. She was shaking and crying furiously. A real nutjob. What had I gotten myself into? I sat down beside her and ran through the whole thing in my head, although it was all too blurry and stupid to really think about. I legitimately feared this girl. I was terrified she'd dream up something horrible and hurt me in my sleep or poison my food. Hell, she could just call the police if she wanted. I was a foreigner and she could tell them anything. It was like sitting on a landmine.

CHAPTER EIGHT

Things didn't go particularly smoothly after that. I could see Min Jung straining to keep herself in check, which made me happy. I knew it couldn't last, but the fact that she was making an effort to be reasonable meant a lot to me. I tried to keep her happy, too, because even though she'd done something awful to me I still felt there was no need to be an asshole. I wanted to make things work with this girl. Maybe I could help her get over the Kimchi Rage... Maybe we'd be together forever. I kept waiting for an e-mail from a hagwon, hoping for a job so I could get away from her for a while. Even a day at work would help. Whatever happened, I could make things run a little more smoothly by giving her no reason to get upset.

My first day of work back in Korea came two days later and it was Kelly who got me the job, although I didn't tell Min Jung. Kelly had asked around the regulars at the bar and one of them hooked me up with a school in Siji, on the far eastern side of Daegu. I would work for ten hours and make three hundred dollars. I said I'd gotten the job by walking about and asking people, and Min Jung didn't seem to doubt me, but I could see the beginnings of curiosity in her eyes. She wanted to believe me and I felt terrible for lying, but what did it matter?

The school was a tiny three-classroom business on the third floor of a cheap-looking building on a skinny backstreet, surrounded on three sides by an abandoned stretch of wasteland. There was no parking, no elevator, and it was barely marked by signs outside. Inside everything was cheap and nasty and smelled of kimchi. The desks and chairs were all marked or broken, there were no board markers in the classrooms, and trash lay everywhere. All the clocks were set to the wrong time and the walls were decorated by stickers that had been stuck on slanted and had since been partially ripped off. I wondered why anyone would send their child there, but when I saw them I realised these were the poor kids. They were dressed in clothes from supermarkets rather than designer stores, with tears at the knees and stains down the front. All the brats I'd taught at Charleston had been spoiled rich kids, dressed like dolls in frilly clothes. Some of them were even on crash diets at six years old – the apples of their parents' warped eyes.

The walls were paper thin and I could hear the other teachers' lessons as I taught. Some of it was as embarrassing as the "I am name is…" style of grammar taught at Charleston. Mostly, though, the teachers played tapes and CDs to accompany illegal photocopies made from mistake-riddled books. Whenever they spoke they did so loudly, but without much accuracy. I wondered what chance these kids had of making it to a decent university.

It was an easy day of work. My co-workers were fascinated by me, having never worked with a foreigner before. None of them spoke much English, but there were all teaching it to middle school kids. It seemed ridiculous, but I think the teachers were only marginally ahead of the students and studying from the same books. They were paying me as much to talk to them and help them with their English as to teach the kids, who also seemed fascinated by me, having never been to a big hagwon before, and having probably never seen a white guy up close.

They were sweet kids – much nicer than the rotten spoiled brats at Charleston. Naturally, they seemed scared of me at first, but once the other teachers assured them I wasn't a murderer or rapist, they settled down and soon we were having fun. There were no teaching materials other than those awful textbooks. Even at Charleston I'd been given flashcards and puppets and posters. Here I had a book and the kids had copies of it, and we had to sit and talk. Talking to six-year-olds without a common language isn't easy, but I managed it and they learned a little.

I finished work at eight and met Jonathon for one beer in Trend before going home to Min Jung, having told her I was working until nine. I also told her I was paid two hundred dollars instead of three, in case she tried to extract the cash from me as payment for her prior generosity. I fully intended to treat her right, of course, but not to pay her back in hard cash. Dinner here, a movie there… That was the plan.

Jonathon was laughing at me for getting myself involved with a Korean girl. "I told you, man," he said. "Those bitches is all crazy. Kimchi Rage!"

"Alright," I admitted. "You were right. She's alright now, though. I have her under control."

"Sure you do… Just wait 'til the next time she goes off. You'll wake up with your dick glued to your stomach or something. Or maybe she'll stuff you in a kimchi pot and bury you."

"Jesus, that's horrible… I already thought of it, though. I'm just going to sweeten her up every time I go to sleep – give her massages, tell her she's pretty, eat some kimchi. Never go to sleep when she's pissed."

"You need to get yourself a nice girl," Kelly ventured. "Min Jung seems crazy."

"She is crazy, but she's also nice. I'm working on moulding her into a sane person. Or at least keeping her at bay until I get my own place."

"Well, don't tell her you stayed with me," Kelly said. "I don't want her comin' round here and startin' shit up!"

"She won't," I said.

"Doesn't she got her own friends?" Jonathon asked. "Bitch gotta get out more, then you can spend more time with me. I hardly ever see you, brother."

"That's a good idea," I said. "She's always talking about her friends, but she never does anything with them. They just speak on the phone all day."

"Then tell her to go have a girls' night out."

"Okay, but you need to be nearby, ready to jump in. If I tell her to go have fun she's gonna go crazy on me…"

"Shit, man, that ain't no way to live. Dump that bitch."

"And be homeless? Besides, I do like her."

"Just be careful, man," Jonathon said. "I don't wanna see you getting hurt."

I told Min Jung that I thought it was strange that she never saw her friends and she seemed to agree. She said they talked on the phone and that was usually enough. I told her to go and do something with them, but I posed it as a vague question and she didn't seem to get too upset.

Again, I could see flickers of paranoia in her eyes. She wondered why I wanted her to go see her friends. She probably thought I was going to bring girls back to her apartment.

When she went to see her friends, I went to see Jonathon. The problem was, though, her friends were also crazy bitches. By the time she came home – and I was home earlier than her, just to keep her happy – her head was full of bad craziness.

"You are see sexy girl!" she shouted and my head dropped. I didn't feel sad or hurt this time. I was just bored of it. I couldn't cope with her madness any longer.

"No, I'm not." I sighed loudly. "What makes you think that?"

"My friend see you with sexy girl!" she threw her coat on the bed and punched me on the arm, then collapsed in a theatrical heap.

Instead of getting angry like I usually did, I breathed deeply and spoke firmly: "Where? When?"

"No matter! She see you!"

"Tell me where and tell me when and I'll tell you why she's wrong. I haven't been spending any time with any 'sexy girls.'"

Min Jung was crying loudly on the bed and I just lay down beside her and pretended to go to sleep. If she'd really believed her friends she would have kicked me out of the house again. There was no reasoning with her and I didn't want her to get angrier, so I lay there listening to her crying for an hour before I fell asleep, making sure to remember never to suggest she sees her friends again.

The next day I asked her straight out: "Why are you so fucking nuts, babe?" and she told me: "I don't know, I can't help it," and she cried again. I felt bad for hating her stupid dumb rages, but if she couldn't help it then it was hard on both of us. I decided to toughen up. As long as she treated me right when the Kimchi Rage wasn't clouding her head, I'd stick by her.

CHAPTER NINE

I worked a few cash-in-hand day jobs for small and sketchy schools and toyed with the idea of opening my own hagwon. I'd use a Korean person's name, of course, because nobody would send their child to a business owned by a dirty foreigner. I mused it over, but then dismissed it as ridiculous when I thought about the logistics. Firstly, I'd need thousands to invest, and if I had thousands I'd probably take that money to a better country and invest it there. I began dreaming of going to the Philippines or Cambodia and opening a bar. There were parts of the Philippines – according to Jonathon, who'd been there before – that were tourist hotspots, but only the poor locals made money off it because no one had bothered investing anything. There were plenty of such places. I imagined myself sitting on a beach and sipping rum while some locals ran the bar and fleeced the tourists. At least some of those tourists would be cute chicks and they'd fall head over heels with the tanned owner of a beachside bar in paradise... That would be the life.

Of course, it was all about logistics. Money was easy to make in Korea for a guy who looked like an American. My day jobs always paid me enough to eat and drink for the next week, and if I didn't have Min Jung's place I probably could have worked harder and paid for a love motel to sleep in each night. Instead, I worked a day or two each week.

After three weeks and no major fallouts with Min Jung, I managed to score a proper job. This one was legal and the contract was for one year. I'd earn over two million won per month – around two thousand dollars. I knew I wouldn't spend nearly that much, and I probably wouldn't stick with the job more than six months, so I planned to take what I could and head to the Philippines after I got bored. If necessary, I'd come back to Korea every year and earn enough to live the beach-life on a beautiful island. The perfect plan.

My new job was out in Siji, far away from the downtown bars and clubs. It was also far from Min Jung, which upset her. I told her I could still spend most nights at her place, or she could come out to mine, and that I was only working out there. My apartment would be in Siji, too, but I didn't have to stay there. She seemed content by these possibilities, and I was happy that we would still stay together and yet cut down on the time we shared.

The school was called JLP and I never bothered to find out what that stood for, if anything. There were many big hagwons in the area, and someone told me that Siji was the second most competitive hagwon district in Korea, after Gangnam in Seoul. I wondered if that meant I'd actually have to work hard. Fuck it, I thought. I yearned for the job that would set me straight – something difficult but rewarding, and not just in a financial way. I'd spent my life either doing nothing or doing shitty jobs. Working in the hagwons for lots of money hadn't been particularly rewarding, either, because I hated the crooked system. If I could find a good one maybe it would turn my life around. I didn't like always being the loser – whether I was the drug-addicted and chronically unemployable waster in Scotland or the homeless and pussy-whipped little bitch I'd become in Korea. I needed something to make me a man.

Of course, JLP was just another school. It was bigger and shinier than most, but it was another goddamn hagwon. The kids, it turned out – as I had once again signed a contract without any investigation – were far younger than I wanted to teach. They were all three, four, or five years old in Korean age, which made them between one and four in real-world age. My contract allowed for a week's vacation of my choosing, plus two weeks of theirs. I had two sick days, which is almost unheard of for a foreign teacher in Korea.

My new apartment was yet another typical one-room place on a street that seemingly housed all the foreigners in the area. I guessed that the city planners decided it would be easier to keep an eye on the outsiders if we were all stuck together on the one street.

Siji smelled better than Manchon or Sam Deok. It was separated from the rest of the city by several miles of countryside and surrounded closely by mountains. I was never more than ten minutes from the greenery of Uksu Mountain. There were parks and little spots of trees all around and, although the natives used them as toilets, they looked pleasant enough. There was a road that ran from Daegu to Gyeongsan, and a few highways connecting other cities, but there wasn't much traffic, and the air generally felt a lot less polluted. It was less crowded and people seemed to move slower. They were generally a little friendlier - not staring as much as the ones downtown and quieter when they talked about me. People rarely pushed me on the pavements or spat at my feet.

My boss – a woman named Ms. Sim – seemed friendly enough. She was surprised that I had nothing with me but the clothes on my back. I told her someone had stolen everything I owned and that I had no money, and she took me out for dinner. She was about thirty and fairly unattractive. Her skin was bad and I could tell by looking at her that she didn't have a boyfriend or a husband, and that her parents were probably on the cusp of disowning her. But I liked her. She looked to be a better boss than Mr. Park.

"When did you come Korea?" she asked me over dinner.

"Six months ago," I said. "I think."

"Why did you leave old school?"

I hadn't explained that yet, so I quickly made up a lie. "They went out of business. Not enough students."

"Oh," she said. The prospect of business failure seemed to alarm her, as though she were being introduced to the idea of her own mortality for the first time. "Very bad."

"But JLP's not going out of business, right?" I laughed.

She didn't look happy. Comedy can be a hard thing to translate. "No…"

"Well, great. I'm looking forward to teaching for a long time." Another lie.

"What about Scotland?" she asked. I knew from experience that when a Korean person says "What about _____?" they mean to ask you "What is _____ like?" or "What do you think of _____?"

"It's cold and rains too much."

"Really?"

"Yes. A lot of rain."

"How much rain?"

"Enough to necessitate the constant possession of an umbrella."

"Korea has many rain, too." She sounded proud, as though striking a victory for Korea in the Great League of Rainy Nations.

"And how about Korea?"

I stopped and thought. How could I avoid lying outright without telling the awful truth? "Er, it's a nice country." Damn, a lie. "I like Korea." Shit, another one! "The mountains are beautiful." Okay, there's something truthful… or at least presumably truthful on account of my having never been into the mountains.

"And the food? Many foreigner like Korean food, but so spicy!"

"Yeah, I like the food. It's not really spicy, either. Chinese, Indian, Mexican… All those places have food that's spicier, and Western people love their food way more than Korea's."

"Really?" She looked as though I'd just insulted her country.

I realised I should have censored myself and just said, "Yes! Korean food is delightful!" but instead I went and told the damned truth. Truth is not something that serves a foreigner well in Korea.

"Why did you come Korea?"

"Adventure," I said. "But also to learn to teach. My mother was a teacher." That was pretty much what I had told Mr. Park, and what I felt passed for an acceptable answer. I wasn't about to say, "Well, honestly I was bored, broke, and horny like most of the guys who come here to work."

217

***

When I began working, many of the legalities were skipped – no degree was shown, no AIDS test administered, no criminal records checked. I wondered just how legal my job was... Ms. Sim assured me that everything was above board and would come later but I didn't believe her. I'd seen no paperwork and I knew from my first job and from what I'd been told by other teachers that hiring a foreign teacher is a great deal of work. I wondered if maybe they'd just told me I was there legally and then were screwing me out of tax money. Maybe they were temporarily employing me as an illegal worker and would get things in order later. Whenever I probed, they said it would just take time. I didn't care, of course, because I had a roof over my head and Min Jung was buying my food and soju.

My first day of work was very different from my first at Charleston. There were no observation classes and no preparatory briefings. I was given my schedule, a teachers' guide to each book I needed to teach, and an hour to prepare. I could hardly believe the schedule – I was supposed to work from ten in the morning until two in the afternoon, four days a week! I was being paid more than at Charleston and for less than half the time! I was nervous because I actually cared. This time, I really wanted to give it my best, to succeed as a teacher and grow as a human being.

I tried to decipher the stupid ramblings and poor English of the teachers' guide. It was like reading the instructions to a piece of complex furniture that needed to be assembled, but had been written by, well, a Korean person. It made little or no sense. Even the things like numbers, that should have posed no problem to someone with minimal fluency in the language, were confusing and riddled with errors. But I studied and prepared and went into my first class with confidence.

There were four tiny children in the classroom, along with one Korean teacher and myself. There was a huge glass window in one wall, through which Ms. Sim and four mothers stared intently. It was strange teaching with another adult in the room, but she didn't speak a word of English and seemed far more concerned with controlling the children than with paying any attention to me. In spite of being nervous about her presence, I actually felt comforted by this. I never got her name, but she sat and mothered the children, who would otherwise have been charging around the classroom. Whenever she needed to, she would change their diapers and simultaneously control the other kids. It was amazing. Discipline had been at least half the battle at Charleston and at JLP I didn't even need to think about it.

The children were four years old in Korean age, which is about three in real-world age. This was their first hagwon and none of them spoke a word of English. They all looked terrified of me and some of them cried at the horrifying sight of my white face, but the Korean teachers did a great job of telling them I wasn't so bad. In Korean, they said "Alexander teacher is your mother's friend," and I laughed because I knew their mothers were just as scared of me.

We began the lesson by learning "Hello!" and then tried "My name is…" Of course, none of them had English names and that was apparently necessary, so I was made to give all the kids names. In total there were four classes and around twenty-five children, which made for a lot of naming. I ran through my family and my friends from back home, before going to the computer and printing out a list of generic Western names. Heartless but efficient.

I never learned the names of any of my co-workers.

They all looked terrified of me, but they were friendly enough. It wasn't an English hagwon, so none of them knew any English, and were simply there to teach the kids Korean and play with them, while I would teach a few English lessons. I think they all enjoyed learning English along with the kids. I certainly enjoyed learning Korean by sitting in on the other lessons, watching them teaching about animals and geography in their native language. I learned a lot in the first few days.

After my first day at JLP I went home to my own apartment and lay down and thought about how lucky I'd been to have found a good job. It seemed that no one I'd met in Korea had a job like this. I imagined myself staying not only for the six months I'd planned, but for the whole year, and maybe even signing a contract for another year. Why not? This was a great job and I needed something steady and strong in my life to make me a better person. Now I had a girlfriend and a job and a place of my own. All I needed was that first paycheque and I'd be set.

CHAPTER TEN

Jonathon surprised me by offering to lend me two hundred dollars to help me out until my first paycheque. It was shocking because he would rarely pay his half of a taxi ride or a dinner, even if he'd been the one to suggest splitting the cost in the beginning. He was a notorious welsher and I didn't even think about asking him for a penny when I was broke. But for some reason he offered and I cautiously accepted, and he gave the money without whining. It was odd. With the little cash I had from teaching the illegal day-jobs, plus Jonathon's money, I could make it until payday without too much straining. I was happy.

Min Jung and I ate out once or twice and she paid the bill. We split our time between my place and hers, and I told her that I finished work at four so that I could have some extra time to myself each day. That first week was bliss. Even the stress of learning new materials and teaching kids who were far too young to be learning a second language – considering some of them couldn't yet speak one language – didn't phase me because I was secure and happy in my life. I drank a few drinks every night but never went to sleep drunk. I fucked Min Jung once a day and that kept us both happy.

After the first week, Ms. Sim told me that things were coming along in the visa process. She again assured me that I was working legally, and although I didn't believe her, I pretended to accept her words. She said she wanted to see my degree.

"I don't have it," I said. That was true. Mr. Park had kept it at Charleston and when I quit I forgot to ask him to return it. Later, when I remembered, I didn't dare ask him. I counted it as lost goods – something I might never need, but that only mattered in the sense that I'd earned it in the first place.

"Why?" she asked.

I didn't want to say that it was in the possession of Mr. Park in case she demanded he return it and he told her what a terrible teacher I was. "I lost it," I said.

"I need the degree."

"I could get a copy," I offered.

"Okay."

Using the school computers I managed to download and print an unconvincing fake degree and filled in the details to correspond with my own academic achievements. It was silly because I could well have filled it in to say "Masters" and "Oxford", but my conscience rested easier knowing that I was telling the truth to an extent. Another few days rolled by without any developments. Then Ms. Sim told me I needed to get an AIDS test and a drugs test because Koreans are brought up to believe that everyone born and raised outside of Korea has

AIDS and abuses hard drugs. She drove me to a filthy and disorganised hospital near downtown and helped me to fill in forms that asked questions like: "Are you mental retardation?" "Do you have many crazy?" and "Have you ever been busted for the crack?" I tried not to laugh as she asked me these things in all seriousness. It even asked questions like, "Do you enjoy sex?" and I of course said "No, I don't" and she looked pleased. It's a big concern in Korea that foreigners are coming into the country and stealing their women, even though most interracial couples are comprised of Korean men and foreign women.

Of course, my blood tests came back negative and I was told everything was on track. Ms. Sim even told me I needed to go back to Japan, just so I could pass through Korean immigration again and get my visa stamped. The school would apparently pay for this trip, and I'd get a paid day off work.

They seemed in no rush to make my employment legal. I wondered if they were pushing for the first month so they could skim some cash off my paycheque. After that, maybe they'd push the visa through. Maybe they wanted me to work for a month and then they'd fire me with no fear of legal action because I'd been illegally employed. I got paranoid. I was enjoying work and I grew suspicious partly because I'd never enjoyed a job before.

With my own apartment and a full-time job, I was able to avoid Min Jung and spend time alone or with Jonathon. Although he protested at the distance, I invited him out to Siji from time to time. Mostly he complained about Siji being too quiet and full of "ESL faggots." I agreed that it was quiet and that the only foreigners were ESL teachers, but I enjoyed it far more than being downtown.

One afternoon he called me after work, on the line in my apartment. "Yo, Alex," he said. "How about you lose some of that money back to me at poker tonight?"

I laughed because Jonathon was terrible at poker. "Sure. But you gotta come out to Siji. If we play downtown someone will tell Min Jung."

"Jesus Christ. What a bitch. You for serious? Man, alright. Alright. The things I do…"

"Who's playing?" I asked.

"A couple of guys I know from base."

"They're not going to trash my apartment, are they?" I was only half joking.

"Don't be stupid. They might be pissed that they gotta come all the way out to the fuckin' sticks to play some poker, though. Oh, and I'm gonna invite Kelly."

"What? Don't do that, man. If Min Jung finds out she'll murder me."

"I told you, Alexander, quit being such a fuckin' bitch. Man up. Anyway, she's just gonna play a little cards. We played cards with her before and there wasn't no problem, right?"

"Please don't…"

He hung up.

A few hours later, Jonathon, Kelly, and his buddies arrived at my apartment. Jonathon had a big poker set under his left arm and some Jack Daniels under his right. The soldiers each carried a bottle of Coca-Cola. Kelly came in behind them, looking gorgeous as always, dressed in yellow. She was smiling coyly and taking in everything with wide eyes.

I asked her immediately if she had closed the bar to come play poker and she laughed. "No, it's fine. I got a friend to watch it." I couldn't imagine anyone else actually working there.

The soldiers turned out to be significantly friendlier

than the usual type. They were well-spoken and down to earth, and I could hardly imagine them rape-dancing girls in Heart. Their names were Andy and Tim and they both came from Colorado. They asked the usual questions: Where did I work? What country was I from? The same damn conversations everyone has in Korea. Tedious. But they were at least friendly and pretended to be interested.

I watched Kelly walk around the apartment as Jonathon counted out chips and the soldiers poured drinks for everyone. She had a smirk on her face and I knew it was because my apartment was even shittier than hers. Although they were both tiny, at least hers had *things* in it. My place had empty walls and empty cupboards. There was no furniture or bed sheets, and the cupboards were empty. It was basically a cave.

"What's so funny?"

"Your place," she said. "I guess I always imagine foreigners living in some big mansion or something. You know, like you see on TV."

"That'd be nice. But this is alright. It's small and crappy but it's at least a place to live. I'm moving up in the world... slowly."

We sat down and played poker. Not much was said as we all went into competitive mode, but after an hour of fast drinking we loosened up. Betting went wild and conversation flowed as we forgot our turns.

It was just then Andy pulled out a little plastic bag from his jacket pocket. I didn't pay any attention until he asked, "You mind if I smoke?" and I said of course I didn't mind. But instead of pulling out a pack of cigarettes he opened the bag to reveal a small amount of dark green weed.

"You okay with that?" he asked.

I didn't know what to say. Of course, I'd smoked weed since I was fifteen and had no problems with it. In the hotel room in Busan back in the summer I had shared a joint with a group of foreigners, and so I didn't care about smoking it in Korea, despite the country's notably harsher laws. But something felt wrong... I was happy in my job and felt that I actually had something to lose, should I get caught. But how would I get caught? I was in my own home, with friends. I'd also just passed the only drug test I was legally required to take.

Before I could say anything, though, Jonathon piped up. "Shit, Alexander's from Scotland. They all smoke down in Scotland, right Alex? They do crazy shit over there."

"Yeah," I said. I had told Jonathon about Scottish nightlife on various drunken occasions but was surprised that he had remembered.

Andy produced a packet of skins and began rolling a little joint as Jonathon laughed and Kelly looked confused. "Where did you get skins around here?" I asked.

"Oh shit, it ain't easy," Tim explained. "But we stock up whenever we get back to America. Andy was back there in the summer and picked up a bunch. I guess some guys just pick 'em up online and others make do without. Whatever, dude, you don't need 'em I guess. Just empty out a cigarette or something."

"Or make a bong," Andy suggested.

Jonathon looked at me and shrugged his shoulders. "I love you, Alex," he said. "These dudes pull out a bag of fuckin' *marijuana* in your house – in a country where you'd probably get executed for it – and you're like 'Where d'you get skins?' Not even interested in the weed."

"It's a bit rude to ask where people get their drugs," I said. "It's not exactly good etiquette."

Jonathon looked embarrassed, and then indignant.

"What the fuck should I know? I ain't smoke that shit."

Andy snickered. "What a bitch. Dude's from Cali and don't even smoke."

Jonathon just shook his head and muttered to himself about "bitches."

When Andy was done rolling we cracked a window and smoked as we played poker. Only Andy, Tim, and I smoked. Jonathon just snorted and said he didn't like it, and Kelly smiled awkwardly and passed without explanation. Nobody pushed her, and I felt bad for smoking myself. I wondered what she thought about it.

At the end of the night, Tim told me that if I ever wanted to buy any weed, I should just speak to him through Jonathon and he'd get it for me. "Really?" I asked. "Isn't it tough to get around here?"

They both laughed hard. "Dude, it's fuckin' *easy* when you know. I ain't sayin' everybody does it, but you'd be surprised. You just don't go around broadcastin' it in a place like this, but yeah, a lotta people are smokin' down. Give us a shout and we'll hook you up."

"I'm broke right now," I said, which was true. "But when I get paid I'll definitely be in touch."

I tried to ride back downtown with Jonathon but his car was too full of shit to fit all of us, so I had to take a taxi. Kelly offered to ride with me, so we said goodbye to the guys and hailed a cab near my apartment.

"So you did that sort of thing back in Scotland?" she asked.

I was a bit embarrassed, so I made a joke: "What, you mean poker?"

"No, the drugs." She wasn't smiling.

"Honestly, yeah. I mean, I'd hardly call weed a drug. You know, it's nothing serious. Things were pretty bad back in Scotland and I did a lot of stupid stuff. I don't deny it. But weed… shit, there's nothing wrong with it. If I can get it here I will."

"Just be careful, Alexander. I don't know a lot about these sort of things but I know you can get in a lot of trouble."

"That's true," I conceded. "If you get caught…"

Again, she seemed serious. "Promise me you won't get caught."

I looked her in the eyes and said, "I promise."

It wasn't even late when we got downtown and Kelly said that she was going to Trend to watch the bar. We'd started poker early and it was only about midnight when the taxi arrived in front of the fire station. Kelly paid for it. "Good luck," she said as we parted.

I walked to Min Jung's house and tried to sober up. I wasn't particularly drunk or stoned, but I certainly wasn't sober, either. What mostly concerned me was that I had told Min Jung I'd be home around nine, thinking that I'd have plenty of time to sit around and relax before going to see her. I was late and didn't have an excuse.

She was furious when she opened the door, and she didn't want to let me in. Although I didn't want to be there, I pushed my way inside and argued with her for a while. I told her a censored version of the truth: That I'd been at my house with Jonathon and two soldiers, drinking and playing cards.

"Why you didn't call me?" she cried.

"I don't have a phone."

"You know my number. Why you didn't use friend's phone?"

She had me there. I could've prevented much of this problem by planning ahead and telling her. But again, I told a version of the truth: "Listen, Min Jung. I lost track of time. I meant to be home by nine, honestly, but I forgot what time it was. I'm sorry."

"Why? Why you lose time?"

"Because… because we were smoking weed. We got a bit high and just forgot. I'm sorry. It was stupid but it was an honest mistake."

"Weed?"

"Yeah, just a little weed. It's no big deal. In Scotland everybody does it. All across the world people do it."

"I know that."

"I'm sorry I was late. But it was just a few guys playing cards. No girls, no going out. We were just having a bit of fun."

"I don't care." Min Jung looked angry but nowhere near her usual levels of rage. She just sat on the bed with her arms folded, red in the face. Then she looked up. "No girls?" she asked.

"No girls."

"You promise?"

"I promise."

CHAPTER ELEVEN

One day Ms. Sim called me into her office – which was more like a lounge in a fancy hotel than a hagwon office. Whereas Mr. Park's had been tiny and filled with the practical items necessary for running a hagwon, in addition to bullshit qualifications and showy books that were never used, Ms. Sim's was decorated in traditional Korean items and had a fountain in one corner that was more than impressive. There were decorative kimchi pots, pebbles surrounding ornaments on the floor and mats, paintings, and statues of Korean people. It was surreal. I'd never even been there before that meeting, as it was hidden behind what appeared to be a cupboard door in one of the classrooms and had another entrance in an entirely different part of the building. This was where business happened, away from the realities of teaching little kids.

We sat on the floor, either side of a small table with little stone cups filled with cold green tea. Ms. Sim was not smiling.

"Alexander teacher, there is problem," she said, looking terribly concerned. My heart sank in an instant and I knew that my world was coming crashing down, just as I'd come to enjoy it. I couldn't say a word so I simply stared at her. I could feel the edges of my mouth dropping and my throat closing up.

"Did you work at..." She looked at a piece of paper in front of her. "Charleston Academy?"

I sat for a long time, just staring into her eyes, pleading silently with her to put the paper away and forget everything. I nodded.

"So you understand?"

"I think so…" I didn't know how to lie my way out of this situation. I didn't understand the visa process or Korean law well enough to create some story that would make everything go away. I didn't even know what exactly it was she knew.

"Do you know Mr. Park?" she asked.

I wanted to point out that there were literally millions of people in Korea called "Mr. Park", but I didn't. I just nodded again.

"There is problem with your visa. You…" She was obviously struggling with the words. A big problem with working in English academies in Korea is the language barrier. When serious issues are raised people get frustrated by their inability to convey their exact message. "You leave Charleston in bad way?"

"It was complicated," I explained. "There's more to it than you could possibly have written on that piece of paper."

"It say here you leave Charleston in bad way."

"Charleston was a bad school. I had no choice but to

leave."

Ms. Sim paused for a few moments and thought about what I'd said, what she thought, and how she could put that information across in comprehensible English. "It is not good feeling," she said.

"I understand. But it's more complicated than just leaving a school. There are details that I know you haven't been told."

"I don't understand, teacher."

"I'm saying that there are things that you need to know that you aren't being told – things that are relevant to my position here at JLP."

"It is a problem, teacher. If Mr. Park not happy with you, you don't get job in Korea."

"Isn't that up to you?"

"No."

"But I'm already employed here."

"It is… difficult. There are many thing to think about."

"But I'm a teacher here. I've worked here for three weeks, I have an apartment… The kids know me and I'm enjoying myself! You can't just turn around and change all of that."

"It is not my power, teacher."

"What do you mean, 'It's not your power'?"

Ms. Sim looked upset. She didn't want to have this meeting and she couldn't adequately put forth her sentiments. She muttered quietly to herself in Korean, trying to find the right words. She was getting frustrated and I felt the hope dying inside me as I realised nothing constructive was coming from this meeting.

"I mean, teacher, that it is for other people to think. It is not my power."

"I thought…" My argument died there and I gave up. "I'm a teacher here! I like my job…"

"I'm sorry, teacher."

"No, please. Why?"

"Mr. Park say you bad teacher. He say you did not do contract. That mean you cannot get job in Korea. I'm sorry."

"But he's a lying… idiot!" I refrained from using an expletive, in some vain hope of impressing her.

"He is rich man."

"How can I fight this?"

"What?" She thought I meant I literally wanted to fight him - which I would have enjoyed, but obviously didn't mean.

"I think he's lying and I want to change it so that people don't believe him. I want to keep my job here. I want to stay in Korea."

"You cannot fighting, teacher. He is rich man."

"That's bullshit!"

"Teacher, please."

"Sorry."

"There is no more."

CHAPTER TWELVE

I was absolutely devastated by the news that my time at JLP was over. There was no arguing, though. It was all done and I was screwed. I'd never be able to get another permanent job in Korea because that traitorous scum Mr. Park had blacklisted me. I thought about hunting him down and slitting his fat throat, but that would hardly do me any good. Pretty soon my tourist visa would expire and even staying on Korean soil would be illegal. Until then I would just have to work whatever shady day jobs I could find. After that maybe I could try and get another tourist visa, but the authorities might get suspicious. What about the next time or the time after that? Eventually someone would have to refuse me entry and I'd be stuck in Japan again. Japan is an amazing country, but you need a lot of money to enjoy it.

Min Jung wasn't happy. She didn't understand why I

couldn't work and she wanted to phone my school and the authorities and demand answers, but I wouldn't let her. It was pointless and embarrassing. She kept asking me "Why?" and I kept telling her a censored version of the truth – that basically I hated my old job and Korea and that I quit and went to Japan. It had been a foolish choice and now I was paying the price.

"What about in the forward?" she asked, meaning the future.

"I don't know, babe. I don't know."

"I want live Daegu!"

"I thought you liked Japan... You said you wanted to travel."

"So?"

"We could go back to Japan, babe... Get decent jobs, live in a civilised country..."

"Why you always run country to country? England, Korea, Japan, Korea, Japan! You never happy... It crazy!"

"I'm not fucking English, Min Jung! Fuck, that's like calling you Japanese!"

"I not Japan person!"

"Then don't call me English!"

"Don't shouting!"

"Sorry... But why do you care so much about Daegu? It's the ugliest, most boring city in the world."

"It my home."

"So? Fuck home."

"Home important, Alexander."

"Home is wherever you decide it is. I was born in Scotland – not England! – and I'm pretty damn sure that's not my home. I spent twenty-two years there and I don't plan on spending any more than an occasional week in that country. Some people would call it my home but I'd disagree."

"I am Korean. Korea is my home."

"Look how many Koreans *don't* live in Korea... How many of them live in America? They live abroad because Korea sucks – which is something you seemed to believe when I first met you."

"I don't care!"

"Min Jung, let's think about this... What options do we have? I'm going to be an illegal immigrant soon, and I'm already working illegally. If I get caught they'll kick me out of Korea."

"Because you was stupid."

"Yes, because I was stupid... But let's not dwell on the past. Tell me, what options do we have?"

"I don't know. You fuck everything."

"We could move to Japan or go somewhere else. I don't think Korea's an option."

"I don't want go Japan."

"Well, I don't really have a choice, babe. I have to leave eventually and if we're going to stay together as a couple, you're going to have to come with me."

Min Jung didn't reply. She just rolled over on the mattress and curled up. I stroked her arm until she hissed at me and I left the apartment, thoroughly depressed. As crazy as she could be, Min Jung had done a lot for me during our short time together and I hated having to put these huge burdens on her. It was unreasonable to think she would leave her country just for me, but it was either that or we split. I felt like a total loser – helpless, pathetic, and leaching from the girl I once kind of loved.

I went to Trend and told Kelly what had happened. She was far more sympathetic. I bought a drink and then she bought me a drink as a few soldiers shot pool in the dim light of the bar. I ignored their loud, ignorant, and boastful talking and watched Kelly as she fiddled with the computer, choosing songs and reading the news. I knew Jonathon would show up and I wanted to talk to him.

"You'll be alright, Alexander," she said. "You're a clever, handsome guy. You could get a job and they'll just pretend it's legal. Right?"

"I don't know. I don't want to get deported. That sort of thing could haunt a guy and I don't really need any more hindrances in finding a real job and a country to call home."

"You'll be *fine!*" I could tell Kelly was already drunk. When she said "fine" it dragged on for two or three seconds and her pupils seemed to shoot off in different directions. I felt like grabbing her and just hugging her hard and telling her to stop drinking herself stupid. Then I laughed out loud at that thought – the idea of someone like me, who'd at various stages in a very short life managed to become totally addicted to a number of substances – telling another person to slow down.

"Thanks, Kelly, but I do believe I'm absolutely fucked."

"Trust me, Alexander. You'll be fine."

"How are you?" I asked, flipping things around.

"Me?" She laughed – a short, loud snort of a laugh. "I'm fine."

"Then excuse me for being a little concerned, but I'm no longer sure that 'fine' is something I want to be."

"Huh?"

"You don't seem to be doing so well, Kelly."

She suddenly looked very sad. Her head dropped and she could no longer make eye contact with me.

"When I look into your eyes I see a whole lot of sadness. You smile and talk and try to save idiots like me, but behind that – inside the real you – is someone that's hurting from something I don't care to speculate about.

It worries me. Even though I sit here and whine and bitch about how much I hate this country and my own stupid life, I do think about you and what it is that's hurting you, Kelly. It worries me. Sometimes I get so lifted by your words – like when you tell me everything'll be 'fine' – that I just think to myself that you'll say these things when you're looking in the mirror and you'll turn out, well, fine."

Kelly put a hand to her nose and began to cry silently. Her little body jerked with each tear she shed. She turned and tried to make herself smaller, trying to dissolve into the background. I stood up and walked around the bar and held her from behind. She took my hands in hers on her stomach for a moment, then turned and cried into my shoulder. The soldiers looked over and then went back to their game, uncaring and probably just waiting for the right moment to order a drink.

"I'm sorry," I said. "I didn't mean to upset you."

She cried silently and held me tight, her nails digging sharply into my back.

"Why don't you go home for a bit and rest? I'll look after the bar."

She didn't move but I could feel the nod of her head against my chest. I kissed her on the top of her head and then held her away from me. I lifted her chin so that she had to look me in the eyes. She tried to look away but I wouldn't let her.

"I'll help you. I don't know how and I'm not good at this sort of thing because I'm usually a wreck and people are busy trying to save me, but shit, I'll do my best. We'll talk later and you'll tell me everything and we'll figure this thing out, whatever's wrong. Okay?"

She nodded again but she didn't smile. She just looked down and then slipped out of the bar.

Jonathon came in about an hour later and laughed at the sight of me behind the bar, serving the few other customers who were sitting around quietly.

"Damn, man, Kelly's got you workin' here now? Shit, where is that lazy bitch?"

"She wasn't feeling so good," I said. "I told her I'd watch the bar if she went home."

"So that means we're drinkin' for free tonight, right?"

"Same rules apply."

"Hell no! I thought you were my boy, Alexander! Besides, didn't I lend you two hundred dollars? Get me a rum and Coke and I ain't payin' a cent for it."

"I'll gladly buy you a drink, Jonathon, but it's not on the house. I'm not taking advantage of Kelly when she's away."

"Shit, she'd be suckin' up all the booze herself if she was here. What's the difference?"

"The difference is I'm not ok with it. I'll buy you a drink but you're not getting free stuff just because she's not feeling well. Okay?"

"Goddamn, man, when did you get so moral?"

"I don't know. It just doesn't seem right to rip off a person who's been so nice to me."

"Alright, alright, I understand. Shit…" He trailed off into mumblings about injustice, but I could tell he knew he was in the wrong.

I poured Jonathon a strong rum and Coke and put five thousand won of my own cash into the register.

"So how's the new job, man? I never see you anymore since you've been out in the sticks. Fuckin' Siji, Alexander! That's too far away! You may as well be livin' in Seoul with Oliver."

"It's a ten-minute drive…"

"Whatever, man."

He sat there, shaking his head at the injustices the

world constantly threw his way.

"It didn't work out. The job."

"What?" He laughed. "You're kiddin' me, right?"

"Nope, I got canned. It's over."

"Shit, man, what happened?"

I told him everything. It didn't take long.

"Damn, man! Well, I guess you shouldn'ta run off to Japan like a little bitch, huh? Shit, though, that sucks."

"Yeah, I'm pretty depressed about it."

"Fuck it, man, we'll get you a new job. Then you can gimme my two hundred bucks back."

I snorted. "How? I can't legally work in Korea."

"Marry Min Jung," Jonathon said instantly. "When you're a citizen you can do whatever you want." I wondered how long he'd had the idea of marrying a Korean girl for citizenship stuck in his head. He really would become the White Korean.

"No."

"Why not?"

"Are you joking? We've been fucked for ages. If I had somewhere else to live we'd probably have split up long ago. I'm constantly surprised when a week passes and we're still together."

"So shit! Tell her you'll give her ten percent of your pay for a year if she marries you, then divorce her later."

I thought about it. It wasn't the worst idea. I'd be honest and upfront with her about everything and it might just work. But maybe it wouldn't. Her parents would never let her marry a dirty foreigner. She'd probably be put on a list of impure Koreans, barred from all good jobs, organ transplants, and educational opportunities.

"Or shit, marry an American bitch and get a job on base with me. I could find you something like *that*. I hardly work… You know, I've told you. The easy life."

"Do I really have to get married?"

He laughed. "No, it's just the easy way. You don't wanna leave Korea just yet, right? You ain't gonna leave me here alone?"

"No."

"Well then, you're probably gonna have to marry someone. What about Kelly?"

"Y'know, I'd rather marry her than Min Jung."

"Well, go talk to her. Marry her tomorrow and get your job back. Once you're a Korean you can do whatever the fuck you want. Fuck that old boss of yours... What's his name?"

"Mr. Park."

"Of course, Mr. Park... They're all called Mr. Park... Y'know, you could go up to him and punch him right in the face and you'd be fine. You're married to a Korean bitch and you can do whatever, man. If you're a foreigner they'll fuckin' deport you for anything."

"I'm pretty sure I'd still be a foreigner..."

"Whatever, Alexander, but you'd have the law on your side."

"I might just take my time and go back to Japan."

"Don't do this to me, man."

"To you?"

"Dude, how many people do I know in Korea? How many friends do I got? You guys were it! I had a million friends in this country over the past five years but they all go, Alexander. Every last one of them. In my first year I'd talk to everyone I met – a hundred percent. The second year, eighty percent. The third, thirty percent. Now... Shit, I don't know. I don't got time for no one! I can't bring myself to make friends 'cause I hate losin' them. You're all I got now, Alexander. Don't fuckin' go and leave me here."

"Come to Japan with me."

He sighed. I knew he was comfortable in Korea, in

spite of hating it so much. It's easy to live in Korea. Nobody enjoys it, but it's easy. What's difficult is re-entering the real world – where your skin colour doesn't immediately get you a job and where you have to think about rent and taxes, and worry about buying groceries and only going out to drink once a week, if that. Once you've escaped all the problems of reality by hiding in a small city on the wrong side of the world, it's hard to go back.

"What about California? When are you going back to reality?"

"Fuck reality, Alexander! Korea's my reality. Until we pull outta this place and let Kim Jong-il and the Chinese roll down here, I'm gonna be here ploughing some yellow ass and taking weeks off whenever I choose to sit on beaches all around Asia. I hate Korea, Alexander – the people are the worst in the world – but god*damn* it's easy."

We both stayed silent in contemplation.

After a while, Jonathon said, "Ah, fuck it. Let's go to Busan tomorrow, man, just you and me. I'll take a couple days off work and we'll chill on the beach."

"I'm broke," I said.

"You got something, right? Ten bucks train ticket and a few dollars for soju, right? We split a motel – it's twenty each. A few bucks for food..."

I laughed a little and shook my head. Jonathon always knew how to persuade me. He made everything sound so simple and free from consequence. When he spoke with the intention of persuading someone to do something it seemed as though nothing else mattered.

"Sure," I said.

"Cool, let's go real early – like midday or something."

"Midday's early?"

"Fuck yeah, man. I don't usually start work 'til one."

"Alright."

"So go home, tell your bitch you're dumpin' her ass for two nights, then sleep at mine and we'll bail in the morning."

CHAPTER THIRTEEN

I told Min Jung that I was going to Busan with Jonathon and she said she didn't care. Or rather, she shouted the fact and turned away from me, and I knew that we might never see each other again. If I'd asked her it would have been different. She probably would have said "no" and then we would have argued and I'd have called Jonathon to apologise and change plans, but I wanted to go to the beach. It wasn't summer anymore but I've always loved the seaside and it was one thing I knew would cheer me after all this bullshit.

Jonathon's new apartment was a nasty little dive near Camp Walker that he'd taken after splitting with Mina. With no one to help him with rent he'd been forced into giving up the big place and getting the same kind of crappy one-room as everyone else in the city seemed to tolerate. It was just as dirty as his old place, except that being smaller it held a smaller volume of dirt and consequently smelled better. He no longer had a rooftop for barbeques, and the kitchen was too small even to hold the amount of filth that his old place had.

I slept on the floor amid a mess of DVDs and clothes until nine, when the sunlight woke me and I woke Jonathon. He suggested going on base for breakfast and I agreed. Using my invalid Alien Registration Card he signed me on and we entered a place that was even more foreign to me than the rest of Korea. Camp Walker was surrounded by high walls, barbed wire, and heavy weaponry. Inside everything was camouflaged, built with breeze blocks, and depressing. All the big, dumb jock-types I'd seen in Effort every night were clustered here in uniform, wielding guns for no apparent reason. Did they really think there was going to be an attack?

I felt paranoid. As a man who has spent most of his life breaking laws I've always had an aversion to police and authority figures in general. These guys with guns scared the crap out of me. I felt just as conspicuous as I did outside the gates – I was skinny, short, and had long hair. Everyone on base was tall, muscular, and buzzed. It was a place of comical, pathetic masculinity. They eyed me carefully, wondering if I was some kind of terrorist. And why not? There were posters everywhere with propaganda I had only seen in military documentaries from decades before I was born – telling the soldiers to not trust anyone, to not say a word about their job, and to always be ready to die for the cause of freedom. I was terrified.

As we walked about in the warmth of the morning sun Jonathon greeted damn near every soldier in sight. He seemed to know the first names of everyone on base, which was hardly surprising since he'd been there for five years. He knew all of their kids, too. These poor teenagers would skulk around, locked behind giant walls and gates, trapped in a life their parents chose. They looked ready to shoot themselves, and there was no shortage of guns should they choose to do it.

We went into a restaurant at the top of a hill, imaginatively called "Hilltop." Inside there were the same big guys in uniforms wielding guns unnecessarily, eating American-style breakfasts. I looked at the menu and was grateful that the military took care of its own in some respects because the prices were pretty cheap. We ate two big American breakfasts and then drove in Jonathon's car to Dongdaegu station. I was glad to leave that weird and unnatural place behind.

In Busan we took a taxi to Haeundae in spite of my protestations. "I can't afford fucking taxis!" I shouted, but Jonathon said he hated subways and it was alright. I took that to mean he would pay for the taxi but of course he didn't. I wanted to say something but I owed the bastard money anyway and didn't want that issue to be raised.

At Haeundae we immediately went to a 7-Eleven and bought some supplies – four bottles of soju, ten cans of Budweiser, a bag of ice, and two bars of ice cream. That would suffice until the late afternoon. Things were more expensive around Haeundae than in Daegu or even the rest of Busan, but it was still relatively cheap. It was a fraction of the price it would have been in Scotland or Japan.

"So when you gonna pump Kelly, man? Shit, that bitch be askin' for it forever!"

"It's not like that," I explained. "We're just friends."

"She's hot, man. You could do worse."

"I know. I like her and I wouldn't mind, but I'm with Min Jung, and even when that dies – which it will do real soon, I'm sure – Kelly's just a nice chick. I want to keep her in my life as a good friend."

"How many non-crazy Korean bitches d'you know?"

"I know, she's about the only one..."

"Exactly! So get on it, man!"

"She's a fragile girl, not just a cheap fuck. If I ever did anything I'd do it right – date her, take it slow... But I've got no job, no money and I'm probably gonna get kicked out of this country pretty soon. It wouldn't be right to sneak in, fuck her, and then just disappear."

"Goddamn, man, you've changed. What a pussy."

I thought about it and he was right. I had changed. I no longer had the urge to fuck random girls and never see them again. I yearned for something more. I began thinking about the girls I had fucked in the past and how awful I had been to them. I hoped that their lives were full of happiness – even the ones with whom things had ended badly. My own personal gratification was no longer the most important thing in the world.

"No, I've not," I lied.

We sat on the beach and talked for hours. It was warm but not hot. The crowds of summer were gone and now there was only the occasional dog-walker or couple. There were a lot of foreigners on the beach, too. It seemed strange because maybe thirty percent of people on the beach were non-Korean in a country where only one percent of people were non-Korean. "Koreans all just do the same shit," Jonathon explained. "When TV tells them summer's stopped they all stay at home. Group mentality. It's either a million Koreans here or none."

We walked along the beach and climbed on the rocks for a while, and then walked back, all the time just talking about nothing of any grand importance. We became drunker and drunker. At about five we bought

more booze – the same shopping list as before. We drank
that by eight and huddled a little closer on the sand as the
cold became noticeable. Jonathon – who had a wardrobe
full of clothes at home – was dressed to withstand the
cold. I, on the other hand, was in shorts and t-shirt and
shivering badly.

At nine we found a motel and sat watching crappy
Korean porn on TV, sipping soju and beer. I'd seen
glimpses of K-porn before but never as much as this. I
was appalled.

"Is all Korean porn about rape?" I asked Jonathon,
who I figured would be a borderline expert on the subject,
given his apparently insatiable lust.

"Yup," he said. "Koreans love rape. Man, they can't
show bush here – no pussy or fuckin' anything – but they
can show a guy raping some poor bitch in the office.
Every fuckin' Korean porno is just some guy raping
some poor bitch. Why d'you think all them Korean girls
make that squealin' noise when you fuck 'em? It's 'cause
they know guys here love rape and they wanna make the
man feel like they ain't willin'!"

"Is there a lot of rape in Korea?"

"What d'you think?!"

"Yes?"

"Hell yes, Alexander! There's a ton of rape in this
country! It's disgusting. These tiny-dicked guys grow
up in this super-oppressive macho bullshit society bein'
told women ain't nothin' but sluts and they go out raping
bitches all over the place."

"Seriously?"

"Yeah, man. Then *if* they get arrested – which they
never do – they get, like, a slap on the wrist. Sometimes
the woman even gets in trouble for bein' raped. Shit,
man, it's fuckin' sick. I know I fuck a lotta girls in Korea
and it always looks like, *Oh, Jonathon doesn't care*

about females! - But that ain't true! I tell girls 'I wanna fuck you, if you wanna fuck me that's cool!' I'd never do something nasty like guys here. Shit, no! This is a macho, violent, sexist fuckin' country, Alexander. I hope it fuckin' burns!"

"You drunk?"

"Oh yeah."

My perceptions were severely blurred by the time we turned off the porn and headed back to the beach. On the way we stopped for more booze and snacks and another convenience store – this one being further from the beach and much cheaper than the first.

"Let's find some bitches," Jonathon said.

"On the beach?"

"Not to fuck with, just for drinkin'."

"Lead on," I said.

We walked along the promenade at the top of the beach. The sand was deserted but there were groups of people out for an evening walk up on the path. There were a few non-Korean faces, a lot of couples, and groups of old men. There were no unescorted women, and we were forced to sit back on the sand on our own.

"Shit, this sucks," he said. "I just need the possibility of sex to have a good time."

"It doesn't matter, man."

"You know how many bitches I've banged since Mina?"

I wondered. Knowing Jonathon it could have easily been a hundred, yet he hadn't talked about any girls and that was unusual. Whenever I saw him he was alone or with a group of guys. "I don't know," I told him. I wanted the conversation to change because nothing good was going to come from bringing up Mina's name.

"None."

"Seriously?"

"I know! Fucked up, right? I can't even get it up since she left." I didn't know what to say to that remark, so I kept quiet. "I loved her, Alexander. I loved that bitch."

"I'm sorry, man."

"Loved her…"

I said nothing, not sure how to kill the topic and move on to something different. My feeble, booze-addled brain tried to think of something to say that would change things as Jonathon sat and waited for my response.

"Man, that shit made me think. I cheated on that bitch a lot and in the end I couldn't deal with it happenin' to me. She threw all this logic shit in my face and I threw her out, but in the end it made me see things a little different. I don't really wanna fuck all these pretty little bitches, y'know? It's nice to think about it and I'm always thinking about fuckin' them, but when I do there's nothin' there, man. Y'know?"

"I understand. There's got to be something more than casual sex."

"Don't get me wrong, casual sex is great! But I guess I over did it or somethin' because now I'm just tired of it. Maybe it's a stage – like I'll get my game back on real soon or somethin', but now I don't feel like it."

"There's nothing wrong with that. Maybe it's a stage or maybe you're growing up. Maybe it was just what you needed to get onto a different level of relationship."

Jonathon laughed hard and loud into the night sky. "Listen to you! Goddamn, Alexander, you sound like a talk show host! Bein' all sensible and shit…"

"Yeah, fuck it. You're right. Sensible doesn't suit me."

He laughed again. "Are we gettin' old, Alexander? It feels like we're gettin' old! I mean, I've known you, what? A few months? Six months or somethin'? I don't know… Not long enough. But goddamn we've changed.

I think we're *bad* for each other! You're makin' me think about shit instead of just doin' it… Goddamn, man. Goddamn."

"Remember out there in the water with Jenny? When she jerked you off?"

"Shit, yeah! Then the next morning in the motel? That shit was fucked, Alexander. Fucked. How did that even happen? We need to do that shit again…"

"It's too cold. Winter's coming."

"There's always another summer, Alexander."

"Maybe there is."

We walked shirtless along the beach in search of women, swigging from our beers and carrying the bags of booze we'd picked up at the convenience store. The air was cool, far too cool for going shirtless, but it felt good. It felt fresh and clean, washing away so much of the dirt that had stuck to me over the past months. It was the second time I'd been to Busan with Jonathon and each time felt like a cleansing.

Of course, there were no single women, and no groups of women. Mostly it was old men sitting on the beach or walking on the promenade, and the occasional couple holding hands. The boyfriend would always hold his girl tighter when we drew near, sensing our desires. We talked mostly about old times as we went, saying things like, "Hey, remember that time in Starz…" and then recounting memories that for most people would be nothing. But when we spoke they seemed like significant, if not spiritual, events.

We stepped down onto the sand again and decided to walk along the water's edge, and soon we were stopped by the shouts of an old man. "Hey, foreigners!" he called in Korean. I'd been in Korea so long by this stage that a shout like that no longer seemed particularly rude.

David S. Wills

"Foreigners! Come here!"

We peered through the darkness at a table of ten old Korean men. In front of them were dozens of empty soju bottles, and around their feet were dozens of unopened ones. They weren't scowling at us as I'd expected. They were smiling and beckoning us over to their table. We looked at each other and shrugged, then joined the old men, who seemed very pleased to have foreign guests at their table.

They spoke excitedly in Korean about "foreigners" and after a while one of the men – who was ever so slightly more red-faced than the rest – asked, in English, "Where are you from?" He gave each word tremendous emphasis. We told him and he translated our answers into Korean for the benefit of his friends. Naturally, "Scotland" was translated into "England." Every now and then Jonathon would speak in Korean, but then he'd stop and I was never sure if he was being bashful or if – as he'd alluded to before – he thought himself above speaking Korean. Regardless, the old men seemed amused by our presence. It was the first time in Korea that I'd ever really been made to feel welcome.

We must have sat there for hours, laughing and drinking. Not much was really said. It seemed like the old men were beyond communicating even with each other, and Jonathon's translations of their speech yielded little worth mentioning. Mostly we just raised our paper cups and said "Geonbae!" and then filled them again. Every single time the cups were filled we would use two hands and obey all the little quirks of the culture that had become normal to us in such a short time. Strangely, the old men marvelled at it. Whereas once I would've guessed that they couldn't fathom dumb foreigners understanding their customs, I began to feel that maybe they were just surprised we cared. Maybe they were

252

honoured that people from all the way around the world would come to their tiny little country and drink with them in the middle of the night.

We were still drinking when the sun rose and still drinking hours after when people began to return to the beach in small numbers. Four of the old men were asleep in their chairs and two seemed to have disappeared altogether – probably home to their families. Silence had been upon us for many of the hours that had passed. We just sat there sharing drinks and smiling at each other. I wondered from time to time if they were just being polite and were waiting for us – the guests – to leave. But I was reminded of the thousands of old men I'd seen in Korea who sat all day with their little green bottles, talking occasionally and mostly just watching the world pass by. I'd always taken their stares as contempt but never thought to smile back, just to see. Never thought to sit with them and share a drink or try to talk.

CHAPTER FOURTEEN

We slept on the KTX and when we stepped onto the platform at Dongdaegu I felt strangely at peace with myself. I wanted to tell Jonathon how I felt but I knew he'd think I was insane. I had no job, no apartment, no money. Really, I was in a lot of trouble. But I felt content, like I had for the first time actually experienced life on the other side of the world. Until then I had merely been watching through my own little peephole.

"So I take it you'll be crowding my spot from now on," Jonathon said as we walked out of the station and along the road to his car, which he had parked on a little side street only five minutes from the station.

"I hate to be a bother, but I don't think I have any other choice."

"It's cool, man. I figured it'd happen sooner or later."

"Still."

"What about Kelly? I mean, I guess I'm cool with you crashing on my floor but if you could rest your head between those sweet pillows it'd probably work out better for you, if y'know what I'm sayin'."

I laughed and shook my head. "I'm a liability that she doesn't need."

We got back to Jonathon's apartment at midday and I crashed on his floor as he took the little bed. We slept until nightfall, and then Jonathon took me back on base for food and made me spend my last ten dollars on our dinner – ten of the two hundred he'd given me weeks before. "Don't worry, Alexander," he said. "You don't need to pay rent anymore." I said nothing about the fact that I'd never paid for rent in Korea.

After that we took a taxi downtown and he snivelled about me not paying for cab fare, and I remarked that I didn't even want to go, given that I had no money with which to purchase even a single drink. But Jonathon didn't care. He'd never cared about anyone's desire to go downtown. All that mattered was that people went. It was interesting that he was so obsessed with downtown even though he no longer had a solid group of friends there.

We walked straight to Trend and settled ourselves at the bar as Kelly greeted us with her usual sad smile. The place was empty. Effort had been the foreigner hangout of the summer, then Trend had its brief moment in the sun, and now, presumably, some other scummy bar was serving dozens of military brats and whiney ESL teachers. I understood, though, and so did Kelly. Everybody went out drinking five or more nights a week and so it didn't take long for a place to get boring. In my short time in Daegu I'd already seen bars and clubs come and go – both in terms of popularity and as viable businesses.

"So how come you guys weren't in here last night?" Kelly asked us. She was drunk already.

"Damn, Kelly. You miss us that much?" Jonathon asked. "You need to get some more customers up in here. Get a DJ or something."

"You think I can afford a DJ?"

"With how much you chargin' for these weak-ass drinks I bet you could."

Kelly laughed. She obviously liked Jonathon's bitching, even though I knew he was always at least half serious. "Maybe if you guys brought some friends with you we might be able to work something out."

Jonathon snorted and shook his head. "Ain't nobody worth drinkin' with no more," he said. He was smiling when he spoke, but he wasn't joking. "Just me and Alex, Kelly, and you should be fuckin' psyched we drink in this dump anyway."

Neither of them looked at each other as they spoke. They both kept their eyes on the little TV set above the bar, which ran stupid Korean dramas without the sound. As usual, it was just loud hip-hop that came from the speakers.

"Maybe you should play some decent music," I said. "Not everyone likes hip-hop."

Kelly shrugged the idea off, but Jonathon said, "Shut the fuck up, Alex. What else they gonna play? K-pop? Shit, that's the only other thing anyone 'round here likes anyhow."

"Fuck it," I said. "It's only nine. No one comes out 'til later anyway. Don't worry about it, Kelly."

We sat in silence, sipping our drinks, which, in spite of Jonathon's complaints, were free. Jonathon kept sighing loudly while Kelly closed her eyes every now and then, drifting off into drunken thought.

After we finished our drinks, Jonathon opened his

wallet and bought two more, then dragged me over to the pool table. We shot a couple of games without speaking, then he leaned in close and said, "Stay with Kelly tonight, man. You need it."

I protested. "I can't do that. I'll just come back and stay on your floor…"

"Dude, just fuck her. She hot, she's lonely, she's got a fucking bed for you to sleep on…"

"Actually, she sleeps on the floor."

"Whatever, man. Just fucking do it. Live with her for a while. Work here or something. I don't mind you crashin' on my floor but for your sake, Alexander, just fuck her."

I protested again but he pushed me away and walked quickly out of the bar. Kelly was still watching TV and didn't notice him leave. It was still quiet., but there were a couple of teacher types at the bar and a few soldiers eying the pool table from the moment Jonathon walked out.

I went back to the bar and sat down.

"Where's Jonathon?"

"Went home."

"Oh. You need another drink?"

"No money."

Kelly smiled and went about getting me another rum and Coke. "I have faith in you, Alexander. You'll get your shit together one day, and when you do you'll probably buy all your new friends rum and Cokes at Trend, huh?"

"Yeah, Kelly."

An hour later I was still sitting there, watching Kelly watching TV. She stood with her left hand on her right elbow, sipping from a glass of vodka and Coke. Now and then she'd move to make someone a drink and she'd always look surprised. She'd give them a cute little smile to say sorry for having not noticed them sooner, and then move slowly and awkwardly. The customers were too polite to say anything, but they looked at each other knowingly. She was drunk and she wasn't good at hiding it. Most of the guys hit on her and I was sure they stuck around just because they knew she'd be wasted by closing time and maybe they'd have a chance of taking her home. The girls were a little meaner. They were mostly fat white chicks who were just jealous because their men couldn't take their eyes off of the cute drunk barmaid.

I offered, once or twice, to tend the bar for her, but she said no. It wasn't busy enough and she was still able to move slowly from bottle to bottle and she seemed to think that she was giving out the right change.

Mostly, though, I sat and sulked. Being downtown made me sick. It was only soldiers and teachers littering the bar, drinking and laughing and having stupid conversations about nothing of any importance – "Oh my god, like, I totally can't believe they don't say 'God bless you' here!" I was starting to hate everything about Korea, including the foreigners. Why couldn't these assholes talk about anything intelligent? I missed my friends back in Scotland. They were all pretentious drug-addicts, but they were interesting and literate. I missed Sarah, with whom I hadn't even shared an e-mail in months. I missed being able to smoke weed until six in the morning and talk about poetry and art. I missed going to art galleries, taking pills, and watching old French movies in abandoned buildings. I missed live music and weird architecture, house parties and libraries. There was nothing interesting or exciting about Korea.

Thomas and Jonathon had been the only people in Korea with whom I'd held meaningful or intelligent conversations. We talked politics, art, and life. It was stupid stuff but it kept my brain ticking over. The rest of the expat crowd, though, seemed beyond dull.

I listened to those morons talking shit and wondered what sort of person washed over to Korea. They were all dumb rich white kids facing life on the other side for the first time and failing to deal with it. I was one of them and I didn't like that. Surely it wasn't just the dregs of Western society that came over to further pollute an already wasted spot of land. Were the foreigners here ruined by Korea or were they just the losers that couldn't cut it in the West and who took their only marketable skill – their native language – and brought it to the one place that was willing to pay? What a depressing notion.

Korea was a new frontier – a place of excitement and wealth in the imagination of anyone who'd never been; a harrowing memory for those who'd become embittered by its unpleasant reality. But instead of hardy settlers searching for a place to call home we were all just running away for a while, hiding in a place our friends back home couldn't even point out on a map.

When Kelly began closing down the bar I helped her, but by this time I was damn near suicidal. I began seriously contemplating the possibility of killing myself. It wasn't the first time in my life – not by a long shot. No, I'd spent a lot of my time in Scotland musing the possibility of ending it all because of loneliness and poverty. Yet in Korea life had always seemed temporary anyway, and suicide always seemed like a grand overreaction. If something wasn't right it wouldn't last, so there was no need to do anything drastic. I could always flee… I was always thinking about escaping, as though that were the great answer to all of life's problems.

I wondered what would happen if I ended it all in Korea… Would my parents have to pay to have my corpse shipped back to Scotland? That would be expensive and an unfair burden to place upon them. I couldn't do that.

What if I left a note that said I wanted to be buried in Korea? Obviously I wouldn't *want* to be buried in Korea, but what difference would it make? I'd be dead. People would spit and stare at my headstone, and the Korean media would probably stake out my grave with cameras to make sure I didn't zombify and come back to further damage the nation's morality...

We closed up and walked to Kelly's place, our arms around one another for some reason. It just seemed natural. It was cold and I kept my arm around her shoulder and she held hers around my waist. She was like a friend or a sister to me and I wanted to keep her warm, but I also felt immensely comforted by the close presence of another human being in such a time of depression. Kelly's beating heart and warm scent kept me from just falling down on the pavement, curling up, and dying.

We didn't talk, though. We walked in silence through the dark, cold, and dead streets. The stench of Korea lingered nastily in the air like it always did. When it was hot it mingled with my sweat and stuck to me, and in the cold it seemed to nip at my skin, biting me and trying to crawl inside. A few old men staggered drunkenly from alleyways, spitting and coughing at us as we stepped over the puddles of urine they left everywhere.

At Kelly's place we opened the door and stepped inside, then kissed and fell onto her mattress. I hadn't planned on making any moves, and I didn't expect anything to happen, and yet it was entirely unsurprising when it did. It was sudden, but it just happened as normally as if we'd not done it. We took turns lying on top of each other, not fucking but kissing and very, very slowly undressing. It was in some ways the least sexy foreplay I'd ever experienced, but at the same time it felt so natural and loving that it moved me more than any others. Even before we were naked it felt as though we were fucking.

"I love you," she whispered in my ear.

"I love you, too," I said back to her, and I meant it.

Afterwards, we lay on the bed and I held her as she purred on my chest. We lay awake, listening to each other breathe, until the sun rose in the gaps between the nearest apartments, straining through the smog.

Kelly looked up at me and smiled her gorgeous little smile without a trace of sadness - a thing that lit up my life and erased every problem, concern, and trouble from my mind. "Aren't you tired?" she asked.

"Not really," I said. "Why? You want to go again?"

She giggled. "No... Well, maybe..." She bit her bottom lip and stroked my thigh. "I was wondering what you wanted to do today."

"I don't mind," I said. "I just want to be with you." Indeed, I could think of nothing better to do than stay with Kelly. Just lying with her felt so much more natural and honest than anything I'd ever experienced.

She kissed me and climbed up on top. "I mean, what do you want to do *with* me today?"

"Well, *this* is a good start. I wouldn't mind doing *this* all day!"

"Ooh, me too!"

"Might get tired, though..."

"So what do you want to do in Korea? I mean, I'll take you anywhere, show you anything... I want you to stay here with me forever and I think that if you actually go out and see the nice things in this country, maybe you'll be happy here."

"Maybe you're right," I said.

"So what do you want to do?"

"Let's go see a temple or a mountain or something... Hell, you're the expert here. You tell me... What's best to see?"

261

"How about I blindfold you and just take you somewhere?"

"How about you blindfold me and *then* take me somewhere?"

"Ooh, alright!"

CHAPTER FIFTEEN

I didn't look at my watch all day. Time ceased to be of any consequence. But not too long after the sun had risen, and well before it hit that point in the sky that said it was midday, we set out to see what Kelly called "the real Korea". When she said those words and showed some optimism I never doubted her for a second. Usually my cynical side kicks in and I laugh silently at anyone when they grow enthusiastic about something I dislike, but I trusted her fully.

We stepped out into the cool morning under the calm sun and walked along the street holding hands. We took a bus to Dongdaegu station and then transferred and took another towards the mountains north of the city. During my time in Daegu I'd merely stared at the mountains, thinking of them as walls holding me prisoner in this awful place. I'd long since stopped thinking of the beauty they might have held.

We stepped off the bus among smaller, older buildings on a steep road. Old people milled about in North Face gear, marching up towards the tree line. Everyone was dressed as though they were ready to climb Everest. Kelly and I stood out in our shorts and t-shirts and sneakers. People stared at us but we didn't care. We were both smiling, lost in each other and in the fresh air that clouded the mountain.

We walked up the hill and away from the buildings and soon we were under the trees. The road wound upwards, covered in the autumn spread of leaves and pine needles that lay damp underfoot. The trees were thin and a stream trickled down alongside the road, and at times we would trek down and climb on the rocks and cliffs that marked the stream's trail. Little fish darted about in the freezing water while chipmunks and squirrels tore up and down the tree trunks, watching us intently.

The higher we went, the smaller the path became – changing from a road to a paved path to a little rocky trail to a set of stairs cut sharply into the rock and winding slowly up towards some invisible peak. All along the route there were old people in their North Face gear. No one wore anything less than a full outfit, complete with hiking pole and giant visor.

After a while we came upon a temple. It was my first visit to a Buddhist temple and it was gorgeous. The air was dense with incense and some chanting coming from the trees, and all about us were purples and reds, humbled before the otherwise encompassing greenery of the mountainside. The roofs of the buildings were slate grey and curved upwards, supported by the reddish-brown walls, which contained golden Buddhas, flowers, and fruits. Coloured baubles hung and swung in the breeze, catching the sunlight and casting pink, green, and yellows shadows upon the ground. Grey stone pillars stood with some purpose I couldn't fathom beside a massive ornate bell, which was guarded by four dragons. It looked as though if rang it would either bring the mountain crashing to the earth or it would shatter into dust and simply blow away.

We walked around the temple very slowly, trying not to disturb anyone. I came to realise that this was a fully functional temple full of worshippers I didn't want to offend. They were all at peace and busy with their prayers and I was just a confused spectator – a traveller passing through. What business did I have even to be there? I imagined the masses of tourists that must pass through, taking crude photos and trivialising the beliefs of those on their knees.

Beyond the temple there were two routes from which to choose – the busy route and the not-so-busy route. We chose the busy route and agreed to descend via the quieter of the two when the time came. It would be best not to get lost on the way to whatever it was we were going to see.

The busier path was indeed the steeper of the two – a stairway cut into the rock that climbed up the mountain like a ladder for a long, long time. Old people passed us in both directions and it amazed me. What could be up there that dragged them from their lives and compelled them to climb this outrageous mountain? My skin was drenched in sweat and it was showing through my clothes, yet these elderly folks – these adverts for the North Face – were marching at ease. They leapt from boulder to boulder both up and down, sure-footed as mountain goats.

Halfway up the climb we came upon a ledge carved into the cliff and there was a women there selling boiled bugs and corn. The smell perverted the air into something unbreatheable and so we moved on hastily.

"Before America came and brought us their candy, people in Korea ate bugs for fun," Kelly told me.

"Do they taste good?" I asked.

"No," she said. "But people still eat them. It's a tradition."

We carried on up until we reached the top – where we found a shop that sold Buddhist merchandise and was run by nuns – and beyond that was a sight for which I was ill-prepared.

On top of this giant mountain sat a statue of a Buddha wearing a hat that balanced magically atop his head. Light shone between the top of the skull and the giant stone hat – some ancient illusion. Up here the wind that was unnoticeable anywhere else ripped across the summit and yet the giant stone hat just sat peacefully atop Buddha's head as it had done for many hundreds of years. Incense clouded the air and those coloured baubles flapped about, obscuring the entire sky, and all around us people knelt praying to their deity and chanting, spinning beads through their fingers. I was between them and their Buddha and I could actually feel the energy of their prayers passing through me and whipping around me.

It all became too much. The atmosphere was so intense I could barely breathe and I ran to the side of the platform on which all this was happening and looked out – and there it was, for the first time: Korea. All around me, thousands of feet below, was Korea in its magnificence. Mountains tumbled down from this one, rearing their rocky cliffs above the sea of green here and there, undulating, broken only by the occasional river, for as far as the eye could see.

Kelly stood behind me and put her arms around my waist as I stared out lost in the sight, my hair whipping back in the wind and caressing her face. I couldn't speak. I wanted to tell her what I thought but I couldn't. She knew. She'd brought me here because of it.

I could feel everything washing away from me. All the shit I'd been covered in by my wretched life in Scotland, the abuse I'd taken in Korea, and the poverty I'd experienced in Japan – it all just washed from away me as I stood in the wind with those soft arms around my waist and her breath on my neck. All the evils of the world drifted from my mind, drawn back, perhaps into the Buddha or the candles or the incense, or wished away by the prayers of the followers. I didn't know. I just felt immensely cleansed.

I began to feel saddened and guilty by all the hate I'd allowed myself to feel for Korea and its people. It had not been a welcoming place by any means but I had failed to rise above it. I'd failed to give myself a fair chance; failed to seek out the beauty in the country. When I'd first come here, I'd fallen into a trap and taken the easiest life I could and followed it almost to my doom. I had waited for the beauty of the country to find me and it didn't and I blamed it, when really it should have been me who'd gone out in search of what I wanted to see. "I've been so stupid," I said quietly into the wind.

A tear fell from my left eye, which was strange because I never cried. I didn't even cry when I'd told my parents I was leaving and they'd cried. It was just one tear but it fell and I felt better for it having fallen. In a heartbeat the wind dried it and left nothing there but a tingling sensation that washed over my head, through my hair, down my spine, and out towards my fingers and toes.

"It's so beautiful," Kelly said.

"It is," I replied. "I could stay here forever."

CHAPTER SIXTEEN

We took the bus back from the mountain grinning the grins only those foolishly in love dare grin. The bus was, of course, packed and so when we were lucky enough to grab a seat Kelly sat on my lap. I held her as we stared out the window and avoided showing any overt displays of affection. Regardless, the old men and women on the bus stared in contempt. We were not so lost in one another that we could ignore the hate, but we pretended for the duration of the ride that it wasn't a big deal.

"Why do you guys come to Korea?" she asked me after looking out the window for a long while. "I mean, I guess the military come here because they have to, but what about you guys – you know, teachers?"

I thought about it for a while, then said, "I suppose there are many reasons. I had a couple of friends who came here because one or two of their parents were

Korean and they were curious. Some people come for money. Some come for adventure…"

"What about you?"

"I guess it's a combination. Not the first, of course. My parents weren't Korean, but I suppose there was no one grand reason for it. I heard about it when I was in a bar one night…" Kelly laughed. "Seriously, I was drinking with a friend and she told me that you could make money in Korea. So I suppose money was the big thing."

"We always see you guys on TV looking rich," Kelly said. "So it's always strange that people come here to make money."

I laughed. "Not all white people are rich. Some are even poorer than me. But there's more to it than money, though. Life can be a little boring at times. I think a lot of people come here for fun. I know we're meant to be teachers but I think it's just an escape, a sort of gap year."

"'Gap year'?"

"Yeah, a lot of people take a year out of work or studying just to have fun, to experience life. I think that Korea is like that for people, except instead of saving up to do it, you make money the whole time."

"I was wondering because, you know, the bar is mostly just a foreigner bar these days. I never even knew any foreigners until I opened it. Then suddenly it was like the hot place for all these military guys and teachers…"

"And what did you think of foreigners when you first met them?"

"Honestly, I found it a little scary. And maybe I still do. I mean, some of these guys are pretty crazy. Foreigners are just so different."

"Yeah, I guess we don't do ourselves any favours when we're here."

"It's a little embarrassing sometimes. What do they say? 'Culture shock'? Foreigners are so different when they're out."

"You ever date a foreign guy?" I asked.

Kelly looked away and nodded. "Yeah," she said. "I mean, not properly or anything, but so many guys just asked me out when the place got popular and I ended up going on a date or hanging out with a couple them. They were all real assholes, though."

I wanted to know more about what they did to make her look so upset, but I refrained from spoiling the pleasant day. "I'm sorry," I said.

Back in Daegu we walked hand in had to Kelly's apartment and fucked before she had to go open the bar. We talked like I'd never talked with Min Jung. In fact, never had I talked with anyone like I talked with Kelly. I began to realise the obvious: that what I'd felt for other girls had only ever been lust.

We ate dinner and went to open the bar at around seven. "There won't be anyone there," she said, "but I always open at seven."

"We'll get the bar back on top," I said, although I wasn't sure how. "We'll be fine."

At the bar, Kelly set about cleaning up. Even though the nights were quiet, the bar got filthy and she was never in a fit state to do much cleaning when the last customers left. We had to clean the little bathrooms, sweep the floors, empty the ashtrays… Until then I'd thought Kelly simply poured drinks.

"We can make this place something," I told her, after thinking through a couple of silly ideas in my head. "We could start doing food – like Western food – or maybe get some live bands in here… You need a website or something to stick pictures of drunk people on. They'd love that."

Kelly looked at me and smiled. "I wish I had your energy, Alexander."

"My energy? Ha! I'm the laziest person I know."

"I thought the same about myself," she said. "Maybe we'll make a good couple."

I thought about it and lost the stupid grin that had been spread across my face since we'd first fucked the night before. I didn't dare say anything, but Kelly knew what I was thinking. "We'll be fine, Alexander. You'll get a job. Shit, if you don't we'll get married." My mouth fell open. "I mean, like, I'll be your girlfriend but we'll be legally married. You know, just for the visa. If it doesn't work out then *whatever*. I'm not crazy like Min Jung. If it does work out then it'll save us the whole drama thing down the line. Simple, right?"

"Right," I said, not really believing her. It all seemed too good to be true.

Our first customers came in at nine. Three soldiers from Walker. I recognised them from Jonathon's barbeque. At least one of them had hit me, I was sure. They didn't recognise me, though. Over the next hour a couple more soldiers came in, then a few teachers. There were a handful of young Korean women who came in together but left after one drink. They looked terrified to be amongst foreigners, and horrified that I – a person who spoke virtually no Korean – was serving them. Some of the guys looked pretty disappointed to see me sitting behind the bar, holding Kelly and laughing with her. It was obvious that some of them came just to look at her.

"Maybe I should sit on the other side of the bar," I said. "You'd probably get better tips."

"That's one thing about a bar," she replied. "Booze pretty much sells itself. It doesn't matter if they wanna fuck me or not."

At about ten o'clock two foreign men came in. One was a young Asian-American and the other a bald white

271

man of maybe forty or older. They were friendly and asked me why I was working behind the bar, and I told them that it was a favour for a friend – I wasn't working illegally. They certainly didn't look or act like the usual customer, but they bought a Corona each and sat down at a table near the bar.

"Those guys aren't very subtle," I told Kelly. "They won't stop staring at you."

Kelly furrowed her brow. "I don't think they're staring at me," she said.

The men sat at the table for half an hour, and after the first five minutes they didn't do much staring. Either they'd clicked that we were aware of their stares or they'd seen what they needed to see. We stopped worrying about it and went back to talking quietly about the future.

Then everything went horribly wrong. The door opened and five police officers entered the bar. Three of them were armed, three of them wore a grey uniform and two wore suits. They marched into the room and stopped. Quickly, the two foreign men stood up from their table and pointed at me. The Asian-American one said something in what sounded like fairly crude Korean, and they all poured behind the bar.

I put up absolutely no fight and they weren't aggressive in arresting me, but they were firm. Naturally, every person in the bar watched as I was cuffed. It was strange to be stared at by foreigners.

The two foreigners stepped up to the bar and the Asian-American one told me, "We have been informed that you are a user and distributor of narcotics and we have a warrant for your arrest."

Cops. Kelly had been right.

"Okay," I said. "What are my rights?"

The Asian-American cop, who appeared to be the only one of them willing to communicate with me, said, "Er, I don't know, to be honest with you. I guess you have the right to remain silent, but I wouldn't."

"Okay. What about a lawyer?"

"I suppose you could."

"Should I?"

"Probably not."

"Okay."

I felt like I was about to shit myself. The sensation was almost overwhelming. I despise being the centre of attention, and there were so many people in the room talking about me – all watching and trying to guess what awful thing I'd done.

"We will be testing your hair and urine for THC, and then we'll search your apartment, if you have one... We can't seem to find a record of that. But I can assure you that you're going to prison for a while unless you cooperate completely."

"Shit."

"Yeah." The guy smiled. In fact, I noticed just then that he'd been smiling since I met him, and not in a malicious way. All of the cops were smiling – but they were awkward smiles. "You'll be alright, though. Just tell the truth and you'll get a fine or a deportation notice. Nothing major."

Something snapped in my head just then and I stopped feeling so afraid. I smiled and laughed a little and made some jokes with the police officers as they tried to calm the panicked Kelly. I was marched out into an unmarked police car, with all seven officers surrounding me as though I was a dangerous criminal. Most of them seemed happy and were joking among themselves.

The car ride to the city's central police building took about fifteen minutes, during which time I joked with the Asian-American cop. The white one looked sullenly out the window. I wondered what they were doing here...

The Asian guy seemed to be acting as my translator, but the other dude evidently couldn't or wouldn't speak Korean. I wondered if they were FBI or just American cops working to help Korea deal with its drug problem.

At the police station I was marched in formation up to the CSI lab and put in a chair in front of what appeared to be an interrogation table. There was an electric drill in front of me, and I jokingly asked if it was for me, but no one laughed and the smiles dropped from their faces.

The questions began quickly enough – where did I get the weed? Did I have any left? Did I sell any? Did I smoke with anyone?

I knew what to expect. I'd overheard foreigners talking about Korea's attempt at stopping drug distribution. They have the right to send smokers down for years, but they instead use the law to find the suppliers. They threaten you, and in many reported incidents, they will torture suspects.

"Listen, I know why you arrested me," I explained, hopelessly. "Some girl told you about me, right?" I looked at them, but they were pros: no reaction. "I bet she did. Min Jung, right? She's a liar and a crazy bitch. You can't believe her." Still they sat and watched me, except one elderly cop who was writing in a book. "We dated and she went nuts, then I just know when we broke up she called you guys. Seriously, I have nothing. No weed. Go ahead and search me." I knew that there was a chance that the small amount of weed I'd smoked with Jonathon's buddies might be traceable in my blood, but I hoped not and hoped they'd realise I was innocent when my pockets showed up empty.

Two of the Korean cops spoke, and the Asian-American one translated for them. They explained that it didn't matter who told them, that it was a good source, and that I was in a lot of trouble.

I thought it strange that by this stage they still hadn't searched me. The number of police officers suggested they considered me some drug lord, but they hadn't considered that maybe I had a weapon on me... or, more likely, a bag of pot.

"I'll pee in a cup," I said, "You can search my pockets, whatever. I don't have anything on me. This is ridiculous."

They asked a few times where I bought weed and when I smoked it, and if I'd ever taught while high. I told them again and again that I was innocent, and after twenty minutes two young men marched me to the toilet and told me to pee in a plastic cup.

Only ten minutes later, after asking me general questions about my time in Korea, the pee cup came back with a sticker on the side that allegedly said it had tested negative for THC. I breathed a sigh of relief and laughed. They knew that meant I *had* smoked weed and it just hadn't showed up.

"Where d'you live, Alexander?" We've got a warrant to search your apartment.

"How did you get a warrant if you don't even know where I live?" I asked.

He blushed a little and said, "It's easier here."

"I don't have an apartment," I said. "I'm a tourist. I'm staying with friends. I used to live near Manchon, back when I had a job. I already told you that."

"We know you smoked marijuana..."

"You can't *prove* I smoked anything," I said.

He shook his head and looked at the bald cop, who was staring blankly at the doorway, not listening to a word.

"We were told you smoked marijuana and that you were here illegally. Neither of those is as big a deal as you probably think. Every now and then they trot some poor bastard out for the cameras, but honestly they don't care. Alright? You admit to smoking pot and tell them where you got it, and you won't hear from them again. You can stay here and find yourself a job and do whatever you want. All they care about are the dealers. The big shots up in Seoul. They do a lot of bad stuff and you can help us..."

"So you want me to confess to something that you have absolutely no proof of me doing?"

He looked at one of the old cops and said something in Korean. The Korean officers talked amongst themselves for a while, then conferred with the American. "Listen," he said. "You already told us you're in the country on a tourist visa. Now I find it hard to believe you've been here this long without a job... It's not gonna be difficult for us to find out where you worked. After that you'll get a fine and a deportation notice, and your employers will probably get in a trouble, too. So unless you want them to suffer because they were nice enough to give you a job, then I'd tell these guys what they want to hear."

"The way I see it is that if I keep my mouth shut then you've got nothing on me. My ex-girlfriend is trying to get me deported because she's a fucking psycho. I don't know who you are or who your friend is, but it seems that the Korean police are putting altogether far too much stock into the words of a girl who isn't even close to sane."

The Korean cops were all talking among themselves furiously, trying to figure out what I'd said. They'd probably heard the word "fuck" and picked up on my anger. The American obviously didn't want to translate, and was looking down at his clasped hands, shaking his head.

"Look," he said, trying again. "Alexander. I saw your face when we picked you up at the bar. You may be acting tough now that you've seen the results of your urine test and now that you think you're in the clear, but I saw that fear in your eyes. We all did. It wasn't just your eyes, it was your whole body. You looked hopeless. When I said we were going to test your urine and your hair and search your apartment, you looked ready to shit your pants. I know that you smoked pot and I honestly don't care. None of us do. We just want to know where you got it from."

"I want a lawyer," I said. It hadn't occurred to me up until then, but it was so obvious. "I want a lawyer."

He turned and spoke to the oldest Korean, who shook his head. "No," came the translation of that universal gesture.

"We're just talking… Things are different here. I'm sorry if this seems unfair," he explained. "We're just after the bad guys, like I said. Guys like you get tied up in this sort of thing all the time and it all gets pushed under the rug… But only if you *talk*. Tell them you smoked. Tell them that you did it once and that you're sorry and then tell them where you got it. Alright?"

I thought about those two soldiers at my apartment. If I said that I smoked with two soldiers whose names I never got, would they believe me? Would they leave it at that? I dismissed the thought quickly.

"They *know*, Alexander. Maybe their THC test didn't show it, but they know, and they'll prove it eventually. They can get you in a ton of trouble, or they can let you off with a slap on the wrists. It's totally up to you."

The bald cop was still staring blankly at the door. The others were watching me, and one was still making notes in a book. I wondered if he could speak English. Presumably the notes he was writing were based upon the conversation.

"I'm sorry," I said. "I don't smoke pot. Never have,

never will."

He let out a big sigh and turned to the Korean cops, who knew already what I'd said. It was pretty obvious. He shook his head and the oldest cop said a few words in Korean that seemed to make the rest of them look regretful. The American turned back to me, also looking pretty saddened by what had been said.

"That bar we found you at. Trend. Owned by a girl called Yoon Seo Kim. You work there, huh?"

I knew immediately where he was going.

"Our source told us we'd find you there. It looked to us like you were working behind the bar, and yet you told us you only have a tourist visa…"

"Don't…"

He sighed again and looked back at the old cop, who nodded. "We can prove without any doubt that you are working in Korea because we saw you. All these guys," – he waved his arm around the room and some of them smiled, not understanding what was being said – "saw you working behind the bar. Without the correct visa that's illegal. My partner and I sat there for thirty minutes and watched you serving drinks. You can't deny that you were working there, and I somehow don't see you magically producing a work visa.

"So… You know where I'm going with this, right? No one here wants this to happen, believe me. But if you can't tell us the name of a distributor of marijuana, we will charge you with working illegally. What's more, and I'm sorry to do this… We'll charge the owner of the bar with hiring an illegal immigrant. That's pretty serious, Alexander. She'll lose the bar."

The bald cop was looking at me now, but I didn't look back.

"Once," I said. "One time."

"Where d'you get it?"

"You're not going to believe me…"

"Just give us something. I don't want the alternative, either."

I couldn't look up. Couldn't make eye contact with anyone in the room. I hated myself. "A few weeks back, with a couple of guys from the military. I don't know their names."

"That's a start. Now how about the truth?"

"Honestly, I met them once."

"How?"

"What?"

"How did you meet them? You don't just call up Camp Walker and ask for a bag of pot… How did you meet two soldiers and end up smoking weed?"

I began to realise just how well the cop had trapped me. He'd tricked me into admitting that I'd smoked pot, which didn't seem so bad compared to the alternative. But now I realised that the story would have to be told, or at least a plausible fake story. Everything was linked – Jonathon had been there, Kelly had been there, I'd been working – probably illegally – at the time. If I told the truth then no matter what the cops said, I was incriminating myself more and more, and threatening various others.

"Downtown," I said, thinking quickly. "I met them in a bar…"

"Which bar?"

"Effort," I said, knowing that it was a believable place to meet two soldiers, and kept Kelly's name a little further from the truth. "In Effort. A couple weeks ago."

"When, exactly?"

"I don't remember. A few weeks. I was drunk, some guys offered me a bag of weed…"

"How much?"

"I don't know, a little bag. Small. Couple of grams? I

don't know this stuff."

"What price?"

Having never actually purchased weed in Korea, I didn't know a believable price. "Twenty dollars," I said. "I mean, twenty thousand won."

The bald guy looked up and laughed. "That's cheap," he said. "I take it was no good?"

"I don't know," I replied. "I never really smoke. It was just once, like I said, so I don't know good from bad."

Both of them grinned. They knew *that* much was bullshit.

"So what happened?"

"I said I didn't have any money. They said they were going out for a smoke anyway, and I could smoke with them."

"For free?"

"Of course."

"And you didn't buy any?"

"No."

"You know, if you *did* buy some, then it makes no difference. We don't care if you bought weed or smoked weed. We just want to know about these guys. The dealers."

"I didn't buy any."

The bald cop looked at his partner and raised an eyebrow, then turned and stared off at the doorway once again. I wondered how much he'd been paying attention. Maybe he was taking it all in, after all.

"So they offered you a bag of pot for twenty thousand won, and you declined, then smoked with them anyway."

"Yes."

"Had you ever seen them before?"

"No."

"And have you seen them since?"

"No."

"I don't suppose you can tell us anything more useful. For example, did they say they worked at Walker?"

"I don't know. I don't remember. Like I said, I was drunk."

"Okay, I can believe that," he said, doubtfully. "But you sure as hell didn't go outside and smoke with these two soldiers without hearing either of their names. I mean, you meet someone for the first time and you at least exchange names, right? Whether you're Korean or American or whatever."

Fortunately, I couldn't even recall the names of the soldiers I *had* smoked with. But I couldn't make names up quickly enough. My mind went blank.

"I dunno," I said. "I was drunk."

"You didn't get their names…"

"I admit that I probably did, but honestly I don't recall."

Thankfully, this last statement came over with sincerity and both American cops seemed to believe me. At this point the one who was translating turned and explained the story to the Korean cops in some detail, giving me a little time to think. I'd already dug a hole for myself, but they'd trapped me. I couldn't let them take Kelly's bar.

One of the Korean cops asked a question that evidently the rest found obvious. The American translated. "So what did they look like? You said they were American… Were they black or white, or did they look like me?"

"White," I said. "Both of them."

"Okay. Now we're getting somewhere. Two white soldiers… Can't be more than a few thousand of them in Daegu." He laughed, and I realised that maybe he actually didn't care that much. He seemed to believe my story, or at least parts of it, and was accepting that maybe he wouldn't get much of a lead out of me.

It went on like this for around an hour and a half, with me mostly repeating the same facts. I kept my story simple and close to the truth, without naming names. I made sure to answer "I don't know" to any complex questions, and they never caught me out as lying.

Another hour passed by as one of the cops typed the information into an ancient computer, and then a copy was printed. I didn't understand a word of it, but the Asian-American cop assured me that I should just sign it and walk out of the police station.

"So what happens next?" I asked, after signing the document.

"Well, you'll have to appear in court to testify against the two young men," he said, assuming that they'd actually apprehend these nameless soldiers. "You probably won't do any prison time... A year at most. I think you'll probably just get probation."

"Probation?"

"You'll be told to leave the country."

"Deported?"

"Pretty much."

They drove me to Kelly's apartment at three in the morning and told me not to go to the bar. Of course, I didn't have a key, so when they drove off I walked back to Trend. The bar was empty and there was a strange girl watching the place. "Where's Kelly?" I asked. She said something in Korean that I took to mean, "She's not here."

Distraught, I walked back out onto the streets to find her. It was a one in a million shot, but in Daegu it's funny how often you walk into people you know. For all the crowds and chaos of little winding streets, friends seem to bump into each other all the time.

I walked around the usual streets, then decided to pop

my head into each of the bars and clubs. It had been a long time since I'd been in any of these places. The only place I'd been since leaving Korea was Trend. But not much had changed except the faces. Every foreigner bar was filled with new teachers – drunken idiots that reminded me of myself. The nightclubs were full of soldiers and young Korean kids trying to imitate their heroes. Guys rape-dancing women and women giggling and tottering about on giant heels.

And there I saw her: Min Jung. She was standing with her friends in the foyer of Heart, all of them playing with their phones. I'd never even seen her friends before, but as I stood at the entrance and stared in at them, they spotted me and told Min Jung. She looked up and gave me a deathly stare… but then it turned into a sneer and she said something to her friends, who all laughed.

She walked over to me, still sneering, and asked, "How is new girlfriend? She still love you?"

"Fuck you," I told her. "Don't ever talk to me again."

I turned and started to walk away as she screamed, "You don't stay Korea for long! Manhole!"

I found Kelly at her apartment several hours later. She was lying unconscious on the bed, beside a bottle of sleeping pills. I shook her, telling myself that she was just asleep – that the stress had been too much and that she'd slept it off – but I knew what had happened.

I picked her up and carried her out to a taxi, then took her to hospital. No one cared to tell me what had happened. Their glares said they thought I had driven her to suicide with my dirty foreign ways, and I suppose in some respect I had. I had been foolish enough to break the law in another country and even though it was a spiteful whore who'd turned me in, I was the idiot and the criminal. It was my fault I'd been arrested, and it was my fault Kelly had tried to kill herself.

After a few hours of sitting and being stared at and told absolutely nothing, I asked a doctor if he spoke English. "My wife," I said, hoping that he'd take me seriously. "She's called Yoon Seo... I need to know if she's okay. Please help me."

The man smiled and said he'd find out, but when he returned he wasn't smiling. I thought for a moment that she had died, but he just said, "She's okay. But I heard she attempted suicide? Maybe you shouldn't see her."

I sat up all night in the foyer of the hospital, enduring the stares and taunts of the patients and visitors, and in the morning she appeared. When I saw her I jumped to my feet, but she looked at me as though she never wanted to see me again.

"Kelly!" I shouted. It was not like me to raise my voice in a public place, but I was caught off guard. Her father was with her, and as I ran over as he tried to shepherd her away. "Please, Kelly, talk to me..."

Her father turned and hissed at me, and Kelly just turned away. "I'm sorry," I said, and then, for lack of any better idea: "It wasn't my fault."

It was a stupid thing to say but I was desperate. She turned and looked at me, crying now, and said, "There's a reason Korean people hate foreigners. It isn't 'cause you look different or come from far away. It's because you come here and fuck up, Alexander." Her father tried to pull her away but she stood her ground. "Look at you, all of you. When we're young we wanna be like you guys like you're so cool or something. We see you and point and wanna talk to you. But you have no responsibility. You come to Korea and act like you're children when you're supposed to be teachers. We stare at you 'cause you're acting like idiots."

I tried to think of something to say to defend myself, or even to defend my friends and fellow immigrants, but I couldn't. I just pleaded, "Kelly, I love you. You know I love you and before last night you loved me too. Even if only for a short time... I'm not asking you to marry me or even to forgive me, but let's at least talk it out. Please."

She turned to me and her father let go of her shoulders. "Okay, let's talk. In fact, I'm going to talk and you're going to give me a one-word answer... Did you sleep with me and tell me you loved me, then act like we were going to be together forever, and then less than a day later get arrested?"

"I didn't plan on..."

"One word."

"Yeah."

"And you promised me – you promised! – that you wouldn't get arrested. Remember?"

"Yeah."

"And that means you're probably getting sent back to Scotland because you have no job and a drug conviction. You're basically the epitome of what Koreans think when they see a white guy on the street, Alexander. You're *it*. You're the foreigner they fear. And they'll kick you out and we'll never be together again."

"We can fight it," I began.

"'We'? Alexander, I barely know you. We were friends and then we hooked up and said shit like we loved each other, and then we spent just one stupid day together. You really expect me to help you? I've been giving you drinks, finding you jobs, and letting you sleep at my apartment, and I was going to continue helping you. I feel like you're *using* me."

"I'm not, I swear."

"You don't *think* you are, but you are. You used Min

Jung and drove her crazy, then you used me. You come to Korea for the same reason every guy comes here – for sex. Why didn't you have a girlfriend back in Scotland? Probably because you were a loser. And I know that sounds harsh, Alexander, but I bet it was true. You've never even been in a proper relationship, and you think that in Korea it's going to be different. Why? You're still a loser here, but because you're foreign you're suddenly special."

"Okay, so I'm a child because I always run away from stuff. I ran away from Scotland, and I ran away from Daegu, once. I always run away because I guess I'm weak and stupid and childish… and I don't know what to say to make you stick with me except that I care enough about you not to run away this time. When the police let me go I could've tried to ditch Korea again, but I didn't and I didn't because I thought of you. I love you."

"Do you? Do you actually love *me*, or are you looking for someone to love *you*? I'm not even sure you're capable of loving someone. All you care about is yourself and your own problems."

Kelly shook her head and began turning away. "You're desperate and you think I can save you. Did you ever even try to make my life better, or was this all just for you? I'm sorry, Alexander. You were lonely and I was lonely, but there was really nothing there, was there? Just forget about it and run away again."

I stood and watched as her father walked her out of the hospital and out of my life. She'd said so much that I just stood and stared blankly at the door for several minutes, before eventually stumbling out into the cold day. Winter was coming on quickly. My time in Korea had just about ended, only I wasn't sure how I would get out.

THE END

NOTE ON
ROMANISATION

Throughout the novel, the author uses some common words of Korean and makes reference to various Korean places and names. In this text, the system of romanisation (transcription and transliteration into the Roman alphabet) uses the Revised Romanization of Korean (RR) system, rather than the older McCune-Reischauer (MR) system. RR is currently the officially recognised system of romanisation in South Korea (MR is still the system in North Korea), and as far as possible this novel makes use of RR to avoid confusion.

Therefore, the airport is referred to as Incheon, rather than Inchon, even though both spellings are still commonly used. The southeastern port city frequently spelled as Pusan is referred to in this novel as Busan.

Taegu is spelled as Daegu, and so on.

The names of Korean characters, however, are spelled according to popularity and common use. Due to the changing of Romanisation rules over the years, Korean names are typically romanised according to what the bearer of said name considers an accurate approximation when used by a speaker of English, and what fashion has dictated as proper. Consequently, the commonly used family names Lee and Park would be spelled as they have been used by Korean Presidents and other popular figures, rather than I or Bak, as they would in RR or MR. Hyphens and spaces are also used according to custom. The characters Mina and Min Jung both have common Korean names, but are spelled and formatted according to preference, rather than any rigid set of rules. They could as easily be spelled Mi Na or Min-jeong, but again in this novel they are spelled according to the most common usage.

ALSO AVAILABLE FROM BEATDOM BOOKS

Scientologist! William S. Burroughs and the 'Weird Cult' (2013)
World Citizen: Allen Ginsberg as Traveller (2019)

COMING SOON

High White Notes: The Rise and Fall of Gonzo Journalism (2021)

www.ingramcontent.com/pod-product-compliance
Lightning Source LLC
Chambersburg PA
CBHW071256170626
46809CB00001B/238